Florence Engel Randall

The Place of Sapphires

Harcourt, Brace & World, Inc., New York

For

Ray Engel, my mother,

and

Ruth Brody, my friend

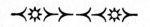 *Gabrielle*

SOMEONE WAS WHISPERING, "GABRIELLE, GABRIELLE," saying my name over and over again, and the voice began my dream. For I was dreaming. I knew I was dreaming the way I knew I was sleeping in a strange bed in a room that was not my own, the way I knew that the roof above had never sheltered me before.

And in my dream it seemed to me that there was the rising wail of the wind and my room was filled with mist. I puzzled over this, for I had gone to sleep with the moonlight shining through the uncovered squares of the windowpanes, and yet I could feel the fog swirl about me, white and cold and heavy, the fog sealing my lips, my eyes and my ears so swiftly, so completely, that I accepted this dulling of the senses as a matter of course. It didn't seem odd now that I couldn't hear the restless murmur of the sea in the distance or open my eyes to the bright moonlight, and with my acceptance inexplicably the room changed, becoming dear and familiar as if I had known nothing else all my life.

The room changed and I changed with it, my identity dissolving as if I, Gabrielle Anne Thatcher, age nineteen, made of flesh and bone and sinew, had no more existence. Another took my place, another whose name was Alarice, although this she didn't tell me. Her eyes and hair and walk were different from mine, she being small as I was tall, fair as I was dark, and yet at this moment in space and time we were as one.

"This is *my* room," Alarice said.

"This is my room," I echoed obediently, her voice, my voice, her thoughts belonging to me. And because this was so, I knew that the dream I dreamt was no longer mine to dream, just as my name was no longer mine to claim. I was not Gabrielle. I was Alarice and this was my room.

I had been tucked in this four-poster bed when I was a little girl. It had a white organdy canopy, and when I pulled down the covers, I pretended I was boarding a ship, and the organdy sails carried me far out to sea. I could see myself so clearly as I was then, sitting up in bed with my hands clasped about my raised knees. My eyes were green-blue and I had fat, yellow braids tied with blue ribbons, and my long-sleeved flannel nightgown was buttoned demurely at the throat.

This was my room. I had grown up in this old house that had been in my family long before my memory began. And as I grew taller and older and wiser, I changed. I unwound the tight braids. I threw away the childish ribbons and I brushed my hair and piled it on top of my head. I brushed my hair until it shone, and when I climbed into the bed with the canopy, it remained a bed and became nothing else. There were no thoughts of the old, long-vanished whalers leaving Stepping-stone and I pretending that I stood like a figurehead in the bow, the wind whipping my long skirt, I, like many another New England woman before me, putting out to sea with the men. Because I was growing older and wiser I lay warm in my bed, and I could see that the white organdy was just the right substance for a bridal dress, and my imaginary ship sailed no more.

On long winter nights I sat on that red rug in front of the fireplace, my legs curled under me, a book open on my lap. The flames leaped high and the logs crackled and the sparks flew. The candles flickered and Mama came in with steaming hot chocolate in big brown mugs, saying in mock dismay, "Alarice,

4

you should have been asleep hours ago," and we laughed because the affectionate scolding and the firelight and the quiet
between us belonged to this hour and to us alone.

My sister never joined us. She was five years older than I, but
the distance between us had nothing to do with age. If she
sought companionship, it was not mine, and if I sought soli-
tude, it could be broken only by someone I loved. And I didn't
love her. Even then I didn't love her, and I will see to it that
she never lives in my house.

Anger filled me and I turned my head on the pillow, my hand
flung out in protest, so that it struck the wall. I could feel the
pain sharp in my fingers and, momentarily conscious, I murmured sleepily, "But I am Gabrielle and my sister's name is
Elizabeth," and I realized that my own bed in my own house
was not placed against the wall as it was here in this temporary
home for Elizabeth and me. My own bed had been in the very
center of the wall, so there was space on either side of it, and I
could breathe without feeling crowded. Even when I had been
in the hospital there had been space around me, except, of
course, when they drew the curtains around the bed, and then I
felt as though I were lying inside a shroud.

But they don't bury people in shrouds any more. Alarice had
been buried in a shroud with her hands crossed over her breast
and her green-blue eyes hidden by the sealed lids, but my own
mother had been buried in her very best dress. Elizabeth had
told me because I had asked. She didn't want to talk about it,
but I had insisted. I hadn't gone to the funeral. Everything had
happened without me—the flowers, the tears, the turned-over
black earth. There was no way I could go. My leg was still in a
cast then, and I had some broken ribs.

"And a mild concussion," Elizabeth had said. "You couldn't
possibly have gone, darling."

"Did they bury her in the blue dress?"

"Gabrielle, please—"

"Did they? Answer me."

"Yes," she said. "Yes."

I looked at Elizabeth and I knew I shouldn't ask any more
questions. It was difficult enough for her to have to bear that

5

overwhelming guilt, but I couldn't be quiet. How was it possible for me to be quiet? I had to know. I had a right to know. "And Dad?" I said.

"His black suit," said Elizabeth, looking very pale.

It was the one he wore to concerts and to the theater, the one he wore when he escorted Mother in her softly draped, flowing blue dress.

He had been buried in his black suit, and Elizabeth brought me here after they let me out of the hospital, here to this strange place.

But I know every inch of this room, I reminded myself. Of course I do. If I were Alarice (and surely I was Alarice), then this was my room, wasn't it? Over and over again my fingers had traced the flowered pattern of the paper on the walls, the paper I had chosen myself with the bluebells and the forget-me-nots stenciled indelibly, forever fresh, forever lovely. My eyes had seen and loved the view from each window, the north facing the sea and the east overlooking the moor. There were sunlit days when I ran across the polished oak floor in my long dress, holding my skirt high above my ankles, running because I was too young and too happy to walk. There were nights when I paced up and down the shining floor, pacing back and forth, although my body ached with fatigue and my eyes burned because they could endure no more tears. And then there were nights like this one when the surf crashed against the rocks and the curtains flapped at the open windows. On a September night such as this, I, Alarice, wept even in my sleep, my throat tight and hard with my grief.

I was crying. I could feel the tears and I was amazed, knowing that my cheeks were wet. Still half-asleep, I wondered why it was so cold. I felt as though I were encased in ice. My tears were frozen crystal beads and my breath was frost, whiter than the mist.

"No," I said out loud, and with the sound of my voice the mist dissolved, the heavy seas subsided and the room held its breath, waiting.

"No," I said again, and at my command all was quiet.

Slowly, with a tremendous effort, I tried to reach for the

6

covers. I knew I must get warm. I felt I would die if I didn't get warm. The ice was so thick. I whimpered a little, deep in my throat, mourning over the thickness of the ice. I beat against it, struggling violently. Blankets, I thought with longing while the ice splintered and cracked around me. Two blankets and perhaps a quilt.

I couldn't open my eyes, for snow lay heavy on my eyelids. And with my eyes closed it was possible for me to see the quilt, the soft quilt that could warm me. It was patchwork, one I had sewn myself, each stitch painstakingly and laboriously made.

But I can't sew, I told myself.

"Yes, I can," said Alarice.

"Yes, I can," I murmured, remembering all those small squares that once had belonged to me, that lovely quilt that was mine. It was bits and pieces of me sewn together with needle and thread, each square a part of my life, each square reminding me of some joy or some sorrow. The red in the center—that splash of red that looked like blood—was once a dress. It was the dress I had worn when I had met Jotham for the first time, and why should one memory only lead to another? I didn't want to remember the day when I took the scissors and deliberately slashed my red dress. I concentrated instead on the white that formed the border. That came from the dining-room curtains (Mama let me keep the remnants), and I also had a piece of the old slip covers from the front parlor, from the sofa where Jotham sat and sipped his tea and ate Mama's little sugared cakes and smiled at me. At the bottom of the quilt was a bit of damask from the footstool where Papa used to rest his feet.

Oh, those long winter afternoons when I sat with Mama's wicker sewing basket on my lap with all the colored threads wound so tight on the spools and the big porcelain darning egg and the sharp-pointed scissors and the bright colors of the materials spread all around me. I ignored the sound of my sister's laughter then, proud that I could turn my head from the gleaming shears so like a weapon. I was pleased with my self-control as I threaded the needle, turning the needle to the light while I closed my ears to any laughter but my own.

What a beautiful quilt it was when it was finally finished. It was soft and light and warm and I knew if I could only find it I would never be cold again.

I reached out, groping, but there was just a sheet thrown over me. My fingers touched it, not recognizing its texture at first, and then knowing it for what it was, and knowing, too, that there was no warmth in it. On this still, hot September night there was no warmth for me anywhere.

I was crying again. The tears melted the snow and I was able to open my eyes.

Shivering, my teeth chattering, I sat up straight, the sheet knotted under my clenched fists, my hands holding onto it as though they were trying to grasp reality itself.

The room was filled with moonlight because there were no curtains to shield the windows. The moonlight lay in long strips on the floor and it shimmered across the foot of the bed. I could see how it danced on the ceiling because there was no canopy above me to billow like the sails of a ship. The cold white light outlined the shape of the dresser and the rocking chair in the corner. I could see the whole room because there was no mist to dull my vision, no curtains to darken the windows and to flap in a nonexistent breeze.

"It's just this room," Elizabeth had said, frowning. "It's odd, come to think of it. Every other room in the house has them."

"What difference does it make?" I said, hating this new need in me to make conversation with Elizabeth. I didn't know what I would do if there were nothing but silence between us. "I suppose we can buy them if you want to, although I really don't know why we should supply things for a house we're only using for a month."

"I suppose you're right," Elizabeth said, walking about as if she couldn't stand still. She ran her fingers across the top of the dresser and she looked into the mirror for a moment. "Is this room all right for you?" she said, not facing me, her reflection staring at my reflection. "I really don't know what made you choose this one. There's another bedroom down the hall across from Maggie's."

"This is the one I want," I said. I tested the mattress. "Why don't you like it? It seems comfortable enough. I just don't understand why Mrs. What's-her-name doesn't see to it that there are curtains at the windows."

Elizabeth turned around. "Maybe they were taken down and put somewhere. I know when Maggie and I came they weren't here. What a mess this place was. Everything was covered with sheets, and even the sheets were dusty, although someone was supposed to come in once in a while and take care of the house. We had some job to do getting things ready. I'll have to ask about the curtains, but, meanwhile, Gabrielle, do remember she's Mrs. Bellingham, if you please."

Elizabeth smiled at me, and I almost expected her to produce that spiral notebook she carries everywhere—the one she tucks under her pillow at night, hoping that inspiration will come hand in hand with insomnia. Along with the infrequent notes she takes for her novel, Elizabeth uses it to jot down marketing lists, telephone numbers and cryptic reminders like "Call S. H.," and then, inevitably, she turns to me and says helplessly, "Gabrielle, who is S. H.?"

Elizabeth is twenty-four and beautiful the way a steel engraving is beautiful, each line and angle sharp and pure. Her fair hair is straight and long and silken, pulled back a little too harshly so that her gray eyes seem slightly uptilted. Only Elizabeth's mouth gives her away. It is too soft to be well defined, and if Elizabeth's features are etched, then her mouth has been rendered in a totally different medium—charcoal, perhaps, with the lower lip smudged, making it a little too full. The cool, remote Elizabeth other people see isn't really Elizabeth at all. Elizabeth is exactly like her mouth, soft, vague and lovely.

And defenseless, of course. She is vulnerable the way my mother was vulnerable. Elizabeth looks like our mother, while I am dark, quick and capable like our father. There are times when I stare at Elizabeth and I want to shake her. In five years, when I am Elizabeth's age, I won't bury myself for a month in a house such as this. Not for any reason. Elizabeth pretends she is doing it for me, but I know better.

But I must be fair. My father always said I had a strong sense

9

of justice and he was right. How do I know what I will be doing five years from now? Did Elizabeth ever think she would be unmarried?

"It's like that old song," she once told me. "You know the one." She hummed off key. "I can't think of all the words, but it goes, 'They're either too short or too tall.'"

"But someone has to be just right," I said.

"Neither too short nor too tall?"

"I'm not talking about height."

"Neither am I," said Elizabeth.

But that was a long time ago, long before the accident, long before our lives changed, long before Elizabeth decided to come to Steppingstone for the month of September.

"It will be good for you," Elizabeth said. "It's a beautiful little island, uncrowded, quiet, just the place for you to convalesce. It's off-season and there will be no tourists, no one to bother us. There's nothing to do but lie in the sun and you can get well and maybe I can get some work done on the book. If we like it, we can even stay another month. I'm sure I can get my leave of absence extended."

I pretended she was fooling me, as if I didn't know any better, as if I didn't know the truth. Elizabeth had said over and over again that we were going away for my sake, but I knew she couldn't bear to return to our own house. She couldn't face those familiar rooms without our parents. She was afraid she would see them walking up the stairs, standing in the kitchen, sitting in the living room, sleeping in the bedroom. She was afraid because she knew she would see them pace through the house, walking side by side, the shadows of our parents touching each other, touching us. If I saw them I wouldn't be afraid, but Elizabeth kept rubbing her arms as if she was cold.

Cold!

But now the cold was leaving me, withdrawing as subtly and as gently as that other presence who had invaded my sleep. I switched on the bedside lamp, pulled the pillow high and sat up in bed.

There was no fireplace on the far wall, although I had seen it in my dream. There was no fireplace for the flames to dance in on a cold winter night, and there was no red rug to place in front of that fireplace that didn't exist, and there was no patterned wallpaper and no disembodied voice to whisper my name. There was nothing but the memory of the dream and the dream wouldn't leave me, even with the light burning bright next to me.

There was a book on the night table, the book I had been reading before I fell asleep, and the marker still held my place. I opened it and tried to read because I didn't want to go to sleep again. If I fell asleep, the dream might return, and I wanted no part of Alarice's grief—whoever she might be—for I had enough of my own.

But I couldn't read and I couldn't sleep and I felt I couldn't stay in that room any longer. I put on robe and slippers and limped into the hall, moving very quietly because I didn't want to disturb Elizabeth. Her door was open—not far—just wide enough so that the light from the hall streamed into her room. I hadn't said a word when I saw she was going to leave the hall light burning all night. I could understand why Elizabeth was afraid to sleep in the dark.

Down the hall another bedroom door was closed. Maggie slept there, for Elizabeth had insisted that Maggie come with us.

"She can cook," Elizabeth had said, as if that were the only reason. But I knew Elizabeth was giving Maggie a chance to stay with us until she found another job. It would never occur to Elizabeth that Maggie had had ample opportunity to look for something else. Months had gone by while I was in the hospital, months while Elizabeth paid Maggie's salary, Elizabeth too soft, too gentle to tell Maggie the truth.

"She loves us," Elizabeth said. "She's been with us so long it would break her heart to leave."

If Maggie loved us so much, why did she still take her money each week? If I had my way, we would have told Maggie we didn't need her any longer. Then we would have gone home, packed all our things, sold the house and never come here at all. It's better to get things over with quickly.

"If something disagreeable has to be done, it must be done

right away," my father always said when Mother kept putting off tasks she didn't want to do. But, in a way, I understood about Maggie, just the way I understood about Elizabeth. Maggie has been with us ever since I was a little girl, and I suppose she does find it difficult to leave.

Standing there at the head of the steps, I realized I should have taken my cane. I hesitated, touching the newel post and thinking about it. Elizabeth hated the sight of the cane, just the way she hated any reminder of what had happened.

"You can walk without it," Elizabeth said, and she was right, but I had become accustomed to the feel of it. The crutches had been heavy and hateful, but the cane was different. When I held it, smooth and cold in my hand, it was like having a third leg. With it I felt rather like an animated tripod, extraordinarily steady and firm and powerful. But I didn't want to go back to my room again.

Alarice's room—not mine—I told myself, and still moving quietly I went down the bare oak steps of the staircase, my feet testing each step. The third one from the bottom creaked, the sound like a pistol shot, and I stood rigid for a moment, my heart pounding, berating myself for not remembering that tell-tale step as if I had gone this way many times before. But how was I to know the creaks and the groans of this house? I had been in it only a few hours. In my own house there is a place in the living room where, if you rock back and forth, you can feel the boards move with you as though, just in that spot, the house was vibrating ever so slightly, and our staircase creaks on the seventh step, not the third.

But I was downstairs now and in the center hall, and the only light was the one behind me, the one Elizabeth had left burning upstairs. I fumbled for the switch and the whale-oil lamp above my head lit up. I could see that the paneling was mahogany and so dark that the wood seemed to absorb the light, making the hall seem dim, as if the light was failing.

"This house was built in the seventeen hundreds," Elizabeth had said when we arrived, Elizabeth using that new voice of hers, that artificially gay, bright tone that told me how uneasy she felt. It was the same voice she had used in the hospital and again on the train. She had chattered on the ferry while the wind whipped our faces. She had prattled as the taxi bounced over the cobblestoned streets of the town, the sound of Elizabeth's voice and the sound of the wheels on the rough stones making me want to clap my hands over my ears. Elizabeth talked and talked while I concentrated on the old shingled houses and the white picket fences and the tall elms almost meeting across the road. And then we were in the open country, the fields and the white-capped bay moving past as though we were standing still. It was getting dark. My eyes burned and Elizabeth didn't stop talking, Elizabeth describing Steppingstone to me, giving me a history of the island as if I cared about it, as if I really wanted to know when it had been settled and the names of its pioneers.

"Some came here to teach the Indians and they remained because they fell in love with the land. You'll love it, too. I know you will, Gabrielle. There are coves and fields and quiet beaches, and when you're well, we can take long walks. It's not a large island. It's only three miles wide and fifteen miles long."

"Why did they call it Steppingstone?" I said idly.

"Because it looks like one, I guess. The Indians said that a giant used it as a steppingstone on the way to Martha's Vineyard."

Elizabeth's voice going on and on, talking about the island, talking about the house, Elizabeth using words to distract me. Like waving a rattle in front of a baby, I thought, amused, watching her pay the driver.

He set the suitcases on the front step.

"Put them in the hall, please," Elizabeth said.

"I have to be getting back," he said.

"It will only take a minute," Elizabeth said.

He dropped them right inside the front door. I saw him glance up the stairs. "Going to stay long?" he asked.

"At least a month," said Elizabeth.

"Hmm," he grunted, and then he got back into the taxi and drove away.

"All hand-hewn," said Elizabeth, ignoring him. She touched the portal, stroking the wood. "Truly old New England. Silver-shingled on the outside and hand-polished on the inside."

"If it's so beautiful," I said crossly, because I was tired and not at all interested in a guided tour of the house just then, "why doesn't Mrs. Bellingham live here herself?"

"Because the house is haunted," Elizabeth said lightly.

"Don't be silly," I said.

Haunted, I said silently now, remembering my dream, re-membering Alarice. I thought fleetingly of turning back. It would be easier to walk through this strange house in daylight, with the sunlight streaming through the multipaned windows and the good smell of bacon frying and Maggie humming in the kitchen and all the doors flung open wide. Instead, as if my fingers had a will of their own, as if I had done this many times before during bygone sleepless nights, I turned on the light in the front parlor.

There was a small, overstuffed love seat, a black marble fire-place, two old wing chairs and a faded floral rug. Through the arch the back parlor yawned like a dark, open mouth.

Leaving lights burning behind me like a marked trail, I crossed the hall to the dining room. The table was round and mahogany like the paneling in the hall, and the scrollwork on the curved legs was deeply inlaid. There was a mahogany-and-satinwood Sheraton-style sideboard dominating one end of the room, and cotton lace covered the very center of the table. On the top shelf of the open corner cupboard was a cobalt-blue cup and saucer. "The orphaned survivors of a set of Meissen," Elizabeth had said. Like us, I had thought while I pretended to look at the other shelves, which were filled with flowered cups. Elizabeth and I were orphaned survivors, too, only I didn't know which of us was the cup and which was the saucer. Dreamily I tried to decide which I'd rather be until Maggie had called to me.

Now the crystal chandelier tinkled faintly as I walked across the room. The passage to the kitchen was familiar as the kitchen itself was familiar, for here earlier this evening Elizabeth and I had sat at the round table drinking coffee while Maggie fussed.

"Such a long train ride and the ferry and then that awful jeep they have a nerve to call a taxi," Maggie scolded. "Look at the shadows under your eyes, and I bet you haven't had a bite to eat."

"I'm not hungry, Maggie."

"She wouldn't let me drive," Elizabeth said. "It would have been easier if she had let me take the car."

I looked at Elizabeth, but I didn't say anything. It didn't matter that the car she now drove was new. If she wanted to forget why I wouldn't ever drive with her again, it was because she couldn't bear to remember.

If the kitchen had been modernized, it had been by my grandmother's standards, not mine. The stove was gas, but it stood high on legs, and the sink was blue porcelain, recessed deep in a high-arched alcove. The refrigerator was small—"But it's adequate for our needs," Maggie had said—and the linoleum seemed smooth and unworn as if, after it had been laid, no one had dared to walk across it.

There was a narrow hall off the kitchen leading to another room and a bath, "Which is the maid's room," Elizabeth said, "but Maggie will sleep upstairs because she's one of the family."

I didn't go down that hall just as I hadn't entered the back parlor. I stood very still for a moment and then, the lights burning behind me and the lights leading the way in front of me, I limped through the dining room and the main hall and up the stairs again.

I stared at the closed door of my bedroom, puzzled, positive I had left it open, and then I shut it behind me, thinking only of the lights that would burn all night.

There was comfort in the thought of those blazing lights. I held onto it while I walked over to the far wall, while I ran my fingers along that wall, searching for a fireplace that didn't exist. I held onto it while I peered out the window, seeing the restless sea in the distance, the sea wall looking foreshortened and oddly close in the moonlight. I held onto it while I got into bed

15

and tucked the pillow under my head. I tried to think of nothing but the burning brilliance of the lights, but all the time I tried to concentrate on them like a beacon in the dark, there was another image weaving in and out of my mind so that one moment it would be hidden and the next it would creep into the open like some furtive creature winding its way through tangled underbrush.

Alarice! Who was she? Had she ever paced this floor? Had she slept in this bed? Had she lived and loved and wept in this house or had I only imagined her, an image created in a dream? Who was she who had invaded my mind and my senses so completely that I had awakened with the singing syllables of her name still vibrating in the air?

Who was Alarice? I didn't know. I only knew I was not Alarice, although her anger had clenched my fists and I had felt her tears stream down my cheeks. I was not Alarice, although she had walked with me through this house tonight. I was not Alarice. I was Gabrielle and I was afraid.

I CAN'T REMEMBER EVER BEING AFRAID BEFORE. NOT even when I was a child and filled with fears that seem in retrospect to be not more than little tremors of apprehension. Then, at night, I kept the bedclothes pulled high under my chin. I knew if I left my arms outside the blankets *something* (it had no name) would clutch at my fingers while I slept. It was necessary for me to close my eyes the minute I got into bed. My mother always left the hall light burning (like Elizabeth does now), and because I was afraid to sleep with my door shut and kept it slightly ajar, the light created shadows where they had no right to be. I worried over my algebra mark and whether my father loved Elizabeth more than he did me. It was tacitly understood in our house that Elizabeth belonged to Mother and that I was Father's, but parents are unpredictable at best, and I thought Elizabeth very beautiful. I would stare into the mirror, overcome with fear, hating my peaked eyebrows, my rounded chin, the dark smudges that underlined my eyes even then. But although I had many fears, I realize now that I knew nothing of fear itself.

To be afraid—really afraid—is total involvement like being

really in love. I have never been in love, but I have imagined what it is like and now, of course, I know what it is to be afraid. It affects not just the mind and the senses, but all the other organs of the body as well. Your skin becomes moist and clammy and the touch of your own soundless breath chills it. Your throat dries so that it is impossible to swallow, your scalp itches and your heart pounds.

Now, lying here with the bedside lamp still burning beside me, although the morning sunlight flamed through the uncovered windows, I knew I was still afraid. My neck ached and I rubbed it, my fingers kneading the tense muscles. Evidently I had fallen asleep again in a half-reclining position with my head propped awkwardly against the pillow, but I had no memory of it. That troubled me because Elizabeth said there were many things I could no longer remember.

"It will come back to you," Elizabeth had told me, her voice gentle. "There's nothing to worry about, darling. Doctor Inness says it's very common in cases of this kind. Your mind has just decided to block out anything painful."

"That's not true. I remember everything that happened in the hospital, except when I was unconscious, of course, and I remember everything just before the accident," I said, deliberately staring at her until she flushed and turned her head away. "Everything right up to the moment it happened."

Elizabeth had been driving and my father had been sitting next to her, his arm across the back of the seat so that his fingers just touched her shoulder. I sat in the back with Mother, hating the way his hand moved almost as if he were caressing Elizabeth, so I concentrated instead on the back of her neck, which is soft and white and smooth like the nape of a child. I saw the way her hair caught the light and the way her hands rested on the wheel. If she hadn't glanced at my father just then ("Keep your eyes on the road, Gabrielle," my father always cautioned *me*), she could have seen that the car in front of us was slowing down, ready to turn at the exit, but Elizabeth looked sideways, saying something in that soft voice of hers that made my father laugh, and I shouted, "Watch out!"

Elizabeth braked. She glanced in the rear-view mirror, her

eyes meeting mine for a moment, and I knew she was calculating the speed of the cars behind us and the speed of the cars traveling in the left-hand lane, and then because she was Elizabeth she made the wrong decision. It would have been better to have crashed into the car ahead. If I had been driving, I would have risked it. We had slowed, and I knew the bumpers would have taken most of the blow, but Elizabeth swung into the other lane, hoping to avoid an unavoidable collision. I closed my eyes, knowing instinctively what was going to happen and knowing, too, that I didn't have the courage to meet disaster with my eyes open.

I could feel the car spin. We must have hit a wet spot on the road, and we skidded until we spun around facing the oncoming traffic, and far away, as if it were happening to someone else, I heard the shattering of glass and felt the impact. And then it seemed to me that I was no longer made of flesh and blood, but was part of the broken car. I was jagged glass splinters and crushed, groaning metal and ripped, shrieking rubber, and I thought with regret that since I was no longer human, I would never know what it was to love. I didn't think of my parents or of Elizabeth then. I could only keep my eyes closed, trying to hold onto my own identity, my own span of consciousness, knowing it was all I had left.

"You'll be all right," the doctor had said. His name was Gordon Inness and he wore tortoise-shell glasses that seemed to reflect the light so that I can't remember ever being able to look into his eyes. If I were drawing him, I would make a rectangle for his face, exaggerating the square, firm chin, and I would put two large circles in the center of it for his glasses, and I would put no eyes behind the glasses at all. I would trace a line for his mouth, and then if I were feeling really hateful, I would crumple the paper and throw it away. Just the way I would like to throw away all those months when I lay there and they stuck needles in me and sometimes I remembered and sometimes I didn't. Not that it mattered, of course. There were a lot of things that didn't matter then.

"You'll be all right," Elizabeth had echoed, hovering over me. Her eyes weren't hidden and I could see them very clearly.

They were gray, with little flecks in them. "Like pepper," my mother once said fondly. "Just like someone sprinkled pepper on Elizabeth."

But I knew better. It wasn't pepper. It was nothing as down to earth, as mundane, as pepper. It was magic. If there is such a thing as a witches' Sabbath, then Elizabeth was born on it. If the mandrake root could have a child, it would be Elizabeth. Of us all only Elizabeth walked free and untouched. I don't know how that could be, but there wasn't so much as a scratch on the smoothness of her cheek. Her skin was unflawed, her bones left whole and strong and straight, but I don't hate her the way Alarice hated her sister. I don't hate Elizabeth at all. I love her. I have always loved her. I don't blame her for the death of our parents. It was an accident and accidents can happen to anyone. I don't blame her for my broken leg or my bandaged head or the intravenous feedings or the tubes they put up my nose and down my throat. I don't blame her for my cracked ribs or the plastic surgery that changed my face. Not that I was beautiful before the accident. No one ever said I was beautiful the way they said Elizabeth was beautiful.

"You were born long and dark and skinny," said my mother. "When I first saw you, I wept."

"Didn't you love me?"

"Of course I loved you," said my mother, surprised. "It's just that I imagined all babies looked the way Elizabeth did."

Elizabeth was fair when she was born and her hair was yellow silk and her skin was white-and-pink satin and she had a hole in her right cheek that my mother called a dimple.

"But Gabrielle is my girl," my father said.

I didn't tell anyone I didn't blame Elizabeth. I didn't tell Elizabeth and I didn't tell Doctor Inness. He kept asking me questions, but I never discussed Elizabeth with him. It sounds so sanctimonious to say you don't blame someone when she was obviously at fault that I felt it was better for me to say nothing.

But I was afraid. Even with the lamp still burning beside me and the sunlight lying in patterned squares on the oak floor I was afraid. I didn't want to think of Alarice again. I was determined not to think of Alarice and yet, lying there, I tried to imagine exactly where the fireplace had been on the far wall and whether it had been hidden by plaster and paint, each layer measuring the years. In front of that fireplace Alarice had sat on a red rug drinking hot chocolate out of a brown mug, shutting out her sister, hating her sister.

As I hated Elizabeth?

"No," I said out loud.

"Supposed to be a bad sign when you start talking to yourself," said Maggie, flinging the door open wide.

I sat up straight. "But you talk to yourself all the time. I hear you."

"That's because I'm getting old," Maggie said, smiling at me. I had always thought of Maggie as a large, brisk woman with dark eyes and hair, moving so rapidly that "It makes me tired just to watch her," my mother had said. But the Maggie who stood in the doorway had gray hair and the lines under her eyes and around her mouth were etched deep and there were round brown spots on the backs of her hands. She moved toward me slowly and, looking at her, I thought, How small she is. What made me think she was tall? Why haven't I ever seen her clearly before? And because she made my throat ache with pity, I shouted at her, "Why don't you knock? I've asked you a million times not to walk in on me like that, Maggie."

She snorted. "Knock? When I've practically diapered you?"

"That's not the point. It's a matter of privacy," I said stiffly.

"It seems to me you didn't want much privacy last night," said Maggie shrewdly.

"What are you talking about?"

"Marching around the house in the dead of the night and leaving all the lights burning."

"It's hard enough for me to walk around all day without doing it all night, too," I said. "And if you think—"

"Well, then—whoever did it left your light on, too," said Maggie, turning off my bedside lamp. She leaned over and touched my cheek with the back of her hand. "What is it, Gabrielle? Couldn't you sleep?"

"I told you it wasn't me," I said stubbornly. I threw back the sheet and then slowly, very slowly, I swung my left leg over the side, bracing myself with my hands.

"Let me help you," said Maggie.

"It's all right," I said, biting my lip, trying not to laugh. "It doesn't hurt too much, Maggie," I added bravely. "It's getting better, really it is."

And then I inched my right leg over until I was sitting on the edge of the bed. Maggie stood very still, watching me, blinking rapidly the way she does when she's trying not to cry.

"You see, it wasn't me," I said. "I fell asleep while I was reading and that's why my light was on."

"Well, I didn't do it," said Maggie, frowning, "and it wasn't likely to be Elizabeth."

"Why shouldn't it be Elizabeth?"

"She doesn't scare easy," said Maggie quietly.

"Don't tell me that," I said angrily. "She's afraid to sleep in the dark. Anyone can see that. Even you can see that, Maggie. Your precious Elizabeth leaves the hall light burning and her door open—"

"She does it for you. The door is open in case you call her, in case you need her. You know that."

"I don't know that and I don't need her," I said rapidly. "I'm fine. Sometimes, like now, I hurt a little, but most of the time I'm fine, Maggie. What did you mean when you said Elizabeth doesn't scare easy?"

"Because she brought you here. Because she insists on taking care of you."

"I don't understand," I said.

"I know you don't. Gabrielle, darling—"

"I'd like to get dressed. Why don't you go away and leave me alone?"

"If that's what you want," said Maggie, looking troubled.

I resisted an impulse to put my head on her shoulder. There was no comfort for me in Maggie's arms and both of us knew it.

"Breakfast in bed?" said Maggie.

I shook my head.

She bent down and picked up my slippers.

"I don't want them," I said. "And stop looking at me like that." I stood up and hobbled across the room barefoot. "Is Elizabeth awake?"

"She's been up for hours," said Maggie. "It's ten o'clock. She wouldn't let me wake you before this. She said you needed your sleep. In fact," said Maggie slowly, "it was Elizabeth who mentioned the lights to me. She was worried about you."

"Such a fuss about the lights," I said, standing in front of the dresser. I picked up my hairbrush and looked at it. Alarice, I thought, with her long hair and the blue ribbons and then the strands unwound, tumbling about her shoulders and the hairbrush held in those long, white fingers, Alarice brushing her hair until it shone.

"All right," I said, putting the brush down again. "So I left a few lights burning. So I walked around the house last night. I admit it. Are you satisfied now? What difference does it make?"

"If it makes no difference, why did you lie to me?"

"Because I didn't want to tell you I couldn't sleep," I said softly. "I didn't want to worry you, Maggie."

"Oh, darling," she said, relieved. She sat on the edge of the bed and clasped her hands. "Are you hungry?" she added hopefully. "How about pancakes?"

I touched the hairbrush again. It was cold and smooth and hard in my hands. "No," I said.

"You must force yourself to eat. That's the only way you'll get your appetite back. How are you going to get strong unless you eat? You had no dinner last night and now—"

"Maggie!"

"These things take time. You mustn't grieve so, Gabrielle."

"Is that one of the rules?"

"What do you mean?"

I glanced at her sideways. "Like 'Don't kick your feet under the table, Gabrielle, and don't talk with your mouth full and don't tease your sister.'"

"But that was when you were a child," said Maggie, puzzled.

"And now I'm grown up and it's 'Don't cry. Don't think. Just pretend nothing has happened.' If I cry, my eyes will swell and my nose will get red and my lips will thicken and I won't be beautiful any more and that would be a shame, wouldn't it, Maggie?"

"All right," she said, standing up. "I won't talk about it. I should have known better. I should have remembered what you were like when you were little. Stubborn and willful and with those temper tantrums when even your poor mother could do nothing with you. You'd be screaming in your room and she would come downstairs looking white and tired, but I was smart then. I would tell her to leave you alone, that you'd get over it by yourself. I should have listened to Elizabeth when she told me not to discuss anything with you, but why should I listen to Elizabeth when I don't take my own advice?"

"Haven't you anything to do in the house?" I said. "It seems to me that there must be plenty to do in a house this size."

She flushed. "It's healthy to get everything off your chest. I was just trying to help. That's all. I know when I've something on my mind if I just talk it out I feel better. Maybe it doesn't solve anything, but it certainly makes me feel better. I should have remembered you were different."

"I'd like to get dressed," I said rudely.

She stared at the closed door. "I thought I left it open," she said.

"It doesn't matter. Just close it behind you," I said impatiently, and then when I heard the latch click, I stroked the back of the hairbrush with my finger.

Over and over again, morning and night, day after day, Alarice had sat in this room brushing her hair She flung it forward until it covered her face, a veil of yellow hiding her face, and then lifting the weight of it with her hands she let it cascade down her back like a shining stream.

I tried to imagine it while I ran my fingers through my own hair, trying to tell just how much it had grown. They had shaved it, of course. My head had been bandaged and now the stubble was rough and I didn't need a mirror to tell me how I looked. I didn't need one at all. If I wanted to, I could get dressed every morning without looking into the mirror, and I

24

could get undressed every night without so much as a glance in its direction.

After Doctor Inness had stitched and patched and sewn me back together again and the bandages had come off, he had held up a hand mirror, forcing it upon me, and I had looked at his long, blunt-edged fingers with the nails so clean and cut straight across, and I had thought idly, How tan his hands are. When does he find time to lie in the sun? How can a man who keeps his eyes hidden ever see the sun? And then because I wouldn't take the mirror from him, he had laid it face down on the bed.

"When you're ready, Gabrielle," he had said. "It's all right. Really it is."

Who was he to tell me it was all right? How could he know? Had he put me back together again like a jigsaw puzzle, saying to himself, "Oh, yes. Here's a bit of an eye and that must be a section of the nose and"—swooping down triumphantly—"the mouth goes just about *here*."

After he had left, after I was alone, I forced myself to pick up the mirror. I felt very calm, suddenly quite detached, as if someone else had entered my body and was cleverly stage-managing the whole thing for me in a most efficient manner. Which was really very perceptive of me, for the girl in the mirror was a stranger and therefore just the reflection of a stranger. The eyes were the same, dark brown, and I recognized the way the eyelashes curled and the color of the lashes themselves, thick and black, and the lids heavy over the eyes, but the nose, which was once straight, was now slightly uptilted, and the chin line was firmer, as if some of the flesh underneath had been chiseled away. "We'll carve a bit more off here," Doctor Inness had said thoughtfully, and now there was a scar running from the jawbone to the back of the ears. "Which will fade," Doctor Inness had said hopefully, "and we will draw the skin a bit tighter over the cheekbones and perhaps the smudges under the eyes will go away," and then, pleased, he had rubbed those scrubbed, tanned hands together and there was nothing now except the neat, pink scar to show that this was a completely new face, nothing to show that this face didn't belong to me at all. That was the horror of it. I think I should have been almost relieved if I had turned out twisted and ugly but still recognizable. It wasn't fair to turn me into a new person before I had a chance to become accustomed to the old one.

I didn't have to look in the mirror in order to dress in the morning and undress at night, but I did. This face puzzled me. I had a tendency to forget overnight what it looked like so that it was necessary that I study it anew each morning. Because the eyes were the same, because of the color and the shape of the eyes, it wasn't completely strange. Every once in a while I would catch a glimpse of the old Gabrielle the way one suddenly sees a familiar face in a crowd, but the moment I moved toward her, she would disappear again.

I gripped the edge of the dresser (Alarice's dresser?), and I looked into the mirror and the girl in the mirror frowned at me. Doctor Inness's jigsaw puzzle had been put back together again so neatly that the seams hardly showed. Standing there with the sunlight burning through the bare panes of the window, I, who knew where all the cracks and the jagged edges were, couldn't see them any more. My hair was growing like a dark cap around my head and I could feel the heat of the sun on my bare arms.

The windows were unscreened and I leaned on the window sill, looking down at the ivy that grew up the wall and at the flower bed at the very bottom with the untended yellow chrysanthemums almost hidden by the weeds and the spindly, neglected asters, limp and lavender. There was a long, unkempt lawn and a graveled driveway filled with clumps of grass, and there was the line of the road that led to the town, and in the distance was the sea wall with two figures silhouetted against it.

I squinted, shielding my sun-dazzled eyes with my hands, and I could see that the woman was Elizabeth. There was no mistaking her gestures, the quick way she moved her hands, the way she turned her head. It was Elizabeth standing close to some man, Elizabeth wearing her green slacks and her green pull-over standing very close to some man. He bent over as if he were about to take her in his arms and I drew back quickly as if I were the one he was about to touch. I closed the window as though that would shut out of the sight of them, and while I showered and dressed, I kept wondering who he might be. Elizabeth and Maggie had been getting the house ready for a few days before I came, but that wouldn't be long enough for Elizabeth to have found a man to laugh with, Elizabeth leaning on the sea wall, dressed all in green, with the sea sparkling green behind her and the sea gulls wheeling and circling over the narrow beach beyond.

"They're either too short or too tall," Elizabeth had said.

But not this one, I thought, going slowly down the stairs, leaning on my cane.

Maggie came out of the front parlor. She looked at the cane and then she looked at me and I watched her blink. She's forgiven me, I thought.

"I'm sorry, Maggie," I said.

She wiped her eyes with the back of her hand.

I put my foot on the step that creaked, the third step from the bottom, and I rocked back and forth for a moment, wondering why stairs are so silent in daylight. Is it because we don't listen for the subtle, whispering sounds of a house when the sun is shining? But it was morning and I was listening and the step was quiet, the old boards very still and quiet. The front door was open and the windows were open and the front parlor was dusted and shining and serene.

I brushed past Maggie and peered through the archway into the back parlor. There was a long, black library table that Elizabeth obviously intended to use as a desk, for her typewriter stood open upon it, and there was a black leather couch and two armchairs, and pushed against the far wall was a mahogany upright piano, the keys yellow with age.

Alarice's piano, I told myself, thinking, I will get it tuned. I will play the piano again. I could almost feel the keys smooth under my fingers, the ivory keys moving under my fingers, and I wondered whether Alarice had sat on that piano stool in the morning, her hair tied back with a blue ribbon, Alarice playing the piano while her sister stood in the doorway watching her, hating her.

Alarice. I shook my head. She was a dream that had lingered long past the time for dreams. If she had lived in this house, she had left it long ago, and what had happened here was no concern of mine Steps are silent and dreams are gone in the morning light and the only reality was Elizabeth falling in love.

"There's someone with Elizabeth," I said indifferently, keeping my face turned away from Maggie. "Do you know who it is?"

"I didn't notice," Maggie said. "Where are you going, Gabrielle? I want you to eat your breakfast. How are you going to get well and strong if you don't eat?"

I let the screen door slam behind me and I stood on the front steps and Elizabeth saw me. She flung up her hand and waved and the man said something to her and the sunlight danced on his glasses. I could see how the sunlight shimmered, rainbowing on his glasses, and I gripped the cane tight in my hand because now I knew who he was.

✧

I TURNED AWAY FROM THEM THEN, FOLLOWING THE driveway that led to the road. I wanted to run. If only I could run away from Elizabeth, I knew just how it would be. I would fling the cane from me and watch it roll along the ground, the cane just a useless stick like any other lying in the grass or half-covered by drifting sand or even camouflaged as part of a bush, and then I would run the way I used to run before the accident happened, running so swiftly, so lightly, so easily that no one would be able to catch me. Skimming the ground, moving faster and faster until I floated and the wind whistling past and I, laughing at the wind, running until I circled the island three times, my speed increasing until I was nothing but a flash of light sparkling momentarily in the lens of Doctor Inness's glasses, and, dazzled, confused, he would never know which was the sunlight and which was me.

Instead, however, I moved slowly, concentrating on my feet and trying to shut out the sound of Elizabeth. There was the cry of a sea gull and blending with it, almost a part of the bird's raucous scream, Elizabeth's voice rose on the syllables of my name.

It was the way she used to call me when we were children. "Gabrielle, where are you? Gabrielle, what *are* you doing? Ga-*brielle!*"

And I, resisting the temptation to giggle, ignoring her, pretending she didn't exist. Sometimes, when she was too insistent, it would be I who would cease to exist. I would withdraw, willing myself to dissolve as if my bones could melt and my flesh disintegrate and I would move far away from Elizabeth, although her hand clasped mine. Some days have more magic in them than others and if, in spite of my concentration, I still felt myself standing next to her, the flesh wrapped tight around the solid bones, I had to conjure an imaginary wad of cotton, stuffing my ears with it until Elizabeth, desperate, infuriated, would shake me.

"You heard me," she would say through her teeth, her eyes reddening as if she were about to cry. "I know you heard me. Why are you pretending? Why do you do this to me?"

Now, by the time I had reached the road, she had stopped calling me. I wanted to turn around, but I kept my back very straight and I held the cane firmly in my hand. Were the two of them still standing there watching me? I wondered. Was his hand about her wrist, his fingers tight about her wrist, keeping her from following me? Who was he to keep Elizabeth away from me? I was the only one who could do that, and I stood very still for a moment thinking about Doctor Inness and what I could do to him.

His glasses, I thought. I will smash his glasses and, with his eyes naked, he will be vulnerable. It would be an accident, of course. These things always are, and who should know better than I that accidents do happen? He would come to the house (naturally he would come to the house. There would be no other reason for him to be on this island unless it was to see us), and he would take off his glasses for a moment, whipping out his handkerchief to polish them. I would brush against him and the glasses would fall to the floor and I, stepping on them, grinding the lens under my heel while the sole of my shoe crushed those tortoise-shell earpieces and I crying out in dismay and he accepting my apology because there was nothing else he could do and all the while his eyes would be bare for everyone to see—Doctor Inness half-blind and helpless without his glasses, the harsh light stabbing his naked eyes.

I smiled at the thought. I felt better. I looked up at the sky and because it was so clear and so blue it made my throat ache, I looked down at the ground. There was the road hard under my feet and then the gravel of the driveway. I was not at all surprised to find myself walking back to the house, and when I looked up again, there were Elizabeth and Doctor Inness standing on the front doorstep waiting for me.

"Where in the world were you going?" said Elizabeth. Her face was flushed and stray little tendrils of hair floated over her forehead and the charcoal drawing that was her mouth looked blurred as if someone had smeared it. "I called and called—"

"I heard you," I said sweetly. "That's why I came back, Elizabeth, because I heard you. Why, Doctor Inness," I said, leaning on my cane, "how wonderful to see you again. What are you doing here?"

"I thought I told you—" He frowned. "I have a vague recollection of discussing it with you, but I could be wrong." He looked at Elizabeth. "Didn't you tell her?"

"Tell me what?" I said. "What didn't you tell me, Elizabeth?"

"Let's go into the house," she said quickly. "Maggie has the coffee on and you must be starving, Gabrielle. You haven't had a thing to eat."

Doctor Inness held the door open and I followed Elizabeth into the hall.

"What is it that everyone thought they were telling me and didn't?" I said.

"It's not important," Elizabeth said. "Please don't get upset. It's just that this is Gordon's house."

Gordon, I thought. When had she first called him Gordon? Had she stood next to my bed in the hospital, watching me as I lay there unconscious, my sister reaching out her hand to my doctor? When had it happened?

"This isn't Doctor Inness's house," I said angrily. "It belongs to Mrs. What's-her-name—"

"Bellingham," Elizabeth said automatically.

"She's my Aunt Constance," said Doctor Inness. "Great-aunt, to be exact. I thought that this would be a good place for you and Elizabeth to stay for a while, Gabrielle. Aunt Constance never uses this house, and whenever I come to Stepping-stone, I usually go straight to the inn. It never seemed worth while opening the house just for the weekend." He coughed and looked uneasy. "But maybe it wasn't such a good idea," he said, turning to Elizabeth. "When I told you about it, I thought it was just a joke. I never took her seriously."

"Don't start now," Elizabeth warned.

"Don't start what?" I said.

"Nothing," Elizabeth said. "It's really nothing."

"Like my forgetting?" I said. "I didn't forget, you know. I remember everything you tell me and you never told me—" I hesitated, took a deep breath and deliberately stessed the words —"that Mrs. What's-her-name was Doctor Inness's aunt. You never even discussed coming here with me You never asked me if I wanted to. You just announced it as something all settled and I'd like to know what you two are talking about."

"The coffee's getting cold," said Maggie, walking into the dining room. "I poured it and if you want to talk, it seems to me it's just as easy to talk sitting down."

"I'm not going anywhere," I said, leaning on my cane. "I'm not going into the kitchen. I'm not budging until you tell me what this is all about."

Elizabeth looked at Doctor Inness and she shrugged her shoulders as if she were an adult about to humor a recalcitrant child.

But I'm not a child, I thought, glaring at her.

"You tell her," said Elizabeth.

Doctor Inness put his hands in his pockets as if he didn't know what else he could do with them. "My aunt doesn't approve of your being here," he said. "At first she thought it was a good idea. She agreed with me when I said that the house had been closed long enough, and she was positive that because you were strangers there would be no danger for you here, but now she has changed her mind. That's why I came. To tell you she doesn't want you to have the house."

Alarice, I told myself, my heart suddenly pounding with excitement. The cane felt slippery in my hand. She knows about Alarice and she's afraid.

"Why?" I said innocently. I opened my eyes wide. "Why shouldn't we stay here? I like it here. Don't you like it here, Elizabeth?"

"It's all right, Gordon," she said. "Really it is. Maggie and I were here almost a week before Gabrielle arrived and everything was just fine. Nothing at all has happened that could possibly worry your aunt, and if anything did, we could always leave. Besides," said Elizabeth doubtfully, "I don't believe in such nonsense, do you?"

"Of course not," he said. "You don't think I would have let you come here if I thought there was anything wrong with this place, do you? It's just that it *is* her house and she's a very determined old lady and there's not much I can do about it."

"But something did happen," said Maggie, standing in the middle of the dining room as if she didn't know whether to go forward or back. "All the lights were burning last night. When I got up this morning, I found the lights on in every room."

"I did that," I said impatiently. "Really, Maggie, I *told* you I couldn't sleep and that I walked around the house and left the lights on. Don't make such a fuss about it."

"At first I believed you when you said you couldn't sleep, and then I remembered how you looked when I asked you about the lights, your face going all white and pinched. Walking around the house doesn't mean anything in itself, but you left the lights burning behind you because something scared you," said Maggie. "Otherwise you would have turned them off like any sensible person. Don't tell me."

"I'm not telling you anything except I'm starving," I said quickly. "I haven't had any breakfast and the coffee is getting cold, and I don't know about the rest of you, but *I'm* going to eat."

My cane led the way into the kitchen as if it were pulling me along and Doctor Inness and Elizabeth followed me. I sat down and Elizabeth sat next to me at the large, round maple table, the old, scarred table freshly polished by Maggie, a table made for laughter and talk and companionship, with no sharp points or edges anywhere to keep people apart. Elizabeth was so close to me that I could smell the scent she wore, that delicate, subtle fragrance of lilac she loved so much, and for the first time I felt that our roles were reversed. It had never occurred to me before that if I could leave Elizabeth, it was possible for her to leave me.

I watched Maggie scramble the eggs. "I'm hungry," I had said to her again, knowing that this was one plea she couldn't resist, and now I had to watch her move that horrible, loose substance around in the pan, waiting for it to solidify. I kept stirring my coffee until I saw Elizabeth clench her fists in irritation, and then I put down the spoon. Normally I would have kept on, letting the spoon scrape the bottom and clank against the side of the cup, turning the spoon around and around, feeling amused and detached and wondering just how long it would be before Elizabeth lost her temper. Right now I didn't want to do anything that would upset her, so I put the spoon in the saucer with a decisive little click.

"I don't see why we can't stay here," I said to Doctor Inness. "We will take very good care of your aunt's house if that's what she's worried about, won't we, Elizabeth?" I added virtuously.

"It's not that," Elizabeth said. Her coffee was untouched and her hands were clasped in front of her, resting on the edge of the table. "You know it's not that, Gabrielle. Why should Mrs. Bellingham feel this way about her own house? When I told you this place was haunted, I was only teasing you the way I thought Gordon was teasing me. But Maggie's right. There was no reason for you to leave every light burning downstairs and the one in your bedroom on all night, too. I've never known you to sleep with the light on before."

"I had a dream," I said truthfully. "It frightened me."

"So that you had to walk around the house?"

"Didn't you ever have a nightmare? Didn't you ever wake up feeling restless, knowing you couldn't go back to sleep right

34

away? What do you do anyway? Do you just turn your brain off at night when you go to sleep? No dreams for Elizabeth. I wouldn't put it past you," I said furiously. "You get into bed and you set the clock and then you set your brain and that's it for the night."

"It's that room you're in," said Elizabeth. "There's something about it." She bit her lip. "It feels damp and cold and I don't like it."

"We can fix it up," I said quickly, carelessly. "Curtains at the windows, and the bed needs a canopy on top. It looks so bare the way it is. I think we should get a white organdy canopy and a patchwork quilt, and we can put a red rug right in front of the fireplace."

"What fireplace?" said Elizabeth. She unclasped her hands and almost spilled her coffee. She steadied the cup. "There's no fireplace in that room. What are you talking about, Gabrielle?"

"That was part of my dream." I swallowed hard. "It was such a vivid dream that I even looked for the fireplace when I awoke."

"You dreamt about the room?"

"Just the fireplace," I said.

Be careful, I warned myself. Be very careful or they'll take you away from here.

"There's nothing wrong with dreaming about fireplaces," said Doctor Inness.

"It's lucky to dream about fire," said Maggie. "I remember my grandmother had a dream book. She said fire and water were lucky things to dream about. She used to make me tell her my dreams every morning and then she'd look them up in the book."

"What happened when you dreamt something that wasn't in the book?" said Doctor Inness.

Maggie sniffed. "I never had that kind of dream," she said, scraping the eggs onto a plate. "I was always respectable."

"Were you?" I teased. "Tell us, Maggie." I looked at Elizabeth, smiling at her, trying to distract her. "Have you ever heard the story of Maggie's life? Maggie believes in astrology, too, don't you, Maggie?"

"I just check on my horoscope once in a while," Maggie said apologetically. "After all, they wouldn't put it in the newspaper every day if there wasn't something to it, would they? Besides, it doesn't hurt to take precautions."

Elizabeth shook her head. "If Gordon's aunt thinks there's something here—"

"Stop it." I started to laugh. "You're supposed to be the sensible one in this family," I said. I could feel my mouth tighten as I remembered we weren't much of a family any more. No, I thought. No. Not now. Don't think about that now. "Look, Elizabeth," I said. "If I believed in ghosts and wee spirits and things that go bump in the night, no one would be a bit surprised. It's just the sort of thing I would do. I used to love to play with the Ouija board and I was always convinced its answers were true." I closed my eyes for a moment, remembering the smooth board under my fingers and my hands moving without any volition on my part, my hands following the pointer as the letters were spelled out one by one, my head bent over the Ouija board, knowing that there was magic and I was part of it. And Elizabeth sitting opposite me, our knees touching and the board resting on our knees.

"You're pushing," Elizabeth had complained. "I can feel you push it."

"I'm not," I defended myself. "Look, I'm barely touching it. My fingers are just resting on top of it. I'm no more pushing it than you are and you wouldn't push it, would you, Elizabeth? Go on—ask it a question."

"No," said Elizabeth. "I don't want to play with this any more. I don't like it. It's a stupid game. Do you know what makes it move, Gabrielle?"

"It's the mystic oracle," I chanted. "There are forces in the universe, tides and currents in the universe, that come to us when we call and the Ouija board knows all."

"It's your unconscious mind directing it," said Elizabeth.

"How can it do that?"

"I don't know, but it does."

"Then there are tides and currents and mysterious forces in

my unconscious mind and the Ouija board will spell them out for me."

"Please don't," Elizabeth said. "Why do you take this sort of thing seriously, Gabrielle?"

"Because it's to be taken seriously."

Now I opened my eyes and looked at Elizabeth. "I don't believe in Ouija boards any more," I said. "Why do you act as if *you* do? Don't you see how ridiculous this all is?"

"Gabrielle is right," Doctor Inness said. He reached into his pocket, took out a pipe and stared at it for a moment as if he had forgotten he held it in his hand. "But it isn't the actuality of any manifestation that is important. It is the belief in it. Aunt Constance can't live in this house. There's something about the atmosphere of the place that disturbs her. She has an obsession about it and she refuses to be more specific. I don't know what she imagines happens here, but whether it is all in her imagination or not is not the point. She *believes*. She is convinced there is something wrong with this house. She won't tell me what it is and she won't put the house up for sale. I have never asked her too many questions. She is a very lucid, very sane, very charming woman and if she has one eccentricity, I rather think she's entitled to it. And since she now regrets giving you the house and is making such an issue over it, I'm afraid I must respect her wishes."

"But if you stayed here for a few days," I said rapidly, "and if you saw and felt nothing wrong and told her so, wouldn't that be the best thing in the long run?" I picked up my fork. "I mean we could have the house and you could have the chance to convince her and then maybe she could come here again. It's such a beautiful place, and it's a shame she can't enjoy it and—" I touched Elizabeth's hand. "I want to stay here," I pleaded. "I think we could be happy here, Elizabeth."

"Oh, darling," said Elizabeth, capitulating. "You really do like it here, don't you?"

"Yes," I said. "I'm beginning to feel well again."

"I'm being so foolish," said Elizabeth. She turned to Doctor Inness. "Gordon, Gabrielle is right. Don't you see? It will end

37

up being the best thing for your aunt and it is a shame to leave now. Look at Gabrielle. She has color in her cheeks for the first time and she looks so—" She fumbled, searching for the right adjective.

"Alive?" I said gleefully.

Suddenly I felt hungry. Really hungry. I ate the eggs and they were solid and warm and soft and gold and white in my mouth and there were dust motes dancing in the air. Maggie now sat next to me at the table and the space between Doctor Inness and me was filled.

"It's not a bad idea," he agreed. He filled his pipe and lit it.

"But what about the lights?" Maggie said.

"Talk about obsessions," I said. "Maggie, what's the matter with you?"

"She explained all that. Gabrielle couldn't sleep," said Elizabeth gently. "Really, Maggie, she's right. You're making a fuss about nothing. It was natural for her to be restless, sleeping in a strange bed for the first time, in a strange house. The first night we were here I didn't sleep too well myself if you must know. In any case," Elizabeth added as if she were talking to herself, as if she had forgotten we were in the same room, "there are good reasons if neither Gabrielle nor I sleep well right now."

"You sleep well, don't you, Maggie?" I finished my coffee and held out my cup for more. "I think I'd like some toast," I said, "with lots of butter or maybe some honey. Do we have any honey, Maggie?" I could feel the hunger within me, the gnawing hunger lying coiled within me. Right now I was appeasing it with food, but later, I knew, it would demand other things from me, the mouth opening wide, the little teeth showing, the sharp, white teeth of my hunger waiting to devour all the good things I would feed it.

"It's the sea air," said Maggie, pleased. She beamed at me. "Talk about foolish," she told Elizabeth. "I'm getting to be an old fool. I've been in every corner of the house and I like it and it's about time I had some sense knocked into me."

"I can stay a few days," Doctor Inness said. "I don't see why not. There's another doctor who can cover for me at the office and there's nothing pressing at the moment. That is, if you can put me up."

"You know there are two empty bedrooms," Maggie said. "You can have your choice, Doctor Inness. There's the room across from mine that is right next to Elizabeth's, and then there's that lovely little room right off the kitchen. I could make that one very comfortable for you," she said, looking at him with her eyebrows drawn together.

Elizabeth laughed. "Maggie is telling you in her own way, Gordon, that she thinks it would be better if you slept downstairs. I forgot to warn you that Maggie lives by rigid rules. It was never my parents who waited up for me when I went on dates. It was Maggie and she wasn't too discreet about it either. Instead of staying in her own room and behaving like anyone would, reading or maybe lying awake and listening, she would plant herself right in the middle of the living-room couch, and no matter what time I came in, there was Maggie with her eyebrows pulled together just like they are now and a book open in her lap as if she was there just by accident, as if the living room was the only place in the house where she could read in peace."

Maggie put the toaster on the table with a thump. "Someone had to look after you. I remember what it was like with the phone always ringing and the boys underfoot all the time. One slice of bread or two? How much do you want, Gabrielle?"

How much do you want, Gabrielle? I mocked silently. How much do you want and how much can you take? There's the lovely Elizabeth, so beautiful, so charming, so talented, the lovely, compassionate, tender Elizabeth Thatcher, still unmarried at the age of twenty-four, and there is the very eligible Doctor Inness sitting right next to her, watching Maggie spoon out the honey.

But would Elizabeth marry a man whose eyes were hidden from the world? I wondered. I, for one, would have to see a man's eyes very clearly before I would marry him.

I looked at Doctor Inness intently. Maybe his eyes weren't

hidden from the world after all. Perhaps (and I almost gasped at the thought) they weren't even hidden from me. If that were so, why then couldn't I see them?

"What is it?" he said.

"It's your glasses. They always seem to reflect the light. I was just wondering what color your eyes were."

"Brown," he said.

He stood up and walked around the table. He tipped my head back, his hand firm under my chin.

I shivered. These were the same hands that had reached for Elizabeth, a man's hands holding a woman in passion, in tenderness, in warmth. Why did they change then when they touched me? The minute they touched my flesh, they became merely the appendages of some sterile, neuter creature, the hands nothing more than the hands of a doctor, immaculate, antiseptic and impersonal.

"Look at me," he said. "I want you to follow my finger."

"I can see it perfectly," I said with contempt.

"Is there anything wrong?" said Elizabeth, her voice rising slightly the way it always does when she is apprehensive.

"No, I don't think so," he said. "But it won't hurt to give Gabrielle a checkup. I left my bag at the inn."

"I don't need a checkup," I said. "I had enough of poking and prying at the hospital. You wouldn't have let me out of there if you didn't think I was perfectly healthy, would you?"

"It's just a precaution," he said.

I ate two slices of toast, dripping with honey, and finished my second cup of coffee, and then Doctor Inness said he was going back to the inn for his things.

"Come with us," Elizabeth said.

"I'm tired." I reached for my cane. I held it in my hand. I tapped on the floor with it as if the floor were a drum and my cane were a baton and I listened to the rhythm of the tapping cane and I watched Elizabeth.

"You can walk," she said. "You can walk without that thing."

"Of course I can," I agreed.

"Well, then—"

40

"But I do much better with it."

"Let her be," Maggie said. "Why are you always bothering her about the cane? I don't understand you, Elizabeth. If it makes her feel better to have it, let her have it. I saw how she could hardly get out of bed this morning, just dragging one leg after the other. She doesn't tell you how it is with her. She doesn't complain, but I saw it with my own eyes and I ought to know."

"But—" said Doctor Inness, looking puzzled.

"I want Gabrielle to rest," Maggie interrupted. "She was up half the night."

She wants Elizabeth to be alone with Doctor Inness, I thought. She wants me tucked away, out of sight, so that her precious Elizabeth can tilt her head back and smile at Doctor Inness.

"We won't be long, darling," said Elizabeth. She brushed my cheek with her lips. "Have a good nap."

"I will," I promised, "and don't hurry back. You don't have to worry about me," I said, watching them walk away, Elizabeth dripping honey.

Maggie cleared the table and I left the kitchen. I walked through the dining room, hearing once again that faint, musical tinkle of the chandelier as the crystal prisms swayed, and then I stood in the hall. I looked up the steps. I was as out of breath as if I had been running for a long time. With one hand on the banister and the other gripping the cane, I climbed the stairs. I paused on the third step for a moment as if it were some sort of talisman, and then, smiling, I almost ran the rest of the way, happy to be alone, glad to be left alone, eager to go back into Alarice's room once again.

�֍

I DON'T KNOW WHAT I THOUGHT I WOULD FIND BE-
hind that closed door. A shadow, perhaps, different from all other
shadows on earth, this one having no link to reality, a shadow
that simply existed, moving by itself, gathering substance as it
went. And if there was nothing in that room that didn't belong
to it, no shadow-shape of something intangible, then there
could be the mist again, white and cold, a cone of mist fighting
the warm sunlight that streamed through the windows.

I don't think I expected to find Alarice herself waiting for
me, with that yellow hair coiled high upon her head and those
slim fingers holding the long dress inches above the floor, because Alarice, young as I was young, wanted to be free to run.
And yet I was so sure I would find some trace of her, a subtle
change in the atmosphere that would separate this room from
the rest of the house, the imprint of Alarice lingering long after
she had gone. It was odd that Elizabeth had been the one to
sense it first, Elizabeth, restless, chilled and frowning. "Are you
sure you like this room?" she had said. "It feels damp and
cold." And I, totally without presentiment, feeling no warning
shiver, awakening, the dream within me as I awoke and the ice
solid all around me.

Now I felt eager and yet strangely calm as if this were a moment in time I had been searching for as long as I could remember. I don't know what I expected when I opened the door, but I certainly wasn't prepared to find the room dusted, tidied and empty of any presence but my own. There was the four-poster bed pushed against the wall, and I knew that Maggie had straightened the sheets and fluffed up the pillow before she had folded it, turning it into a small bolster. The blue bedspread was pulled smooth and the dark wood of the headboard and the long, carved posts gleamed because Maggie had polished it. There was the rocking chair in the corner and the dresser between the two windows. And then there was the unbroken, painted-white expanse of the far wall opposite the bed, surely too smooth to hide the rough, bricked-up, plastered outline of an old fireplace, the wall pristine like a sheet of white paper.

"White paper," Elizabeth would mutter, sitting in front of her typewriter. "I simply can't work on it."

"Why not?"

"Because to a writer it means something is finished."

Finished, I said to myself, looking at the empty wall. Why was the dresser placed so awkwardly between the two windows when there was a whole wall waiting to be used? The fireplace must have been in the very center, which was why the bed was pushed to one side, far from the heat of those leaping flames. Alarice, lying in bed, had leaned on her elbow, her hair tumbling forward so that she had to brush it back impatiently, Alarice curled up and warm under the patchwork quilt, with the crackling of the logs and the fire dance to make her sleepy.

"Alarice," I said out loud.

The room was very quiet. All along I had been conscious of the water running in the kitchen, the gurgling of the water rushing through the pipes and Maggie singing as she washed the dishes and now, suddenly, there were no house sounds at all.

I caught my breath. "Alarice?" I said again, but softly this time, and I shuddered even though I knew with a certainty that surprised me that Alarice would not appear.

Not now, I thought. Not like this. Not with me standing here alert, watching for her, waiting for her. Alarice would come with twilight, with darkness, with that drowsy moment just before sleep when the body is relaxed and all the defenses of mind and spirit are gone. Alarice would come like the beginning of a dream so that for a moment I would not recognize her, and when she came she would not be separate from me, she would not stand apart from me as mist or shadow or woman.

"This is my room," I whispered.

There was a faint sound behind me, the unmistakable click of the latch as the door closed. I turned around.

"Maggie?" I called.

I opened the door. There was no one there.

"I will remember," I said fiercely to the empty hall. "I will watch everything I do. I will listen very carefully when they speak to me and I will remember everything they say. If I leave a door open, I will remember, and if I close it behind me, I will remember that, too."

I shut the door again, firmly, decisively, leaning against it before I searched the room, not knowing what I was looking for and yet knowing I must look.

My clothes hung in the closet, the tweed coat, the wool slacks, the dresses and sweaters. "In case it turns cold," said Maggie, and there were bathing suits and cotton shifts. "Because we can still have warm weather," Elizabeth insisted.

I opened each dresser drawer and found my own things folded neatly, Maggie unpacking and putting everything away. There were handkerchiefs and scarfs in the top drawer and cleansing tissues and make-up and my comb and brush, the dresser top cleared because "I can't stand clutter," Maggie complained. There were underthings in the second drawer and the third was empty except for a large black Bible shoved way in the back.

Like a hotel room, I thought scornfully, not touching it. Salvation along with room service.

I left then, deliberately leaving the door open behind me. I even pushed it until it touched the wall.

"There," I said, giving it a little kick. "Let's see if I'm going

44

to forget now." I touched the knob, thinking illogically that perhaps I was wrong to leave it open. Perhaps if I shut it I could keep Alarice where she belonged. I shook my head. If anyone were to close that door right now, it would be Alarice, not I.

I crossed the hall to Elizabeth's room. Her door was wide open as if Elizabeth had nothing to hide, and there on the far wall was the fireplace, Alarice's fireplace, *my* fireplace with the white, carved mantel and the black fire screen and the heavy andirons. In front of it was the red rug, and if Elizabeth wanted to, she could lie in bed and watch the flames leap high.

I stood very still, my heart pounding. I hadn't been in the other bedrooms the night before. I had been much too tired for a tour of the house. Had Elizabeth told me about the fireplace? Was that why I had dreamt about it, the dream superimposing the reality of the actual fireplace on the blank wall of my room? Why couldn't I remember? Had I forgotten this the way I had evidently forgotten that Mrs. Bellingham was Doctor Inness's aunt?

I backed out of the room and bumped into Maggie.

"Oh!" Her hand covered her mouth. "Gabrielle, what are you doing? You gave me the fright of my life. I looked in your room to see if you were asleep and when I didn't find you there I couldn't imagine where you had gone to. I would have knocked," she said virtuously, "but I didn't want to wake you."

"What are you talking about?" I looked across the hall. The door to my room was as I had left it, wide open, pushed so far back that the knob touched the wall. I swallowed. "My door is open," I said. "You didn't have to knock, because my door is wide open."

"It was closed a few moments ago. I left it open just now when I saw you weren't there. What's the matter, Gabrielle? Don't you feel well? Of course you don't, you poor child. You have no right to be prowling around the house instead of lying down. You were up half the night and you need your rest. Now you just march yourself off to bed and I'll tuck you in."

"No," I said quickly. "I'm not tired. Honestly, Maggie, I feel just fine."

"Nonsense," she said, her fingers gripping my arm. "You just come along now. And what did you do with your cane?"

"I left it in Alarice's room."

"Alarice?" She stared at me.

I bit my lip. "My room," I said. "I meant my room, Maggie. I don't know why I said Alarice. I really don't."

"It's because you were reading that Bible," said Maggie.

"The one in the drawer?"

"What other Bible is there in your room? Yes, the one in the bottom drawer. That's the name written on the cover. Alarice Courtney Lysander. Now just don't stand there." She drew back the blue bedspread. "I want you to get undressed and go right to bed. That's the only way to take a nap. Your poor mother (may she rest in peace) used to lie on top of the bed when she napped in the afternoon, but I could never see that myself. When I want a good sleep I get right into bed. Gabrielle, will you stop looking at me like that? What's the matter now?"

"That quilt," I said, pointing. "Where did you get it?"

"I found it when Elizabeth and I first came. I was surprised to see it, I can tell you that. We had to bring all our linens and there was this in the bottom drawer wrapped around that Bible. I would have put it on your bed last night, but it was much too hot for anything so warm and besides I had a terrible time drying it. When I think we left a house that had a washer and a dryer for this place I could really throw up my hands. All they have down in that basement is some laundry tubs, so I had to hand-wash it. But even if I had a machine," she added thoughtfully, "I'm not so sure I would have used it. It's really very old and all hand-stitched, I should imagine."

"It's beautiful," I said. I walked over to the bed and touched the quilt. It was soft and light and warm and I knew now that I had found it I would never be cold again.

I heard the click as the door shut. I looked at Maggie, but she hadn't noticed. Alarice, I thought. I know you're here. I wasn't frightened. I felt strangely elated.

"Now get into bed," Maggie said. She crossed the room and stared at the door, puzzled. "Could have sworn I left it open," she muttered. She turned. "I don't want you wandering around. You need your rest."

"Yes, Maggie," I said meekly.

She sniffed. " 'Yes, Maggie, no, Maggie' as sweet as you please, but don't think I don't know what happens the minute my back is turned." The door closed behind her.

I sat down on the bed. My fingers traced the pattern of the quilt. There was the square of red so like blood and there was the white that formed the border. The stitches were small and even. I could see Alarice so clearly with her head bent and that yellow hair streaming down her back, Alarice, absorbed, intent, the needle flashing and next to her the sharp-pointed scissors that could slash and stab and cut.

Her sister, I thought.

I walked across the room and opened the bottom drawer of the dresser. I picked up the Bible and held it in my hands for a moment, not opening it, just holding it lightly. Then I sat down in the rocking chair and the book was open in my lap. And there on the inside of the cover was her name.

"I'm listening," I said softly. "Do you hear me, Alarice? If you want to tell me something, I'm listening."

I held myself rigid, but the rocking chair creaked as if I had moved.

"Turn the pages," I said. "If you can close a door, you can turn the pages of a book. Show me that you are here."

There was the sound of the car turning into the driveway and then the slam of a door. I heard Elizabeth laugh.

"Now," I said desperately, knowing there wasn't much time left. How could I concentrate on what had to be done with Elizabeth and Doctor Inness in the house? Without hearing them, without seeing them, I knew exactly what was going on downstairs.

They stood in the front hall. He touched her hand.

"No," Elizabeth said coyly. "Maggie's coming and Gabrielle is upstairs."

"What difference does it make?"

"Gordon, please—" She raised her voice. "We're here, Maggie."

"I can see you're back," said Maggie. "You don't have to shout. I can see for myself. You can unpack if you like, Doctor Inness. I got your room ready."

"Is Gabrielle still asleep?" said Elizabeth. Her hair lay damp on her forehead and her mouth was smudged and soft.

"Still asleep? What do you mean, still asleep?" said Maggie indignantly. "Do be quiet. I just got that child off to bed. If you ask me, she's overtired. Just out of the hospital and then that long trip and no sleep last night. It's enough to upset a well person."

"Maybe I'll just see how she is," said Doctor Inness, looking worried.

"Why not let her rest?" said Elizabeth quickly, jealously. "It's the best thing for her."

"Elizabeth's right," said Maggie. "You can see her later. I won't have her disturbed now."

"Now," I said again.

My mind was a room and I drew the blinds until it was dark and still, the room of my mind self-contained and quiet. Like a door closing, I thought, pleased.

I willed Alarice to come. I pleaded with her, but the pages remained motionless and the Bible was heavy on my lap. I rubbed my bare arms. It was so cold. Why was I sitting there shivering in the corner when I could lie down? Maggie was right. I was tired.

I stumbled toward the bed. How soft the quilt was! I was warm now that my hands and my arms were tucked neatly inside it, and nothing could touch me while I slept. With the quilt pulled up to my chin I was covered and I was safe.

That was the way I always slept, with my hair streaming over the pillow. My sister, Consuela, slept with her arms flung over her head, her palms turned outward, the fingers slightly curved. Consuela's hair was dark, and because she was jealous of me, because she wanted Mama to love her, she used to braid it each night the way Mama did. I never watched Consuela braid her hair, but I watched Mama. While Papa sat in the back parlor going over his papers, I would go into Mama's room. I would sit at the foot of her bed and see the way her fingers moved through the long strands and the way she smiled. Mama and Consuela slept with their hair wound tight, but I didn't have to. I could do as I pleased and know that Mama loved me anyway.

Sometimes she scolded me. "How can you sleep like that, Alarice? You look so untidy."

"I like the tangles," I said. "I like the knots. I like to brush my hair in the morning and I like to feel it loose and free at night."

I don't know how Papa felt about Consuela or, for that matter, how he felt about any of us. I don't remember Papa ever kissing me, even though I sat on his lap and put my arms around his neck.

"I'm busy," Papa said.

"But I love you."

"I'm glad you do."

"Do you love me?"

"Alarice—"

"All right." I touched his cheek with my lips. "If that's the way you want it," I said, rubbing my mouth right across his jaw. Although Papa was clean-shaven, each night he had the beginning of a beard and I liked the feel of it.

"Janet," Papa shouted. "Get this child away from me."

"I'm not a child," I said. "I'm nineteen."

"Then you're grown-up enough to know when you're not wanted."

When I was not wanted. What did he mean by that? Did he resent having two daughters?

"He should have had sons," I told Mama. "Then he wouldn't have to worry about showing any affection."

She was in the kitchen rolling pie dough. She sprinkled flour and shrugged. "He's just not demonstrative," she said. "That doesn't mean he doesn't love, Alarice. He just can't show it as easily as you do."

"Does he show it to you?"

"The pie plates are in the cupboard," she said. "On the top shelf."

49

"You're changing the subject," I said.

"And you're prying into places where you're not wanted," she said pleasantly.

Not wanted!

When I was very small, Mama kept my door open at night. We pretended it was in case I needed her, but we both knew I was afraid of the dark. Once, I awoke and saw something very hairy sitting at the foot of the bed looking at me. I screamed and Mama came, and when I couldn't stop crying, she took me back to her bedroom.

"I'll have none of that," Papa said.

"She's frightened," Mama said, holding my hand.

"I'll be very quiet," I promised. The floor was cold and I rubbed the back of one bare foot against the other. "I'll not bother you, Papa, honestly, I won't. If you let me stay, I'll be very good. I'll just get into your bed and lie between you and go right to sleep."

"No."

Mama sighed and made me go back to my own room. In the flickering light of the gas fixture in the hall, I could see that the thing hadn't gone away. It had hidden when Mama had come, but the moment she shut her door, it was there, standing in the corner, grinning at me.

I ran across the hall and pushed open their door. Mama was lying across the bed and I thought she had hurt herself because she was moaning and Papa was bending over her. When he saw me, he said in a rage, "Damn you, Alarice! You get the hell out of here and don't come back!"

When I got into my own bed again, I pulled the bedclothes over my head. I kept a small space open so I could breathe and I lay very still. If I didn't make any noise, it wouldn't be able to find me. There was a scraping sound and I knew it was sidling across the floor.

"Go away," I whispered. "Please go away."

"What are you afraid of?" it said, and then I heard Consuela laugh.

I sat up in bed.

"You should see yourself," she said, doubling up.

"What are you doing here?"

"You made enough noise to wake the dead." She sat at the foot of the bed in the exact spot where the thing had been and said in a conversational tone, "Do you think we can wake the dead?"

"Damn you, Consuela," I screamed. "You get the hell out of here and don't come back!"

I reached for her, my fingers like claws, and she ran, those neat, tidy braids bobbing. I slammed the door behind her and locked it.

"Alarice," Mama called.

"What's going on here?" Papa shouted.

"Go away," I said, only this time I wasn't pleading.

Mama turned the knob, but she couldn't get in. None of them could get in. I had locked them all out. I turned around and faced the dark. I stared into the dark and I heard them call my name and I walked through the dark with my hands outstretched. I was blind in the dark. I couldn't see the hairy thing or the outline of my bed, but it didn't matter. I wasn't afraid any more.

"I'm not afraid any more," I said, and the sound of my own voice woke me.

I was warm and comfortable with the soft quilt next to my chin and my head placed just so on the pillow and the light fading because it was twilight now. I yawned and stretched. I flung back the quilt and ran across the room, moving lightly, gracefully, because I was young and supple and didn't need a cane.

My clothes hung in the closet, all in a neat row—the summer shifts and the warm slacks and the sweaters and the skirts—and none of them would do. I would like to wear a long dress tonight. I would like to go downstairs in a long, sweeping dress and I would hold it high, high enough so that my ankles showed as I ran down the stairs in my long dress. But all my dresses were short and ugly, lopped off above the knees as though they had been slashed by sharp scissors, and I had to compromise, wearing my blue robe, the one Elizabeth had given me when I was in the hospital. "So you'll look pretty," she had said.

Swish, swirl, silky blue robe and the Bible lying open upon my dresser, the pages turning faster and faster. I stood very still for a moment, hearing the rustle of my robe and the rustle of the turning pages and then, when the room was quiet, when neither the pages nor I moved again, I saw the marked passage, the message underlined just for me.

Surely there is a vein for the silver, and a place for gold where they fine it.

Iron is taken out of the earth, and brass is molten out of the stone.

He setteth an end to darkness, and searcheth out all perfection: the stones of darkness, and the shadow of death.

The flood breaketh out from the inhabitant; even the waters forgotten of the foot: they are dried up, they are gone away from men.

As for the earth, out of it cometh bread: and under it is turned up as it were fire.

The stones of it are the place of sapphires: and it hath dust of gold.

Standing there I could see it. Without moving I walked through the dust of gold, and I saw the stones piled high all around me, the walls, the ceiling, the floor blue and green and blue-green, the sapphires sparkling and rainbowing in this place where there was no light, the fire of the stones lighting the darkness, the fire of the stones blazing, and I, beholding them, I, holding them burning in my hands.

"The place of sapphires," I said softly. "Is that where you are?" And then I left the room, deliberately leaving the door open behind me.

I could hear their voices, Elizabeth and Doctor Inness and Maggie talking and laughing downstairs, but I stood on the landing waiting patiently until I heard the door of Alarice's room close behind me.

✷

NONE OF THEM KNEW SHE WAS THERE. NOT DOCTOR Inness, who unpacked his things and smoked his pipe and walked all around the house as if he owned it, and not Maggie, who had taken the spider webs from the ceilings and the dust from the furniture and the floors, and not even Elizabeth, who can be very clever at times. I came down the steps in my blue robe and I knew that not one of them was aware of Alarice.

They were in the kitchen. Elizabeth, of course, was helping Maggie make dinner.

"Why don't you ever help me, Gabrielle?" my mother always complained. "If you'd only be like Elizabeth—take an interest in things."

"You have Maggie, too," I said. "Just how many little helpers do you need?"

My mother would have loved two fair daughters, dimpled, smiling and sweet, two daughters singing in the kitchen, but she had to settle for one. She had to be content with Elizabeth, whose softness and indecision had killed her. She had to be satisfied with Elizabeth, who sang and smiled and possessed my fireplace.

Unless—

I tiptoed across the dining-room floor and the unlit chandelier was quiet, the prisms hanging straight and still. There was a fireplace in the front parlor, and therefore it was logical that Elizabeth's room, which was directly above, should have one, too. Alarice's room—my room—was over the dining room. Tomorrow I would check the outside of the house for another chimney, but now it was getting dark, and if there had been a fireplace in the dining room, it would be behind the large server that blocked the wall.

"What are you doing?" said Elizabeth, and she turned on the light.

I blinked. "Looking for a fireplace."

"A fireplace? What makes you think—?" She frowned. "Is it the one you dreamt about?"

"What do you mean?"

"This morning you said you dreamt about a fireplace."

"Did I?" I said indifferently.

She untied her apron, took it off, looked at it, and then put it on again.

"Perhaps you've forgotten," she said. She walked toward me and the chandelier tinkled.

"I have forgotten nothing," I said.

"Gabrielle." She bit her lip. "It doesn't matter," she said. "It's so unimportant. Why should we argue about a dream?" She smiled at me and the dimple showed as if I had poked a hole in her cheek. "You were right not to get dressed. You look so rested, darling. Did you sleep well?"

"How can I look rested if I didn't sleep well?" I said.

I walked into the kitchen and Maggie turned around. "You don't have your cane," she said. "You're walking without your cane."

"I said she didn't need it." Elizabeth was triumphant. "I knew if she just tried—"

"Well, I did try," I said, "and my leg hurts."

"Gordon says—"

"I don't care what Doctor Inness says." I leaned on the table and then sat down very slowly, trying not to let my weight rest on my leg. "He doesn't know how I feel. He doesn't know a thing."

"Be quiet," said Elizabeth. I saw her glance toward the small hall and I knew Doctor Inness must be in his room.

"I'm no longer Doctor Inness's patient," I said. "He discharged me from the hospital, remember? Or perhaps you're the one who forgets, Elizabeth."

"There's no need to quarrel," said Maggie. "I have a good dinner prepared and I want it eaten. I remember when I was little. Every night at the table my father would start an argument. It got so I used to dread eating. I'd just sit there and listen to them fight and my stomach would hurt with it. One night he even pulled the tablecloth off the table—dishes and all."

"He did?" I started to laugh. "Oh, Maggie, that's wonderful. What a character he must have been. I'd have loved him."

"I bet you would," said Maggie grimly. "But he was no fun to live with, and I made up my mind that, no matter what, for the rest of my life I'd not eat food while anyone—I don't care who—" she glared at me—"quarrels."

"Sugar on the food," I said. "Sprinkle sugar on everything, Maggie. No bitter herbs for us."

"Sounds delicious," said Doctor Inness lightly. I looked up. I hadn't heard him come into the room. "You look very festive tonight, Gabrielle."

"It's my hospital robe," I said. "The one I didn't wear while I was there. Elizabeth gave it to me. You see, there are some things I remember perfectly, Elizabeth."

"Of course you do," she agreed.

"Then why do you tell me I forget?"

"How are the eyes?" Doctor Inness said. He tilted my head back, and again I felt those impersonal fingers touch me.

"Mine are fine," I said dryly. "It's yours that bother me."

"How can they bother you if you can't see them, Gabrielle?"

"It's always the things you can't see that are important."

"I don't understand."

"The sounds you can't hear, the sights you can't see, the things you can't touch," I chanted.

55

"Dinner is ready," said Maggie, and I was glad she had interrupted me. I was being careless and I knew it and I wanted someone to stop me.

I was very charming while we had dinner. I joined in the conversation and I talked about everything that didn't matter as if it were very important, and after dinner I even offered to help Maggie with the dishes.

"It's not the lack of a dishwasher," she muttered, "it's not having a washing machine. How can anyone live without a washing machine?"

"Alarice did," I said.

"Alarice?" Doctor Inness pushed his chair back from the table. "What do you know of Alarice?"

"Her name is in the Bible upstairs," I said quickly.

"She was my grandmother," he said. "I never knew her. She died when my mother was born. She was my Great-aunt Constance's sister."

"Alarice's sister was Consuela," I said.

He stood over me and I had to look up to see him. His eyes were hidden, of course, but I could see how his lips had thinned.

"How do you know the name Consuela? How can you possibly know it?"

"Don't shout," I said. "My head aches when you shout."

"I'm not shouting, Gabrielle. But I never mentioned Consuela to you. How could you know about her?"

"I don't know," I said sullenly. "I just do."

"Impossible," he said.

"It must have slipped out when you weren't aware of it, Gordon," said Elizabeth. "Sometimes that happens."

"No," he said.

"Maybe her name is in that Bible, too," said Maggie helpfully. "Maybe that's where Gabrielle saw it. I know Alarice's name is in there. I saw it myself. I remember looking at it and thinking what pretty handwriting she had."

"Constance Suellen," he said. "If her name is in the Bible, that's the way it would be written. Only my grandmother—only Alarice—called her Consuela. No one has called Aunt Constance that since my grandmother died. She hated the name."

"She hated your grandmother, too." I felt excited. "And Alarice hated her. That's why Consuela can't live in this house."

"That could explain it," Elizabeth said. "That could be the answer, Gordon. The atmosphere your aunt feels is only the memory of hate."

"They were sisters and they hated each other," I said loudly. "Can you imagine such a thing?" I looked at Elizabeth and smiled. "Two sisters hating each other?"

"Stop it," she said.

"Stop what?"

"Stop talking like that," said Elizabeth, looking very pale.

"It was just a question," I said. "I don't see what you're making such a fuss about. I was only asking—"

"If you'd all get out of the kitchen, maybe I could do the dishes," said Maggie. "I don't need any help. I can do them by myself. All I need is a little peace of mind. I'm getting older and if I don't find some peace of mind in my old age, when am I going to get it? I don't know how many years I have left. It's a day-by-day thing right now as far as I'm concerned, and at least let my last days on this earth be pleasant." She took out her handkerchief and blew her nose.

"Oh," said Elizabeth, putting her arms around Maggie, "please don't."

"She just wants sympathy," I said with contempt. "She just wants you to pay attention to her."

"That's enough," said Elizabeth sharply.

"Do you think you're immortal?" I said to Maggie. "You're going to die, you know. You're going to die and I'm going to die and Elizabeth is going to die and even Doctor Inness over there is going to die. All his pills and magic potions won't help him a bit."

Maggie wiped her eyes. "She looks feverish. Look how flushed she is. That child wouldn't act like this if she didn't have a temperature."

"I'm not a child and I'm fine," I said scornfully. "I just don't like it when you talk that way, Maggie. I hate it when you

57

whine. We're all going to die, but we don't have to keep harping on it. We don't have to think about it if we don't want to, and what's more," I added softly, "we don't have to be afraid of it."

"You're not afraid?" Doctor Inness said.

"Not any more."

"Why not?"

"Because it doesn't mean oblivion, that's why. Because something—some part of us—goes on."

"You could come to church with me on Sunday," said Maggie eagerly.

I laughed. "You think I've found religion, Maggie? You think I'm going to sit there and follow the ritual of a prayer book, kneel when I'm supposed to and rise when I'm supposed to? Is that what you think?"

"But you said you used to be afraid," Maggie said.

"That has nothing to do with it," I said impatiently. "Sure, I used to be afraid. I used to wake up in the middle of the night and stare into the dark and shake because I was so afraid. But that was when I was in the hospital. That was when I'd be lying on my back as if I were in a coffin. That was when I'd think of my parents and how they died."

"How did they die?" Doctor Inness asked.

"Gordon," said Elizabeth.

He turned around.

"No more," Elizabeth said. She moved away from Maggie and touched my shoulder. "I don't want any more of this. Maggie's right. Gabrielle should be taken care of—not badgered."

"He's not badgering me," I said. "He asked a sensible question, provided, of course, he didn't know the answer." I smiled. "I thought you knew the answer, Doctor Inness, but I was wrong. My memory isn't as perfect as it used to be. At one time I had an excellent memory. Almost total recall, but now Elizabeth keeps telling me I forget things. But this is one thing I haven't forgotten. I know exactly how my parents died."

"Let's go inside," said Elizabeth. "We can sit in the front parlor and maybe we can have a fire in the fireplace. I love a fire, don't you, Gordon? It's much cooler tonight and I know Maggie wants to clean up and—"

"In an automobile accident," I said. "That's how they died. We were driving along and it was a beautiful day and one minute everything was all right and the next everything and everyone was smashed to bits. Everyone except Elizabeth. Elizabeth didn't get a scratch. Which is really amazing when you start thinking about it."

Her fingers tightened, clutching my arm, and I tried to move away from her.

"But it's better not to think about it," I said. "There are some things that don't bear thinking about, isn't that true, Elizabeth?"

"Yes, darling, that's true."

"I don't know what you're talking about," said Maggie. She crumpled the handkerchief and stuffed it into her apron pocket. "How could Elizabeth—"

"Maggie," Elizabeth shouted, "do be quiet, please! What's wrong with all of you?"

"I don't know what's wrong with the rest of you," Maggie sniffed, "but there's nothing wrong with me. I can tell you that. And now if you'll excuse me, I'm going to do the dishes." She marched over to the sink and turned on the water full force.

"Come," said Elizabeth, holding out her hand to me. "Gabrielle, please come inside. Gordon, do you think you can find some driftwood? I would love a fire. And some music, too. Gabrielle, darling, I'm sure the piano is dreadfully out of tune, although Gordon's aunt did have people coming in and taking care of the house, but, even so, perhaps you would play for us. Firelight and music," said Elizabeth, pulling at me. "Let's have a happy evening."

"Maggie said, 'How could Elizabeth,' and then she stopped only because you made her. Why did you stop Maggie? What was she trying to say?"

"Nothing really," said Elizabeth. "I just didn't want to think about the accident. It's as simple as that."

"Is it?" I swallowed. "Why didn't you get hurt then?"

"You don't remember?"

"There you go again," I raged. "Of course I remember! I remember it perfectly. I can close my eyes and see the whole thing." I caught my breath. How could I accuse her now, when I had protected her for so long? "Maybe you're right," I said. "Maybe it's better if we don't think about it."

"Let's go inside," Elizabeth pleaded. "It's so noisy in here. With Maggie running the water and clattering the dishes like that, it's impossible for us to talk."

"And we'll talk in the parlor?" I said. "We'll sit in the parlor and have a fire and put our feet up and talk happily all evening?"

"I'll see if I can find some wood," said Doctor Inness. "That is"—and he looked at Elizabeth—"if you think you don't need me."

"No," said Elizabeth. "It's all right. Really it is, Gordon."

"He's only good at patching up the flesh," I said. "When it comes to the psyche, he just doesn't have the tools, do you, Doctor Inness?"

"I'm not a psychiatrist, if that's what you mean."

"I'm talking about the soul," I said, "not the mind."

"I know what you're talking about," he said quietly. "Look, Elizabeth, I think—"

"Please, Gordon."

The front door closed behind him.

"Gabrielle," said Elizabeth.

"I'm coming," I said sullenly.

I walked ahead of her, exaggerating the limp until we reached the hall, and then I turned around and faced her.

"My leg aches," I said pitifully.

She sighed, resigned. "Where's your cane?"

I opened the front door. I could see the receding, bobbing beam of Doctor Inness's flashlight. The air was clean and sweet and smelled of salt. I closed the door and leaned against it. "I left it in Alar—in my room," I said.

I turned on the hall light and looked up the stairs. The door to Alarice's room was closed. Is she there now? I thought. Is she leaning on that door as I lean on this one, the two of us separated by time and our places in it, the two of us separated and yet so close? Is she there waiting for me? "Would you get my cane for me, Elizabeth?" I asked softly. "I'm so tired."

"Of course," said Elizabeth eagerly. She ran up the stairs. She opened the door to Alarice's room and I waited, listening, until I heard the door close again behind her.

She is wondering what's wrong, I thought. Elizabeth is standing there looking for my cane and wondering what stray breeze has slammed the door, and then she will see that the window is closed, too, and even with the window closed, the pages of the Bible will slowly turn. Elizabeth won't wait for any message. She won't wait for the pages to stop turning. She will run out of the room, her flesh prickling, and I'll laugh and laugh, knowing that even if she had waited, even if she had the courage to wait, there would be no message for her.

Maggie turned off the water in the kitchen. The chandelier tinkled as if someone had walked across the dining-room floor, but I knew it was because Elizabeth was walking above it; the ceiling of the dining room was the floor of my room. And then the door to Alarice's room opened again and Elizabeth stood on the landing. I saw her lips move. I knew she was speaking, but I couldn't understand a word she was saying.

"I can't hear you," I said.

Her lips moved again and she leaned over the banister. I saw the door to Alarice's room close, but there was no sound.

"I can't hear," I said again, my mouth forming the words, my tongue wrapping itself around the silent, spoken words. "Elizabeth, I can't hear a thing."

I could feel the scream like a tangible thing, the scream hard and painful deep in my throat, but the sound of it was lost in a barrier I couldn't see. And yet it was there. I knew it was there just the way I knew I stood in the hall, just the way I knew that Elizabeth was talking to me. I could see and touch and feel in a world without sound, but if I cried out in pain, who could hear me when I couldn't hear myself?

I moved toward Elizabeth, my arms outstretched. She started down the stairs toward me, but I couldn't hear her footsteps.

"Help me," I cried loudly, soundlessly, and I could feel the tears on my cheeks.

61

There were hands firm on my shoulders and I was spun around. It was Doctor Inness.

"It's all right, Gabrielle," he said. His voice was deep and warm and sure, and it cut through the invisible barrier as if it didn't exist. Everything became very sharp and very clear. I could see the way the light was reflected in the paneling, the light no longer dim, no longer drowning in the dark wood but sparkling as if in a mirror. I could see the strong, clean line of his jaw. I looked at him intently and there behind the glasses were his eyes, brown like the mahogany paneling, deep and warm and sure like his voice, and the light was in them, too, intensified, heightened, so that I could see myself at last in Gordon's eyes.

ELIZABETH HAD FELT IT, TOO. THERE HAD BEEN THAT barrier blocking the steps, and she had brushed against it as I had brushed against it, our words lost in the heavy, dead silence, and I knew as I watched her come toward me that neither of us would ever be the same.

"What is it?" she said. "What is wrong?"

"I don't know," Gordon said. He still had his arm around me and I leaned against him. "I think something frightened Gabrielle."

Not just Gabrielle, I thought shrewdly, watching her.

"I can't imagine what it could be," said Elizabeth.

She was very pale. If I slapped her, my fingers would leave red welts across her cheek.

I sighed. "It was nothing," I told Gordon. "I've been walking around without my cane all evening, and I guess standing here and waiting for Elizabeth to get it was just too much for me. I'm tired."

I swayed and his fingers tightened.

"I couldn't find the cane," Elizabeth said defensively. "I looked all over the room and I couldn't find it anywhere."

"I left it behind the door," I said.

"Oh, that reminds me, Gordon," Elizabeth said. "There's something wrong with the door to Gabrielle's room. It keeps swinging shut."

"I'll check it tomorrow," Gordon said. "Meanwhile I think Gabrielle ought to go to bed."

"I don't think I can climb the stairs," I said wearily. I glanced at him sideways. "I really don't think I can manage alone, Gordon."

"Maybe you ought to change rooms," Elizabeth said quickly. "You could take Gordon's and he could have yours and then there wouldn't be the problem of the stairs for you."

"No," I said. "I like my room."

"But that isn't the point."

"That's where you're wrong," I said sweetly. "That's exactly the point."

"There's no problem, Gabrielle," Gordon said, lifting me high in his arms. "This should do it."

I looked at Elizabeth and tried not to smile. It was just as if I had slapped her. There were two round red spots on her cheeks.

I put my head on Gordon's shoulder. He smelled of tobacco and salt air and soap. "So good," I murmured.

"What did you say?" He set me down in front of the closed door of my bedroom.

"I was thanking you," I said. "Gordon, why did I spend all these months hating you?"

"Perhaps because you were in pain. Does this mean you don't hate me any more, Gabrielle?"

"You know I don't," I said softly. "Did I tell you I can even see your eyes?"

"I imagine you've seen them all along," he said quietly.

I shook my head. "I don't care what eye tests you've given me. I really couldn't see them. I don't know why. I could see your glasses but nothing beyond that. Then when I was so frightened and you came to me in the hall, I suddenly could see them so clearly."

64

"Frightened? But you said you were tired."

"I meant tired. Did I say I was frightened? How silly of me."

"Look," he said, his voice tight, "that's enough." He took a step toward me.

A few moments ago I had been lying helpless and soft in his arms. He had carried me up the stairs and when he had looked at me it was in a new way, the way I had seen him look at Elizabeth. Now he was angry.

"All right," I said rapidly. "I might as well admit it. I was frightened. I didn't want to say anything in front of Elizabeth. I didn't want to upset her." I touched his arm. "Please understand, Gordon. Elizabeth's older than I, but in some ways she's really so much younger, and she might want to leave here. If I tell you, will you promise we can stay?"

"I'm not promising anything," he said grimly. "What was it?"

I shrugged. "I don't know. There was something on the stairs. It was like a wall. I couldn't see it and I couldn't touch it. I just knew it was there. I could feel it. It was outside of me and yet it was inside of me, too."

"You could feel it and Elizabeth couldn't?"

"I don't know." I shrugged. "I think some people are more sensitive, more perceptive, than others, don't you? Elizabeth was much too calm. If she had felt it, wouldn't she have said something about it? I don't think she's trying to protect me, too, do you? Gordon, please don't tell her."

"This damn house," he said. "I never should have let you come here."

"We had to come," I said. "We couldn't go back home, and there was just no other place for us to go. Don't be sorry we're here. It was kind of you to let us come."

I opened the door and he followed me into the room. I could see him shiver. "It's cold."

"There should be a fireplace," I said. "Then I could have a fire."

"The fireplace of your dreams?"

"They're the best kind. You know that. A dream fireplace always burns brightly and never needs fresh logs and all the smoke goes up the chimney where it belongs."

"Gabrielle." He smiled at me. He took off his glasses and rubbed the side of his nose. "Why don't you sleep with Elizabeth tonight?" he said thoughtfully. "There's a real fireplace in her room."

"That won't make any difference," I said. "It won't be any warmer in here tomorrow, and I'm not going to leave this room, Gordon. It's like this always and you just have to get used to it. It's the same no matter what the temperature is outside, no matter what the rest of the house is like. It's the same in the morning and in the afternoon and in the evening and in the nighttime. It's always cold and it doesn't bother me a bit. In the beginning it did, but I'm used to it now." I took a deep breath. "This was Alarice's room, you know."

"My grandmother," he said.

He had his back to the door, and, fascinated, I watched as it slowly, silently swung shut.

"Why is your Aunt Constance afraid to come here?" I said loudly, deliberately.

He stared at me. "I didn't say she was afraid."

"Didn't you?"

"No," he said. "She's not afraid. She's just not comfortable here. Maybe the house has unpleasant memories for her. Anything else is nonsense. There was nothing on the stairs, Gabrielle, and this room is cold because it isn't insulated properly."

"Then why did you say, 'This damn house'?"

"Because I can't stand the waste of owning a house and never living in it."

"She can't live in it and she can't rent it and she can't sell it and I don't understand what made her let us have it."

"It's been years," he said. "So many years. I guess she was hoping you'd find nothing here. I guess she was hoping that it was all her imagination."

"And it isn't," I said. "You know it isn't. She's afraid." I looked at him. "And you are, too," I said, amazed.

"It's a throwback," he said uncomfortably. "Not very scientific, I admit that. There's something atavistic in all of us. I've seen people die. I've performed autopsies and I know what lies there is nothing but inert, lifeless flesh. It's the question that haunts all of us. Is there something else? Something more?"

"And if there is," I said, suddenly elated. "If it's in this house, in this very room, why should we be afraid? Why—if the answer is right here—why shouldn't we look for it? If there is a spirit or a soul or whatever you want to call it, then it wouldn't matter how or when we die. Everything would make sense, don't you see? Why shouldn't we welcome it?"

"Because I don't think the answer is here," he said slowly. "I think that if there *is* something here, it's—" He searched for the words, jamming his hands in his pockets and pacing up and down. "Like an echo," he muttered, "or the heavy, oppressive atmosphere you get right before a thunderstorm when you are sure you can almost touch the air. It's a vibration, perhaps—a lingering vibration of something that has happened before this, but it can't affect us now. It has nothing to do with here and now."

"Then how did I know about Consuela?" I said recklessly, triumphantly. "You said only Alarice called your Aunt Constance that. How did I know?"

I looked at him and I sat down at the edge of the bed. I had made a mistake. As usual I hadn't known when to stop. "Bite your tongue," Maggie used to say when I was a child. "Don't you know when to leave well enough alone?"

"I don't know how you could have known," he said, troubled, "but I do know one thing, Gabrielle. Tomorrow I'm going to take you and Elizabeth out of here."

"I wanted to be honest with you," I said with contempt. "I could have lied. Why can't you be consistent? One minute you call it nonsense and the next you admit that it—whatever it is—exists."

"This is the sort of situation that doesn't call for consistency," he said quietly, "and I'd rather you didn't sleep in here tonight."

"Nothing will hurt me," I said flatly.

"You seem very sure."

"How can a vibration hurt me? How can an echo do any harm?" I said softly, persuasively. "Don't you see, Gordon? If we leave here now, you're only admitting that your aunt was right all these years." I stood up. "The great Doctor Inness," I mocked. "Did you hear about Doctor Inness, the man of science, the rational, intelligent Doctor Inness, who has examined every inch of the human body without ever discovering the existence of the soul? Why Doctor Inness now believes in the supernatural and runs as fast as he can away from a house he calls haunted."

He raised his eyebrows. "It won't work," he said. "I can see right through you."

"That's funny." I began to laugh. "Don't you see how funny that is? That makes me the ghost."

"Maybe you are," he said. "I wouldn't put it past you, Gabrielle."

There was a knock on the door.

Elizabeth, I thought.

I walked over to him. I stood very close to him and tilted my head back invitingly. "What wouldn't you put past me, Gordon?"

He frowned. "A good haunting," he said.

I smiled. "Come in," I called, and then, timing it, I stepped back just as Elizabeth opened the door.

"Oh," I said, confused. Embarrassed, shy, I put my hands against my cheeks, telling Elizabeth without words that her entrance had caused Gordon and me to separate, telling Elizabeth with every gesture that she was interrupting us.

"I didn't know it was you, Elizabeth," I said.

"Who did you think it was?" She looked at Gordon. "I was worried. You were up here so long that I thought Gabrielle didn't feel well."

"If I didn't feel well," I said, "Gordon would take care of me. He would take good care of me. There's nothing for you to worry about when I'm with Gordon, Elizabeth, darling."

"Yes," she said. She put her hand to her throat as though she felt a lump there. "It's just that you said you were so tired. I do think you ought to get some rest."

"I'd like Gabrielle to sleep with you tonight," Gordon said.

"Why?"

"Gordon," I said. "Gordon, please, don't."

"Was there anything on the stairs?" he said abruptly, ignoring me.

"I don't know what you're talking about," Elizabeth said.

"There," I said. "I told you so. Gordon, please stop now."

"When you stood at the top of the stairs," he said, "did you feel some sort of barrier there? Like an invisible wall?"

"An invisible wall?" she said, puzzled. She shook her head. "I felt a little dizzy for a moment, that was all. I remember speaking to Gabrielle, telling her I couldn't find the cane, and then I had to hold onto the banister because I thought I was going to faint. It was an odd sensation." She pushed back the stray tendrils of hair that fell over her forehead. "I'm usually very healthy," she said apologetically. "I can't remember ever feeling that way before."

"Now do you believe me?" I said with satisfaction. "I told you so, Gordon."

"I wish I knew what you two were talking about," Elizabeth said wearily.

"It's nothing," I said.

"I hope you're right," Gordon said. "Just the same, Gabrielle, sleep with Elizabeth tonight."

"This is *my* room," I said.

"I can't do anything with her," he told Elizabeth.

"Why should you be any different from the rest of us?"

"I suppose I can't use force," he admitted ruefully.

"I'll be all right." I touched his hand. "Please stop worrying."

"I wish you'd explain." Elizabeth clenched her fists, and then I could see how she forced her fingers to relax. "Good night," she said gently. "Sleep well, Gabrielle." She turned and opened the door. "Gordon, are you coming down? I'm not a bit tired."

He paused in the doorway for a moment. "Gabrielle—"

"I'll be all right," I said again.

"Sure," he said doubtfully. "Of course you'll be all right," and then, reluctantly, he followed Elizabeth down the stairs.

I held the door open, leaning against it, listening for the

sound of their footsteps, listening for the sound of their voices.

They were in the front parlor. It was difficult to understand what Gordon was saying, but Elizabeth's voice was pitched high. "Aunt Constance?" she said. "Why are you going to call her?"

I couldn't hear his answer. Like a living thing, as if it had a will of its own, the door wanted to close. I braced myself, pushing against it, and it took all my strength to hold it open.

"All right," I whispered savagely. "Have it your own way."

I stepped forward and the door closed quietly, conspiratorially, the latch barely clicking. I leaned over the banister.

"There's nothing else for her to do," Gordon said.

"Your aunt is old. She's almost eighty. She should be left alone."

"Because she's old, she can't be left alone," Gordon said. "If this house is closed up again, she will never know what she's been running from all these years. She has to face this. Just because she's old, she has to face this. Originally I didn't ask her to give this place to you. It was she who suggested it, disguising her motives in an altruistic gesture. And then because she felt guilty and apprehensive after you were here, she changed her mind again."

Their voices faded away and I held onto the banister. Then I heard Elizabeth say, "It's too dangerous."

"She's healthy," Gordon said. "Lord knows she's healthy."

"But what about Gabrielle?"

"What about Gabrielle?"

"Will she be all right?"

"I don't know," he said flatly. "That's a chance we have to take."

"I don't," Elizabeth said. "I don't have to take any chances with Gabrielle."

"You're taking them every day whether you know it or not. We discussed this before and you made your decision."

"Yes," said Elizabeth. "I suppose I did."

"Well, then?"

"Do you think your aunt will come?"

"I think she's only waiting for me to call her," Gordon said.

I could hear their footsteps again. If they walked into the

hall, it would be possible for them to see me. I tiptoed across the landing and went back into my room. I closed the door myself this time, quickly and quietly.

The Bible was on top of the dresser where I had left it. It was open, but there was no flutter of the pages, although I watched it intently for a few moments. The room was very cold, colder than it had ever been. It seemed to be draining all body heat from me like some avid, desperate creature seeking sustenance. I forced myself to move, turning on my bedside lamp before I turned off the main, center fixture, deliberately lighting my way into bed. I wrapped the quilt around me, the quilt pulled under the sheet with me, next to my body. I thought of Elizabeth and Gordon downstairs, Gordon calling his aunt and Elizabeth standing next to him, Elizabeth pushing the stray hair away from her forehead with the back of her hand, her eyes wide and tender, her mouth gentle.

What decision had she made about me? Who was she to decide anything that concerned me?

"She's not going to have him," I said softly.

I was warm now. Wrapped in my soft quilt, I was warm and safe and contented.

"I'll see to that," I said.

The room was very still. I switched off the light. I lay in the dark, my eyes wide open against the dark and then, realizing what was going to happen, I sat up straight.

"Consuela is coming," I said loudly. "Did you hear that, Alarice? Consuela is coming back."

There was a sound, so soft that if I hadn't been listening for it, I doubt if I would have heard it. It was musical and gay and completely irresistible, and sitting there, my own amusement throbbing deep within me, I doubled up, savoring it, loving it, not knowing or caring whether the laughter came from me or Alarice.

Two days later Constance Suellen Lysander Bellingham arrived at Steppingstone. She was almost eighty ("My birthday is next week," she said), but she packed her bags and took a plane and then Gordon and Elizabeth met her at the ferry. I wouldn't go with them, even though they had asked me, even though I knew that Gordon and not Elizabeth would be doing the driving. I wouldn't go anywhere with Elizabeth behind the wheel.

In any case I couldn't go. I had too much to do. In a sense both Maggie and I were getting the house ready for Consuela, Maggie scrubbing, dusting and polishing as if it really needed it, and I concentrating on my own room, admiring the new curtains that hung at the windows and the crisp, white organdy canopy that framed the bed. And on the floor, right in front of where the fireplace should be, was the round, red rug.

"You can have something else for your room," I told Elizabeth insolently. "It doesn't belong there."

She didn't argue with me. I knew she wouldn't. After the quarrel we had I knew Elizabeth would be very careful to placate me.

It took place the morning after I knew Consuela was coming. I had awakened early, feeling happy and refreshed. Nothing had happened during the night, nothing that I could remember, although I had that nagging, illogical sensation that something important had been forgotten. I was up so early that I was downstairs before Maggie. The kitchen was still pristine from the night before, and down the small hall Gordon's door was closed.

He was asleep, then. I tried to imagine how he would look lying in bed, his eyes closed, his hair rumpled. Did he wear pajamas or did he sleep naked? Did he lie on his side with one hand tucked under his cheek? Did he sprawl on his back or did he turn on his stomach? What was it like to sleep with a man? No, not just any man but with Gordon, lying very close to him, my head on his shoulder, my head turning, my mouth moving across his bare chest, my mouth burrowing, my mouth upon his.

I thought about Gordon while I stood there in the kitchen, and then because I had been ignoring it, I finally remembered why I had awakened so early.

I had to get the room ready for Consuela. It was important that the room be exactly as Consuela had known it. When she stood in the doorway to Alarice's room once again, she would be eighty no longer. She would be eighteen and nothing would be changed.

There was no need for breakfast. Why had I gone into this part of the house? Had I been looking for Gordon, hoping he would be awake? I had to get the car before Elizabeth could stop me. I didn't know why she should want to, but I knew with a certainty that surprised me that she would try.

It was easy to find the keys. They were in the back parlor on the library table right next to her typewriter. I slipped them into the pocket of my skirt and then stood very still for a moment.

There was something else. I opened the small drawer in the front of the table, searching, and saw Elizabeth's spiral notebook. I looked at it, tempted, and then closed the drawer. I knew now where she kept it. If I needed it, I knew where to find it. It wasn't the notebook I wanted, it was something else, something that would be vitally necessary after I drove into town. I stared at the uncovered typewriter as if it could help me and I looked at the yellow keys of the piano and I bit my lip.

I was dressed properly. It had nothing to do with the way I was dressed. I would look just right driving into Steppingstone and parking on the main street. I wore a yellow skirt and a white blouse and there was a white cardigan draped over my shoulders, the sleeves hanging loose. I would be just fine walking through the streets of the town, and what else did I want? What else did I need?

There was no use standing there. It would come to me sooner or later, and meanwhile I had to get to the car before Elizabeth awoke.

I went out the front door, very easily, very swiftly, very quietly, and I walked around the side of the house to the garage. I stopped for a minute to look for a chimney, but there was none, which meant, I told myself, startled, that there couldn't have been a fireplace in Alarice's room. The only chimney was on the other side of the house, serving both the front parlor and Elizabeth's bedroom.

And yet there had to be a fireplace in Alarice's room. If I closed my eyes, I could see it so clearly, see Alarice sitting in front of it, head bent, the yellow hair tumbling loose and her arms hugging her knees. I shook my head. There was no point in worrying about the fireplace. Right now I had too much to do.

The garage had once been a small barn. It was shingled in imitation of the house, but the shingles, although weather-beaten, weren't silvered with age. The clumsy, double doors groaned in protest when I swung them back one by one.

I held my breath. The only sound I heard was the distant cry of the gulls as they wheeled and swung over the bay. In the house the sleepers slept and the car was mine.

I slid behind the wheel. My hands were wet. I looked at them, surprised, and then wiped them on my skirt. I put the key in the ignition. My knees shook and my heart pounded and my hands were wet again.

I had to find my handkerchief. But my handkerchief was in my purse, which was in my room on top of the dresser, right next to the open Bible. I had forgotten my purse. How could I buy all the things I needed without money?

Money, I thought, amazed. It didn't matter that I didn't have my purse. I had no money in it. That was because I hadn't needed any in such a long time. When you don't use something, it's easy to forget about it. Whom did I ask for money? Elizabeth? Maggie? Once it had been my father. What was I going to do?

I cursed my own stupidity. I sat there and held onto that wheel with my slippery, shaking hands and cursed. I used words that would make Maggie weep, words that weren't in Alarice's Bible even though it was an authority on hell and damnation.

My hands were wet and now my cheeks were wet, too. I had no way to buy all the lovely things I needed for Alarice's room, but, I thought grimly, I would have Elizabeth's car just the same. I would drive Elizabeth's car along the winding road that led to the town, past the fields burning brown in the September sun, with the bay sparkling and shimmering on my left, and the tall elms almost meeting across the road. That was one thing she couldn't take from me. That was one decision she couldn't make for me.

But I couldn't turn the key in the ignition. I knew how to do it. I knew just how the motor would respond, just how it would feel to have the car move, but I couldn't turn the key. With an effort I managed to lift my right hand and touch it, but then my hand wouldn't obey me any longer. Of its own volition it went back to the smooth surface of the wheel, clinging to it until my knuckles were white with strain.

"Gabrielle!" Elizabeth cried. She flung open the door. "Oh, Gabrielle, darling, I've been looking all over for you." Her eyes filled with tears and I stared at her. She was wearing her old terry robe and slippers flapped on her bare feet and her eyes were red-rimmed as though she had awakened at some time during the night and wept in the dark before falling asleep again. "Gordon," she shouted, "I've found her." She put her hand on my arm. "Come in the house now. You must be hungry."

"I knew you'd find me," I said dully. "You always do, don't you?"

"I don't know what you're talking about."

"You never leave me alone. Why can't you ever leave me alone?"

"Please get out of the car. Come on, darling," she said persuasively. "Aren't you hungry? I'm starved."

"Is that all you're afraid of? That I'll miss breakfast?"

"Here's Gordon," she said, relieved. "Gabrielle's been in the car all this time," she told him.

"One usually takes a car when one wants to drive somewhere," I said coolly. I looked at Gordon. He was in a bathrobe, too, but he had stopped to pull on a pair of slacks before he had left the house. Which means he doesn't wear pajamas, I thought, amused. Elizabeth had called him, Elizabeth hysterical because I had escaped from her vigilance, and he had grabbed the first pair of pants he could find and then, in a hurry, not able to find a shirt and concerned about me, he had simply, ridiculously reached for his robe. Because I suddenly felt tender and relaxed, I was able to open my fingers and take my hands from the wheel.

"Where do you want to go, Gabrielle?" Gordon asked.

"To town."

"What for?" Elizabeth demanded.

"Do I have to answer that?" I asked Gordon. "Can't I do *anything* without having to explain to Elizabeth?"

"You've been sick," Gordon said quietly. "Naturally, Elizabeth feels concerned."

"I wasn't sick. I was in an accident. There's a difference, you know," I said with contempt. "As a doctor you should know there's an enormous difference between getting sick, which is a flaw of your own body, and having an accident, which is caused by someone else's weakness."

"Please come into the house," Elizabeth begged. "We can talk then if you want to, Gabrielle. Let's not stand here."

"*I'm* not standing," I said. "I'm really quite comfortable. If you and Gordon will get into the car, I'll be happy to drive you wherever you want to go. I'm a very competent driver. My father always said so. 'Watch the road, Gabrielle,' he always said. 'Never turn your head. Just keep your eyes on the road.'"

"Yes," said Elizabeth. "I know, darling."

76

"Do you keep your eyes on the road?" I asked her.

"Gabrielle—"

"She's crying," I said to Gordon. "Why is she crying?"

"You're upsetting her," he said. He held out his hand. "Come on, Gabrielle."

"Why am I upsetting her? I'm not doing anything. I was just discussing driving. I was just telling the truth. My father was right. He gave very good advice. Why should that make Elizabeth cry? Or does she cry because she didn't listen to him and now she knows it's too late? That must be it," I said thoughtfully. "That must be the reason she is crying."

"Stop it!" Elizabeth shouted. "Why are you doing this to me?"

"Doing what? What am I doing?"

"Deliberately tormenting me!"

"If I wanted to torment you," I said calmly, "I could do it in more interesting—in much *more* imaginative ways. But I don't want to. I'm your sister and I love you. But you don't love me. You pretend to, but it's obvious you don't love me. You watch me all the time. You don't want me to have any life of my own, any privacy. That is torment if you must know. No privacy, no time to think my own thoughts, no time to be myself."

Elizabeth wiped her eyes. "I'm sorry," she said. "I really am, Gabrielle."

"Then why don't you leave me alone?" I put my hands back on the wheel. "All I want is to drive into town. Is that asking so much? I have some shopping to do. I want to get curtains for my room." I frowned. "Do you have any money, Elizabeth? It's awkward, but I don't seem to have any."

"I'll go with you after breakfast," Elizabeth said eagerly. "It's a wonderful idea. I've been wanting to go into town anyway. We can spend the day there if you like. We can shop and—"

"I don't want you," I said. "I like to choose things myself. I know exactly what I want, and it's not having you look over my shoulder and telling me what to do."

"I'll take you," Gordon offered. "I'll take care of whatever you need for your room. After all, it's my aunt's house."

I smiled. Gordon would drive. How easily he would turn the key in the ignition, and all I had to do was sit beside him and fold my hands demurely in my lap.

"I'll wait here for you," I said happily.

"Breakfast," Elizabeth reminded me stubbornly.

"I'm not hungry."

"You simply can't go off like this without your breakfast."

Gordon looked at Elizabeth and shook his head. "Gabrielle and I will have something to eat in town," he said. "I'll only be a few minutes," he told me, and then he cupped his hand under Elizabeth's elbow and marched her away.

I took my hands off the wheel and slid across the seat. I put my head back and closed my eyes. I kept them closed for just a second, but when I opened them again, Gordon was bending over me.

"We're here," he said.

I blinked. We were parked on a narrow cobblestoned street in front of a row of buildings that were half houses, half shops. All the first floors were stores, the bay windows filled with merchandise, but the upper floors were shingled or whitewashed, with painted shutters and curtains tied back neatly at the windows.

I yawned and stretched. "I've been asleep," I said, astonished.

"The quietest passenger I've ever had," said Gordon.

We had breakfast in the coffee shop on the corner. We perched on red-cushioned stools and drank orange juice, and every time I glanced at Gordon, he turned his head away, pretending he hadn't been looking at me, too.

"Nice day," the man behind the counter said.

Gordon agreed that it was a nice day.

"It's sure quiet in here," the man said cheerfully. "It's always like this after Labor Day. The whole town is dead now."

I could see it so clearly, street after narrow street, house after clapboard house, streets and houses lying very still in the setting autumn sun. Doors were nailed shut and shades were drawn and windows were shuttered and fence gates were fastened tight. Dried, yellow leaves filled the streets, the streets turning yellow as the unswept leaves piled high, the streets filled with dust of gold, and all the townspeople sat quietly behind their closed windows in the dark rooms, sitting bolt upright with wide, staring eyes waiting for the snow to fall, waiting for the ice to melt, waiting for spring to come once again.

Dead, I thought.

The sun felt hot after the cool, dim interior of the shop. The street we walked was near the water front, and behind it the town climbed a small hill, and on top of the hill was a colonial church with white columns and a black, wrought-iron fence circling it, and behind that, I told myself, is the graveyard.

"Gabrielle," said Gordon.

"What?"

"Stop daydreaming."

"All right," I said obediently.

"While you get the curtains, I'll go into the hardware store. I want to fix the door to your room. It probably needs new hinges."

"I'll only be a few minutes," I said.

But I was longer than I thought.

"Why organdy?" the woman in the shop asked me. "They're a nuisance. Have to be starched and ironed. Why don't you get something new like drip-dry?"

"I don't want something new," I said patiently. "I'm not interested in something new. It has to be organdy or it won't be right."

She raised her eyebrows. "Are you summer people? Haven't seen you around here before."

"Not summer people," I said. "Not even leftover summer people. Autumn people. We just came."

"The Lysander house," she said.

"Mrs. Bellingham owns it," I corrected her.

"Always been the Lysander house. Never been called anything else. Besides, Mrs. Bellingham was a Lysander." She looked at me eagerly. "How long do you think you'll stay there?"

"I don't know," I said. I stood first on my right foot and then on my left. "About the curtains—"

"The Sanders' used to go in it once in a while and clean things up. Will took care of the garden and Julie worked inside of the house. They said they didn't like doing it, but Constance

Bellingham made it worth their while. I don't know what it cost Constance, but I told Julie Sanders, I said, 'Julie, just be glad you don't have to live there, and whatever she pays you, just remember it isn't enough.'" Her mouth was thin, but her eyes crinkled when she smiled. "Tell me," she whispered confidentially, "what's it like?"

"What do you mean?"

"You know what I mean."

"Oh, that," I said airily. "Why, it's haunted, of course."

She stepped back. "I thought it was just stories. I didn't really think—"

"Yes, you did," I said. "You wouldn't go there after dark, would you? And you thought the Sanders' were very brave to go there even in daylight."

"But you're there now," she said. "You're there all the time."

"It's customary to sleep in the house you live in," I said evenly. "Now if you don't mind, I'm in a hurry."

"Have you seen—" She swallowed. "Have you heard anything?"

"Sometimes in the middle of the night," I said wickedly, "I hear footsteps in the hall. They walk back and forth, back and forth, and once I thought I heard someone crying."

"There," she said. "I knew it was true."

"Did you?"

"It had to be. Constance can't live there. Everyone knows that."

"Really?" I said sternly. "I was just teasing. You ought to know better than to believe in such nonsense. It's a perfectly lovely place. We wouldn't stay there if there was anything wrong with it, would we?"

"No," she said suspiciously, "I don't suppose you would." She went into the back of the store. "Will these do?" she asked, bringing out the organdy curtains.

"As long as they crisscross, they're fine," I said. "What kind of stories?"

"What?"

"You said there were stories about the house."

"There are stories about any empty house," she said shortly, wary of me, not ready to let herself be trapped again. "Especially this one. Family owns a home and yet when they come to Steppingstone, they stay at the inn."

"It's more convenient. It's such a nuisance opening a house, don't you think?"

"Maybe so," she said grudgingly. She found the material I needed for the canopy, and by the time she had finished wrapping my packages, Gordon had arrived.

"Doctor Inness," she said. "I didn't know you were with the young lady."

"Doctor Inness is staying with us," I said maliciously, thinking, That should give her something to talk about.

"My aunt will be here in a few days," Gordon said quickly, paying her. "Coming, Gabrielle?"

"Why did you tell her your aunt would be here?" I complained as he put the packages in the car. "You spoiled everything."

"That's because I'm beginning to know you very well," he said complacently. "What now, Gabrielle?"

"The churchyard," I said.

He looked at me. "Sight-seeing?"

"Alarice is buried there, isn't she?"

"How do you know?"

"I don't," I said.

"As it happens, she *is* buried there," Gordon said. "Why do you want to see her grave?"

"I just want to. If you won't take me, I'll go myself."

He glanced at me briefly and then turned his head away. We walked side by side up the hill without touching.

He's angry, I thought. The sun was burning the back of my neck, and our shadows led the way, our grotesquely foreshortened shadows climbing the hill in front of us.

I made my shadow face Gordon's. "You're walking too fast," I complained. "I'm getting tired." When he didn't answer me, I said, "I don't know why you're so upset. You should visit your own grandmother's grave once in a while. See if it's being taken care of. Put flowers on it or something. It's the right thing to do."

"Lest the living forget?" Gordon asked.

"How can the living forget?" I said. "We try to, but there's no way we can."

We had reached the top of the hill. The church was across the street.

"I'm not angry with you," Gordon said, taking my arm. "The way I feel has nothing to do with you, Gabrielle."

"Then what is it?"

"Myself, maybe. For being a damn fool. For letting you and Elizabeth come here in the first place and then letting you stay. I can't figure out why I'm doing it."

"It's not your fault," I said. "You can't help yourself. We have to stay and there is nothing you can do about it. If I had told you a few days ago that Consue—" I swallowed—"that your Aunt Constance would come here, too, you'd have said it was impossible, and yet she's coming, isn't she?"

"When I asked her to come and she agreed, I asked what made her change her mind. She said it was because her birthday was next week. Does that make sense?"

"She's old and getting older," I said calmly, without pity.

We opened the gate and followed the narrow path that led to the graves. There was mound after mound of grass and ivy and row after row of old tombstones, the inscriptions eroded and faded, and there was row after row of new tombstones, the names sharp and clear. There they lay, the dead, old and new, all of them beyond time, free of time; the names of the dead carved upon the stones, the names of those who had walked this earth, breathing this air, seeing this sky, knowing what we know and knowing now more besides. There they lie.

The place of sapphires, I thought. If there are sapphires, blue-green sapphires piled high in dust of gold, the place where they lie is far away from here.

He stopped. "Here is Alarice," he said.

We were at the edge of the cemetery. There was the boundary of the iron fence and the empty field beyond and Alarice's grave with the small stone marker.

She's all alone here, I thought. Why is she all alone?

"Where are the others?" I said.

"The Lysander family plot was filled," he said shortly.

"Alarice Courtney Bellingham," I read out loud. "Born October 16, 1892. Died March 5, 1912." I looked at him. "I don't understand," I said.

"That was her married name."

"But it's the same as Con—as your Aunt Constance's."

"Alarice married Jotham Bellingham. When she died, Jotham married Aunt Constance and she raised my mother. Aunt Constance had no children of her own."

"And Jotham? What happened to him?"

"He died when my mother was six years old."

"Is he buried here, too?"

"The Bellinghams have their own plot," said Gordon, pointing. "It's over there."

"With no room for Alarice?"

"I hadn't thought about it," said Gordon.

"And your mother?"

"She came back once when I was a child, but she never came back again."

"They were both in love with the same man," I said softly. "They hated each other and they loved the same man and Alarice won. She married Jotham and she had his child and she was sure she had won, and then Consuela not only got Jotham but Alarice's child as well. How did Alarice die, Gordon?"

"In childbirth," Gordon said. "A very natural death."

"Who told you that?"

"Aunt Constance, of course," he said, surprised.

"Have you ever seen the death certificate?"

"Let's go," he said grimly. "You have a way of twisting and turning things that appalls me."

"There must be a place where they keep records," I said gently, and then I was quiet, letting him think about it, letting him turn the thought of Alarice's death certificate and her lonely grave around and around in his mind.

As for me, I was perfectly willing to go back to the house. I had so much to do that I didn't know where to begin. I had to get the house ready. I had to get Alarice's room ready. I was going to be very busy getting everything ready for Consuela.

Gordon helped me. He found curtain rods in the attic and a frame for the canopy, and when he had finished putting up the rods and seeing that the frame was securely in place, he worked on the door. He examined the hinges and he swung the door to and fro.

"Doesn't seem to be anything wrong," he said after a while, "but it won't stay open."

"You can fiddle with that as long as you like," I said, amused, "it won't make a bit of difference." But he wouldn't listen to me. He just squatted on his heels, whistling through his teeth until I realized he was happy working with his hands and left him alone.

Finally he went up into the attic again and came down with a large, dusty object that, said Gordon, would make a good doorstop. He washed it in the bathroom, using one of Maggie's best towels to dry it and then he braced open my door with a flourish.

"There," said Gordon with satisfaction.

"It's a porcelain cat," I said.

I stared at it with loathing. It was almost two feet high,

although it was sitting down, and it had huge paws, green eyes and a pink nose. Its black whiskers had been painted on, and it sat there, its back against the door, its eyes watching me balefully.

"It won't work," I said scornfully. "Nothing can keep that door open."

"Gabrielle hates cats," Elizabeth said. She had been trying to write. I had heard the sound of her typewriter earlier, but it had been quiet for the last hour. She looked tired and her fingers were smudged as though she had spent most of her time fighting with the typewriter ribbon.

"That's because I'm allergic to them," I explained. "I start sneezing."

"I had a kitten once." Elizabeth pushed back her hair and she left a long black mark across her forehead. "My father gave him to me, but I couldn't keep him because of Gabrielle."

"*Nasty* little thing." I watched the door, fascinated, wondering how long the cat could hold it open. "He scratched me."

"It doesn't matter. It was a long time ago."

"But it does matter. What a good memory I have," I said pleasantly. "I remember it perfectly."

I remembered other things, too. I remembered trying to hold open that door myself, exerting all my strength, all my will to hold it open. But I had been a challenge, flesh and blood against the unknown. How much force would be applied to an insentient, inanimate object?

"Well, this cat won't make you sneeze," said Gordon, "and it's not likely to scratch you, either."

I'd like it to scratch Elizabeth, I thought.

"I want my door closed," I said. "I can't possibly sleep any other way."

"You only use this when you want it to stay open," said Gordon, touching the porcelain cat with his foot. He stared at it for a moment, startled. "It moved," he said.

"Of course it did," I said. "Just push the door back and start all over again."

"The floor must be uneven," said Gordon, puzzled.

"If I only had a desk," I said quickly, trying to distract him.

"What do you want a desk for?" Elizabeth asked.

The cat looked at her, its claws sheathed, its green eyes reflecting the light.

"It doesn't have to be a real desk," I said to Gordon. "I just want something I can write on."

There was a small table in the bedroom next to Elizabeth's, the room Consue—Mrs. Bellingham would use when she came, and it was after Gordon had brought in the table and a straight-backed chair for me that I made Elizabeth give me the red rug.

"It looks lovely," she said, putting her head to one side the way she does when she is pleased. "You're right, Gabrielle. It really belongs in this room."

"Yes," I said complacently.

Inch by inch the cat slid across the floor.

"If we're going to meet the six o'clock ferry—" Gordon looked at his watch.

"I won't be long," Elizabeth said. "I just have to bathe and change. Don't you want to come, too, Gabrielle?"

"No."

"Why not?"

"I have too much to do."

"This room is finished now."

"Then I'll help Maggie."

"But there's nothing more to do, darling."

"*I'll* drive," Gordon said.

"I don't see what difference *that* makes," I said. "I don't care *who* drives. What makes you think I do? If it came right down to it, I could go to the ferry myself and bring Con—Mrs. Bellingham back here. I could do it easily."

"Of course you could," Elizabeth said gently.

"Of course you could," I mimicked.

"Oh," she said. She touched her throat, and when she took her hand away, I looked for the black mark, the long streak like the one she had left on her forehead. Only not black, I told myself. Red! Red like a scratch from the unsheathed claws of a cat, a sharp, red mark drawn across Elizabeth's throat, a jagged,

86

ever-oozing line of blood that even Gordon's clean, clever, knowledgeable hands couldn't heal.

But how could the cat reach Elizabeth's throat? Spirit imprisoned in solid casing, there was no way for it to tense its muscles, no way for it to crouch, tail lashing, no way for it to spring at Elizabeth.

Unless I helped it. Unless Alarice helped it.

I heard Elizabeth say, "Gordon, I don't know what to do."

So that's the way it is, I thought. She appeals to Gordon, eyes wet with tears, Elizabeth abused, abased by her nasty sister, and he turns to her, tender, compassionate, filled with pity.

I clenched my fists. The cat moved again. "Alarice," I whispered.

"What?" said Elizabeth.

"I said I was sorry." I didn't look at Elizabeth. I looked at the cat, concentrating on the cat. "I didn't mean to upset you, Elizabeth." My voice was very gentle. "I really didn't. It's just that I want to be alone for a while and you seem to worry about it. I guess that's the reason you nag me—because you worry. It's sweet of you to be so concerned about me, but I don't think there's anything wrong in wanting to be alone, do you?"

"Seems reasonable," said Gordon, smiling at me.

"I'm sorry, too," Elizabeth said. "I guess I *have* been impossible. It's just—" She wiped her eyes with the back of her hand in a weary, childlike gesture. "I can't help it," she said, sniffling. "You were so sick and now—"

"And now if we don't hurry—" said Gordon, interrupting her, his voice warning her to stop.

My fingers tingled. My head ached. The only sound in the room was the faint scraping as the cat inched across the floor, and yet it seemed to me that I screamed. Alarice, I thought desperately, and the cat moved again.

Elizabeth put her cheek against mine.

"You'll be late." I pulled away. "You'd better go," I said, timing it, shoving her toward the door. She turned just as it swung forward, the door pushing the cat before it. The cat moved faster and faster, its green eyes spiteful. It tumbled on its side. There was a crash and the head fell off, the head wedged in the doorway, the green eyes still aware and watching. Another piece, a section of the broken feet, flew into the air as if it had been thrown and I aimed it at Elizabeth. The claws! I closed my eyes. My nails dug into the palms of my hands. The unsheathed claws and Elizabeth's throat, so white, so vulnerable, so bare, and the blood running and—

"Watch out!" Gordon shouted. "Good Lord! Are you hurt?"

I opened my eyes.

Elizabeth stood there, her hands clasped as if she were praying and her throat white and whole, the column of her throat untouched, unblemished, and it was all for nothing.

The pain was so sharp within me that I bent double with it. There was no sorrow. There was only pain.

"I can't bear it." I opened my hands. I could see the marks my nails had made, crescents in the flesh, an intricate design that was all my own. I lifted my hands and touched my face. My cheeks were wet.

"Don't cry. Gabrielle, darling, please don't cry." Elizabeth put her arms around me. "There's no need to cry. I'm not hurt. Look at me. There isn't a scratch on me."

"I know," I said. I sniffed the faint scent of her perfume. Lilacs! The smell of spring, the buds unfolding and the wet, new leaves beginning; but this was autumn and the leaves were dry and dying and the buds had been forgotten long ago. "I was just frightened," I said quickly.

"I was, too," Elizabeth said.

"This damn door," Gordon said. "Well, it's shut again, that's for sure." He bent over and began to pick up the broken pieces. I looked for the cat's head, but I couldn't see it.

Maybe it rolled somewhere, I thought. Maybe it turned over and over, rolling across the room, rolling under the bed, and it will stay there, its eyes unwinking, its eyes knowing, gleeful and evil.

"Gabrielle didn't like that thing anyway," Elizabeth said. "Did you, darling?"

"You've got to find the head," I told Gordon. "It must be in the room."

Maggie opened the door. She had the cat's head in her left hand and a dustpan and brush in her right. "I just got the house cleaned," she complained. "I just finished cleaning and I heard this awful crash and I knew you must have broken something. I work my fingers to the bone and just when I think I'm finished, you make a mess again." She stepped inside the room and deliberately closed the door behind her. "I'll do it myself," she said.

"I thought I'd help," said Gordon.

"I wasn't talking about the cleanup," Maggie shrugged, "but if any doors are going to be closed around here, I'd rather they be closed by me."

"And opened by me," said Elizabeth. She put out her hand and then let it fall by her side. "I can't do it," she said. "I can't touch that door."

"Why do you blame the door?" I said. "You kicked the cat and knocked it over."

"Did I?" she said, relieved.

"Of course you did. I saw you."

"I'm glad," she said. "When I think of the door slamming with such force—" She shuddered. She put her hand on the knob. "I'll only be a minute," she said to Gordon.

Gordon waited until she went down the hall and then he turned around. "She didn't touch that cat," he said.

"I know," I admitted, "but don't you see, Gordon, if it makes her feel better to think she did—"

"You'll miss that ferry," said Maggie. "You'll dillydally until you miss it and then Mrs. Bellingham will have a fit." She closed the door again behind Gordon.

I sat down in the rocking chair. "You didn't admire the room," I said, rocking back and forth. "Doesn't it look beautiful, Maggie?"

She straightened, her apron full of the broken pieces. I couldn't see the cat's eyes any more. "I don't care what you do with this room. As far as I'm concerned that door can stay shut forever as long as I'm on the other side of it. If I had my way I'd lock it and none of us would come in here again. If this thing got smashed by that door, anything can happen. I don't know why you stay in here. It's cold and I wouldn't stand it for a minute if I was you."

"But you're not me," I said, rocking contentedly.

"And a good thing it is, too."

"Don't you want to be young again?"

"That's not what I meant."

I stopped rocking. "Maggie—"

"It's nothing," she said quickly. "I don't know what I'm talking about. You mustn't pay any attention to me, Gabrielle. I'm just upset over Mrs. Bellingham coming here. There's no reason for her to come, and what's more, there's no reason for us to stay."

"Elizabeth doesn't want to go home," I said spitefully. "That's why we're staying. She wants to be near Gordon, and if she went home, she'd have to face everything all over again."

"All right," said Maggie, "have it your own way," and she shut the door behind her.

I yawned and stretched. Like a cat, I thought. This was the way I felt the afternoon Jotham came to see Papa, that stormy afternoon of the northeaster with the rain running down the windowpanes and I sitting warm and safe in this rocking chair, purring with happiness, and the fire leaping high. I had seen Jotham come up the walk just a few minutes before, his head bent against the wind and his coat collar pulled high. I had wanted to rap on the windowpane. I had wanted to open the window and lean out, just to see him look up, just to hear him say my name. I loved the way he lingered on the first syllable, Jotham saying "Al-arice" as if he loved to say it, but I did nothing. There was nothing more I could do. I heard him knock on the front door and I knew he would hand his wet things to Mama and she would scold him because he had walked from town.

"On such a day," Mama said, "and with no umbrella." She held his dripping coat away from her, dismayed. "Soaking wet. Do you want to catch your death of cold?"

It was easy to know exactly what Mama would say and do. She had a phrase to fit every occasion, but Jotham kept his thoughts to himself and it was difficult to put words into his mouth. I could only imagine him standing there in the hall, looking at Mama the way he sometimes did, his eyes intent and searching as though something about her puzzled him.

"Go right into the front parlor," Mama said, still holding his coat at arm's length. "Mr. Lysander is waiting for you."

And I, rocking back and forth in my own chair in my own room, was waiting for him, too. But I was in no hurry. Not like Consuela, who was always in a rush.

"Jotham is downstairs," she said, flinging open my door.

I kept on rocking. "I didn't hear you knock."

"That's because I didn't."

"When you leave, close the door behind you," I said pleasantly.

"But I'm not leaving."

"Do as you please." I sighed. "The door," I reminded her patiently.

"All right," she said, shutting it obediently. "Why is Jotham here? Why is he talking with Papa? What are they talking about?"

I stood up. "How should I know?" I walked across the room, picked up the poker and pretended I was fixing the fire. I stood on the round, red rug in my warm, beautiful room and watched the coals glow in the grate and all the time I kept my back turned toward Consuela.

"Why did Jotham walk from town?" she said rapidly. "I heard Mama say he walked."

"Maybe it gave him more time to think about me," I said serenely. "Maybe it gave him a lot more time to think about what he was going to say to Papa."

"But you just said you didn't know."

"Did I?" I turned around. In this twilight of a dark day, with the only light in the room the light from the fire, Consuela stood bleak and dark in the dark corner. Her dress was black. Her hair was black. Her eyes were black. The lovely, vivacious, charming, gay Constance Suellen Lysander was a black mouse. Nothing more.

"Alarice!"

"If you must know—" I stopped to laugh. "If you *really*

must know," I said, pouncing, "Jotham came to ask Papa if he could marry me."

Such a little mouse trembling in the corner. "I don't believe you," she said, her voice uncertain.

"That's up to you," I said indifferently.

"He loves me," she said. "I know he does."

"Then why hasn't he asked you to marry him? Why has he asked me? Don't you think it odd for a man to propose to one sister while loving the other?"

"You're lying." Her fingers plucked at her skirt. "You're always lying. You twist everything until it's impossible to know the truth."

"I don't blame you," I said gently. "I can understand how you must feel, Consuela. I didn't mean to break it to you like this. I would have been much more considerate, but it's really your fault for barging in. I would have told you myself, but I wanted to have Papa's permission. You know how old-fashioned he is. Naturally, he would rather the oldest daughter married first, but I'm sure he won't stand in my way once he sees how things are. And then, after Papa agreed, Jotham and I were going to speak to you. If this had happened to me, I would feel *exactly* as you do, although," I added smoothly, "I don't think I would have called you a liar. I don't think I would have been vituperative and called you names. I think I would have made the best of it and tried to be happy for your sake."

She walked toward me, moving very slowly. I backed away and held the poker tight.

"Just tell me how you did it," she said dully. "Just tell me how you managed it."

"I don't know what you're talking about."

"Oh, yes, you do."

I took a deep breath. "We love each other," I said. "Isn't that enough?"

"You've wanted him. I've known that. I've seen you look at him and I knew you wanted him, but Jotham—" She rubbed her eyes as if they burned. "I'll find out," she said. "I'll ask Jotham."

"And humiliate yourself? I know you better than that,

Consuela. You have too much pride. You'll never ask Jotham. What are you going to say to him? Have you thought about that? Are you going to grovel and weep and tell him he really is in love with you? Are you going to tell him you're in love with him?"

"But I was the one he came to see," she said. She rubbed her eyes again and her cheeks were wet. "I was the one he took sailing. I was the one—not you. When we walked together, we walked hand in hand and now you tell me—"

"That he's going to marry me. And you won't ask him a thing, will you? You'll be very polite and sweet when you see him and you'll never, never ask Jotham anything about me."

"Don't be so sure."

"But I am sure. I know you. I know you so well. I can see you now, standing so proud and so regal at my wedding, Consuela the maid of honor, Consuela the lady, never showing how she feels. I can see you now growing old so gracefully, knitting or embroidering through the long, cold winter evenings, the languishing spinster aunt, absolutely doting on my children. Because you will love Jotham's children, won't you, Consuela?" I smiled at her. "But I could be wrong. For your sake, I hope I am wrong. Perhaps you will be very sensible and find someone else. There are other men, you know."

She stood very still. "I've never seen you like this," she said. "I've known you to be cruel, but never like this."

"But I'm in love," I pointed out reasonably. "That makes a difference."

"I'm going downstairs," she said. "I'll see Jotham and I'll find out if you're telling the truth."

"Don't be a fool."

"And what's more," she said, "I'll shut the door behind me."

I could hear her footsteps going down the stairs. She moved slowly as if her legs were trembling. But it wasn't until I heard their voices in the hall that I knew something was wrong. They were laughing, Consuela and Jotham walking hand in hand laughing together, and I flung open my door and started down the steps.

The front door was wide open and it was twilight, but it

93

wasn't raining. A woman stood framed in the doorway, the young, black mouse fading, the black dress now gray, the black hair now white, the young, slim woman now bent and old, and looking at her standing there, even my hatred, even my black hatred, felt old and gray and tired and I said her name softly and with sorrow.

"Consuela," I whispered.

It was impossible for her to have heard me and yet she looked up and smiled.

"You must be Gabrielle," she said, her voice high and sweet.

I was halfway down the stairs. I couldn't go forward and I couldn't go back. I was frozen, caught on this staircase, this span of time, with Consuela in front of me and Alarice behind me. Because that was where Alarice was. Behind me.

I must be Gabrielle, I thought. Consuela had said so and she ought to know. Released, I ran down the steps and took Mrs. Bellingham's hand in mine.

✿

I *must* BE GABRIELLE. I HAD BEEN GIVEN AN ORDER and I followed it obediently. And since I was Gabrielle, it was possible for me to breathe with Gabrielle's lungs, speak with Gabrielle's tongue and see through Gabrielle's eyes. For the next two days I got out of bed and bathed and clothed Gabrielle's body and went through the hours so cleverly that I seemed exactly like everyone else.

"It's wonderful to see you like this," Elizabeth said contentedly. "You seem so well and happy, darling, ever since Aunt Constance came."

Elizabeth called Consuela "Aunt Constance" because Consuela had asked her to.

We were having dinner in the dining room that first night because "the kitchen isn't suitable with Mrs. Bellingham here," Maggie said.

"It's so strange," Consuela said, putting down her fork. "You can't imagine how odd I feel being in this house again."

"I'm so glad you came back, Mrs. Bellingham," Elizabeth said.

"I believe you are," Consuela said, smiling at Elizabeth, "but I'm not so sure I am. When I was very young, I used to think

95

that after you had lived a number of years you automatically obtained a certain wisdom and could make decisions very easily, but now I know that nothing comes easy. I thought that the moment I stepped foot in this house—for your sake, most definitely for your sake—I would ask you to leave, but here I am, still not sure of anything."

"We're very happy here," Elizabeth said earnestly. "We couldn't go back home, you know that, not right away. It would have been too unbearable, and for this transition period in our lives—" She hesitated and her eyes were wet.

"For especially this period," Consuela said. "If ever a house wasn't suitable—I was selfish. I was only thinking of myself and of my own needs. If anything should happen, I would never forgive—"

"We are very grateful that you let us have the house," Elizabeth interrupted. "I can't even begin to tell you how much it means to me."

"I would never forgive myself, but you would forgive me, wouldn't you, Elizabeth?" Consuela leaned forward. "Gordon was right," she said slowly. "You are lovely. I would like you to call me 'Aunt Constance,' if you would."

"Thank you, Aunt Constance," Elizabeth said.

"Anything else seems so formal," Consuela said briskly, picking up her fork again. "Don't you think so, Gabrielle?"

"Yes," I said primly.

"Well, then—?" She looked at me, thin, fragile hands motionless, the dark eyes half-veiled by the heavy lids.

"Yes," I said again.

But I didn't call her anything. When I spoke to her, I never mentioned her name. She told me I was Gabrielle, but she preferred to forget she was Consuela. She thought because she was old and the blue veins were raised and knotted that I, too, would forget who she was. She pretended she was here on an ordinary visit, the mistress of the house once again, presiding over the table, supervising the menus, marching upstairs and down as if she had never been away, as if she had never been afraid to return.

She poked here and there, tidying Maggie's always neat

closets, arranging and rearranging the kitchen cupboards.

"We *never* put the staples on the bottom," Consuela told Maggie. "We always kept them on the second shelf."

Everyone helped her pretend. And since I seemed exactly like everyone else, I helped her, too. She was wrong, of course. Before the kitchen had been rebuilt after the fire, there had been a pantry and Mama always kept the flour and sugar and the potatoes there, but I was Gabrielle and I didn't remind Consuela.

I didn't remind her of anything. I didn't have to.

"She's remarkable," Elizabeth said respectfully, "the way she does things. Her mind is so clear. It's hard to realize she's going to be eighty."

"So will you if you live long enough," I said caustically.

I felt no pity for old age. I felt no sympathy for the infirmities of the old, the bent shoulders, the trembling hands, the aches and the pains and the fears of the aged. If I had to weep, I wept for the young. I wept for the young who lived with the awesome knowledge of their own mortality. I wept for the young who had died too soon. I had no tears for Consuela, who had so much time she could afford to waste it. I had no tears for Consuela moving through the days, stopping once in a while, momentarily aware of danger, seeing desperately, sharply, clearly for just a second before she moved forward heedlessly once again.

She was old now. The months moved by faster, faster, the seasons turning from one to another, the years spinning around her until overcome by vertigo, she had come home again. I could not weep for Consuela facing death clothed in her used, wrinkled, tired flesh. She had worn it long enough. It was time she got rid of it.

She was home again and she went upstairs and down, moving this and changing that. "Over here, Gordon," Consuela commanded. "That chair doesn't belong in the corner," and then, cocking her head to one side, considering, "Perhaps if we pushed the couch over there—"

She was home again and she went downstairs and up, her steps heavy and measured in her sensible shoes with the round toes and the broad, firm heels, Consuela pausing to rest on the stairs, out of breath and exhausted because there was nothing more she could do, nothing more she could find to do that would keep her from thinking, that would keep her from realizing why she had come home.

They sat in the front parlor that first evening, Gordon and Elizabeth side by side on the love seat and Consuela in the easy chair. I was in the back parlor, perched on the piano stool, twisting and fidgeting until Elizabeth said I made her nervous.

"Do settle down, Gabrielle," she said.

Settle down, I thought. It was easy for her to talk. Elizabeth was all settled, nestled so cozily next to Gordon, brazenly placing herself next to him at the dinner table, wantonly forcing herself upon him on every occasion. Gordon couldn't seem to take so much as a casual stroll without finding Elizabeth by his side. Right now she was pushing against him on the narrow love seat, but, I told myself gleefully, if Gordon wanted to look at Elizabeth, it was necessary for him to turn his head. I was right in front of him and I could see that he didn't move. He was watching me instead.

"I think I will go to bed," Consuela said.

"It's early," Elizabeth protested.

"It's been a long trip. I'm tired and I still have to unpack."

"I'll help you," Elizabeth said.

I swung around on the stool. If Elizabeth went upstairs with Consuela, I would be alone with Gordon. I could sit next to him, and because I was next to him, he would turn his head, his eyes searching, intent. But while I was with Gordon, Consuela would walk up those stairs without me. She had to pass my room in order to reach her own and I wouldn't be there to see the expression on her face. Would she be apprehensive? She was old. She knew death was coming and she was afraid to die. That was why she had come back, because she was afraid to die. Her ego screamed in agony, longing for immortality. If the entity that had been Alarice still existed—if Alarice waited for her in this house, then death wasn't annihilation, and anything else could be endured.

Would she stand outside the closed door to my room for a

moment, her hand on the knob, or would she walk past as fast as she could, face averted? Without me, Consuela would unpack leisurely, forgetting death, forgetting Alarice for still another day. She would be happy, prattling to Elizabeth in that high, sweet voice of hers, and Elizabeth would help her, her hands touching Consuela's things. It would be Aunt Constance this and Aunt Constance that, and intimacy established with no barrier of age between them, the two of them would giggle like idiotic schoolgirls. In the midst of laughter, surrounded by light and the solace of the familiar, which of them then would think of me?

Now I walked into the front parlor. "No," I said firmly. "Not you, Elizabeth. You stay right here with Gordon." I smiled at Consuela. "Please let me help you," I said softly.

"I'm quite capable of unpacking by myself," said Consuela, "but I have to admit I would welcome company. Come, child."

We started up the steps, Consuela holding onto the banister.

"Do go ahead of me," she said. "I move so slowly nowadays. It's foolish of you to wait."

"I've been waiting for you for a long time," I said.

"What?"

"I said I didn't mind waiting."

"I really must have my hearing tested," she said apologetically. "I've always been grateful that I never had any trouble with it, but occasionally lately I do find I've been asking people to repeat themselves. I've been very lucky up to now. I suppose I have no right to complain. My eyesight is just fine and I use my glasses only for reading."

Her eyesight is fine, but *I* can't see, I thought, looking up. The mist was forming, a thin ribbon coiling, eddying, and as I watched, it began to pour over the top step.

"No," I screamed silently. "Please don't. Don't interfere. Let me do it my way."

Consuela rested, panting. "I get out of breath," she said simply.

I forced myself to speak. "Are you all right now?" I asked, making my voice concerned and gentle, imitating Elizabeth's sugary tones.

"Yes," she said.

Her eyesight is fine, but she still doesn't see it, I told myself. We move side by side on this staircase and she can't see it. It holds out its wet arms to us. We rise to meet it and still she cannot see.

Suddenly I was glad the mist was there. Consuela and I would walk into that cold whiteness, hand in hand we would walk through it and together we would reach the other side.

We were there at last. The mist closed around us. It was so cold it hurt to breathe.

"What is wrong, child?"

"Nothing," I said. "Why?"

"You look so strange."

I couldn't see her, but she could see me. How was that possible?

"I have a headache," I said truthfully.

"There's some aspirin in my suitcase," said Consuela helpfully. "I suppose I really shouldn't prescribe with a doctor in the house, but Gordon's a specialist and I don't trust specialists, do you? They don't let you stay with them long enough. In my time we got to know our doctor. We didn't have a nose man and an eye man and a skin man and a bone man and a brain man—" she snorted—"and who knows what else?"

She was leading me, her hand on my arm, and I knew we were past the door to my room. I knew she was taking me to her room and I couldn't see the expression on her face. I couldn't see her at all.

"Sit down," she said. I could hear her move away. I could hear the water running in the bathroom. I could hear the bed squeak as I shifted my position and all the time I was lost, the mist following me, the mist part of me.

"Drink this," she said.

The glass was solid in my hand, but how could I raise it to my mouth when I couldn't see the glass and I couldn't find my mouth?

"That's better," said Consuela.

I swallowed. The water was cold, as cold as the mist, as cold as I.

"Just lean back and keep your eyes closed," Consuela ordered. "I have a great sympathy for anyone who gets headaches, not that I have any knowledge of them personally. I never get them myself. But I remember when I was a girl Mama used to have migraine that was so bad she had to take to her bed."

"Not Mama. It was Papa. You've got it all mixed up," I said with contempt. "It was Papa who had the migraine headaches. We were always apprehensive when he came home early. We were never really glad to see him because we always knew what it meant. 'Not another one,' Mama would say, and she'd lead him upstairs and he'd be almost staggering with the pain. Mama would put him to bed, in the bedroom right next to this one, and then she'd close the bedroom door and we'd spend the day tiptoeing around because the slightest sound would put him in a frenzy."

I opened my eyes. The curtain of mist parted and there was Consuela standing at the foot of the bed looking at me.

"Do you feel better?"

"It was Papa," I said loudly. "Didn't you hear me?"

"Don't get up," she said serenely. "It's much too soon. I can manage very well by myself."

"It was Papa," I shouted. "You know very well it was Papa who had the headaches."

"I won't argue with you." She shrugged. "As long as you insist you feel well enough to help, I must admit I would appreciate your lifting the suitcases onto the bed for me. I do get a bit dizzy when I bend over and then straighten up too quickly, but I suppose I should expect these things. After all, I'm not as young as I used to be." She smiled ruefully. "And now, if you'll open it. Just snap the latch. That's it. Thank you, dear."

I could see everything so clearly now. There was nothing wrong with my eyes, but she was deaf. Her hearing would be tested, the sound rising in volume, the needle quivering, the machine measuring in decibels, and all the time Consuela would sit there, bewildered.

"What did you say, dear?"

"Nothing. I didn't say a word."

"I thought you spoke to me."

She was moving back and forth, unpacking her things, settling down in her old room as if she had never been away, putting dresses of black, gray and beige into the closet that once had held flame and pink and indigo, with the top shelf crammed with hatboxes because "I can't stand the sun on my bare head," said Consuela with a sigh.

When she was young, she carried a parasol, Consuela carrying her own shade with her, but it was only an appendage like her long, white gloves, like the fan she fluttered, like the black hair piled high upon her head, the black braids always neat and tidy. It was a sop to keep in Mama's good graces for "No well-brought-up young lady exposes herself," said Mama severely. But when Consuela was out of sight, when she could no longer be seen from the house, down came the parasol, off came the gloves, and sometimes she stepped out of the high-heeled shoes and ran in her stockinged feet along the beach, kicking the sand, her face turned greedily toward the sun.

Now the white hair was cropped short and the clean, firm lines of chin and throat were blurred, wattled, the flesh hanging loose, even the nose changing, becoming thinner, more beaklike and narrow. She stooped, bent as though she carried a weight upon her shoulders, and when she spoke to me she had to look up, although once she had been as tall as I.

"That should do it," said Consuela, turning around. "And now, child, if you'll just put the suitcases away for me. No, not over there. In the back of the closet. That's right. Thank you, dear." She ran her fingers over the smooth surface of the bedpost. "I can't believe I'm actually here," she said softly. "I have to keep reminding myself where I am. It's been so many years—" The finger moved up and down, up and down. "I'm so grateful to you and your sister. If you hadn't come—"

"It's a lovely house," I said rapidly, maliciously. "It was a shame to let it stand empty so long. Why haven't you lived in it?"

The finger stopped moving. Her body was rigid. "I couldn't," she said. "Too many memories, I suppose."

She was lying. She couldn't live in this house because Alarice wouldn't let her. It was Alarice's house and she and I would see to it that Consuela didn't stay. Consuela would find what she was looking for. She would find it and then, unable to bear unbearable beauty, she would run away again.

That is, if *I* let her. She was much too old and much too slow to run away. If Alarice wouldn't let her stay and I wouldn't let her go, what would happen then?

I thought about it, amused.

"Would you like to see my room?" I said.

She looked at me, startled. "Your room?" She coughed. "The room you're in—is it comfortable?"

"I like it."

"Do you sleep well?"

"I always sleep well."

"You don't find it a bit—?"

"A bit what?"

She coughed again. "Never mind, child."

"I'd like to show it to you," I said.

"Tomorrow," said Consuela.

"Why not now? I fixed it up just for you. It's a beautiful room."

"It's been a long trip. And now, Gabrielle, if you'll excuse me—"

"It would only take a minute," I coaxed.

"I'm tired," she said. She swayed. "So tired."

"It's just the way it used to be," I said. "Just the way you remember it. I put back the red rug and there are curtains at the windows and there's an organdy canopy over the bed. Nothing has changed except for the fireplace. I can't find the fireplace at all."

There wasn't just one finger moving restlessly over the polished surface of the bedpost. She held on now with both hands, the knuckles white from strain.

"What do you want from me?" she said. "What is it?"

What did I want from her? I wondered. What had I to do with this old woman? Who was she to me? She was Alarice's sister, not mine. Elizabeth was my sister, Elizabeth who turned her face to Gordon, smiling; Elizabeth, guilty, guilt-ridden, and yet still smiling.

This was Alarice's house, but this was also Consuela's room. Was she safe in her own bedroom? If she locked her door, if she refused to go into Alarice's room and she turned the key in the lock of her door, could she keep Alarice away? Could Elizabeth keep me away? Alarice was mist and mist could slide under a door. Mist could float through a keyhole. There was nothing that could bar its way.

But I was neither memory nor mist. I would have to find my own way to Elizabeth.

"Why are you doing this?" Consuela whispered.

"Doing what?" I said indignantly. "What am I doing?"

She rested her head against her hands. "Who are you?"

I stood very still. My heart pounded. How could she? What kind of question was that?

She looked up. She was so small. I ached because she was so small. If I put my arms around her, she would be like a child leaning against me. I went toward her. I drew her close.

"I'm tired," she said, her voice muffled against my shoulder. "It must be because I'm so tired. It's dangerous to get exhausted when you're my age. Gordon says I must rest every afternoon and normally I do try, but today was an exception, of course."

"Yes," I said soothingly. "I know."

"For a moment—" She freed herself. She tried to stand very straight. "You must forgive me, child. I didn't mean to upset you. It's hard for the young to have patience with the old. You've been so kind and so helpful. I really don't know what got into me."

"It's all right," I said, even though I knew it wasn't. I touched my lips to her cheek. "I'll see you in the morning."

I left her then and went down the hall. I stood at the top of the stairs for a moment, listening, but there was no sound from the front parlor.

Where were Gordon and Elizabeth? Were they still together, sitting on the love seat in this heavy silence, bodies touching?

Or had they left the house, walking along the beach in the dark, walking side by side along the dark beach, their hands clasping while the black water lapped the black sand?

Where was Elizabeth? It didn't matter where she was. I would find her when I was ready.

When *I* was ready. I.

"Who are you?" Consuela had asked.

What an odd thing for her to say. She knew who I was. She had known from the very beginning.

"She's remarkable for her age," Elizabeth had said. "Her mind is so clear." But Elizabeth was wrong. Consuela was eighty. Her eyes were dimming. Her ears were dulling, the world of sound and sight retreating, the world retreating and the old forgetting.

"I had it just a moment ago," Maggie always said, searching for the elusive spool of thread, the lost carving knife, the mislaid napkin ring. "If my head wasn't tight on my shoulders, I'd lose that, too," she complained.

The old forget. Because Consuela was old she had forgotten who I was, but, I comforted myself, I was young and I wouldn't forget.

I opened my door and walked happily into my cold room. The house was so quiet. Everything was so quiet. My bed waited. My soft quilt waited, but for me the waiting period was over. It was time for rest, for sleep, for dreams.

✹

"It's a special occasion," Maggie said. "She's going to be eighty."

"We'll invite some people and have a party for her," said Elizabeth eagerly.

"What people?" I said.

"Gordon will know," Elizabeth said. "He can help me make a list of her friends."

I began to laugh. "They won't come," I said. "None of them will come."

"Of course they will," said Elizabeth impatiently. "Really, Gabrielle, I don't know what gets into you sometimes."

"She's eighty," I pointed out reasonably. "How many friends do you think she has left? Are you going to invite half the cemetery? And none of the others will come. Do you think they are going to step foot in this house after all these years? The dead can't," I said, "and the living won't."

I had told Elizabeth that the dead couldn't, but that wasn't true. What was left of the body Alarice had used lay in a lonely grave, but Alarice would be at Consuela's party.

I leaned back for a moment, thinking about it, seeing Elizabeth addressing the invitations, Elizabeth turning toward

Gordon, consulting Gordon in that soft, helpless way, with her head close to his. And the invitations delivered in person because the time was too short to mail them, Elizabeth going from house to house, stopping to visit with the old ladies rocking on the front porches, stopping to have tea and cake with the foolish, frightened old ladies who wouldn't come to Consuela's party.

"Constance has so many good friends," Mama had said. "It's difficult having to narrow the list, but I do have to eliminate someone."

"Helen Warren," I said spitefully. "As far as I'm concerned you can leave her out."

"I didn't ask for your opinion," Mama said sharply. "It's Constance's birthday and I want it to be a day she will remember always."

And they came to the house, all the young girls in their party dresses and Mama had a chocolate cake with nineteen candles in a circle and one in the center. "To wish upon," Mama said.

I leaned forward and there was Elizabeth sitting at the kitchen table and Maggie was saying, "I'll bake a chocolate cake," and then Consuela came into the kitchen. Maggie and Elizabeth looked at each other like conspirators and didn't say anything else about it because "the party will be a surprise," Elizabeth told me the next day.

"Did you invite Helen Warren?" I asked.

"As a matter of fact, I did," said Elizabeth. "I wish you had come with me today, Gabrielle."

"It was foolish of you to have asked me. You know I won't drive anywhere with you."

"You can't keep staying in this house," she said, looking worried. "It's not good for you."

"I like it here," I said. "It must be good for me because I don't use my cane any more. Have you noticed that I walk without my cane?"

"Yes," she said, "but—"

"And you told me how well I was looking, didn't you? I feel just fine, Elizabeth."

"Everyone was glad to be invited to Aunt Constance's party.

There are so many old friends still living and so many people in town who have known her through the years. You should have been with me."

"You had Gordon. That should have been enough for you."

"Gordon didn't go with me."

"Then he should have. The devoted nephew should have gone with you."

"How could he?" she said, startled. "How could he have possibly gone with me?"

"What a silly question," I said. "By the way, where is he now? Is it possible that you are actually sitting in one room of this house without Gordon by your side or have you allowed him to escape from you for a while?"

"He left this morning," she said. "There were some things he had to do at the office. He won't be back until the night before Aunt Constance's birthday."

"He could have said good-by."

"The call came last night after you were in bed. He didn't want to disturb you. I told you this morning at breakfast, don't you remember?"

"You're a liar," I said. "And don't shout at me. I don't like it when you raise your voice. I don't shout at you, do I?"

"I wasn't shouting," she said. She shook her head. "You forgot. I told you and you forgot."

"Are you starting that again?"

"Gabrielle." She turned away. "It's because I love you," she said, her voice low. "Whatever I do, it's because I love you. You know that, don't you, Gabrielle?"

Hypocrite, I thought. She stands there, pleading, anxious, expecting me to believe her. She killed my parents and she would like to kill me and she stands there, her eyes wide and candid, those eyes with the little flecks in them, filled with tears.

"I don't know you love me," I said, "and I don't know what you're doing. There would be no way for me to know what you're doing or what you're thinking. I can't follow you around all day or all night, too, for that matter. I can't get inside your head. I can't follow you right inside your head, so how would I know you love me and how would I know what you're doing?"

"It's impossible to talk to you," she said. "You take everything and twist and turn it to suit your own purposes."

"You will keep your voices down," Maggie scolded, coming into the room. "Mrs. Bellingham is upstairs and she doesn't have to hear you. I'm ashamed of both of you. What are you quarreling about?"

"The guest list for the party," I said. "You have to be very careful whom you invite to a party like the one we are going to give. You have to screen people and know exactly what you're doing. And then I'm worrying about the present. I have to give her a very special one, don't I?"

I began to laugh, thinking about the birthday present I would give Consuela.

Maggie's lips tightened. "It's time for your nap," she said.

I spent my afternoons seated at the small table Gordon had given me. There was a fiction that I was an invalid, and Elizabeth insisted that I rest every day after lunch. It was her way of getting rid of me, so that she could be alone with Gordon, but I didn't care. She could be with Gordon all she liked. She could walk along the beach with him or she could go fishing with him or she could sit in the front parlor with him. It didn't matter where she was or what she did. She would never have him.

Elizabeth and Maggie thought I was napping, and perhaps I was, sleeping upright in the chair with the paper spread before me and the pencil held loose and relaxed in my fingers. Sometimes it seemed to me that I really did sleep through the hours while the pencil traveled swiftly, guided by a hand surer and stronger than mine. I awoke cramped, exhausted, and the pencil rolled across the table while I tried to read what hadn't been written. Surely in the upper right-hand corner there was a faint impression, the first tentative formation of a vowel? Searching the blank pages, crumpling them angrily in my hands, I could almost remember the words, knowing that sheet after sheet of paper had been filled while I slept, and yet, eyes open, eyes properly focused, I could see nothing.

Sometimes I remained alert, willing the pencil to move, not knowing what it was I wanted to say, and yet knowing that it had to be said. It was all inside me, sweet and bursting inside me, the contained no longer containable, the inexpressible crying to be expressed.

How many afternoons had I spent like this? I wondered. How many days had passed since Consuela had come? What time was it? I hadn't wound my watch. It was nothing but an ornament on my wrist. There was no clock in the room because no clock belonged in this room. What concern of mine was the tick-tick of a mechanical device? There was no way time could be measured, and why was it so dark? Why should I be sitting at this table in the night, when it should be afternoon with the sun shining?

I rubbed my eyes, but the room was still dark. There was no sun and there was no moon. Where were the stars? Was there a house and an island and the sea? Or was there only the void and infinite space and the tangible, choking blackness?

I held out my hands with longing. If I kept my door open, this wouldn't happen. An open door is a friendly thing. There would be light from the hall if the light still burned in the hall.

I stood up and walked across the room, my hands still outstretched. I was looking for something, my fingers moving up and down the wall, searching. Puzzled, I stopped. Mama always kept an oil lamp next to my bed and candles on my dresser, but I didn't need a light to find my way through this house. I didn't need a light to find my way to Jotham. And because that was so, I was no longer afraid of the dark.

I opened my door, amazed to find the hall lit so brightly. I blinked for a moment. The door struck me then, not hard but lightly, like a warning tap on the shoulder, and I was forced to move. I padded down the steps in my bare feet, silently, softly, aware of Mama and Papa in their room and Consuela in hers.

Jotham was sleeping in the small back room downstairs. "So we can have an early start in the morning," Papa had said.

"I'm going with you," Consuela announced.

"Why can't you be like Alarice?" Jotham said, pretending to be annoyed. "She doesn't want to go fishing with us."

"She gets seasick," Consuela said with contempt.

I smiled at Jotham. "I just don't want to be a bother," I said gently. "There are times when men have to be by themselves."

And now Jotham was by himself, sleeping in the small room off the kitchen. He had spent the evening with Papa, the two of them seated at the dining-room table long after Mama and Consuela had finished clearing it. Papa opened a bottle of brandy and they had "almost finished it," Mama had said angrily.

"We're both fine," Papa had said thickly. "That boy's got a good hard head on his shoulders. Make a fine husband for Constance Suellen."

Be quiet, I told them savagely, silently. I closed my door and put my cheek against the hard, smooth wood and imagined Consuela lying in Jotham's arms.

Be quiet, I told myself now, and as if I had lived through all this before, I knew exactly what had happened.

At first I had thought of knocking on his door, standing like a ghost outside Jotham's door in my long, white gown, rapping timidly at his door in the middle of the night.

"Who is it?" he would say, his speech slurred from sleep, from the brandy.

"Alarice."

"What?" He would stand there, his hair rumpled, belting his robe about him.

"I have to talk to you."

"Can't it wait for morning?"

"No," I would say. "Oh, Jotham, no."

And then—what? He would send me away. He wouldn't be drunk enough, foolish enough, to let me in with Mama and Papa and Consuela sleeping upstairs.

Besides, he didn't want me enough to let me in. He didn't love me enough. He didn't love me at all.

And that is why I didn't knock. I stood outside his door in the dark passageway and I didn't knock. The knob was cold in my cold hand and it took a long time to turn. The door creaked and I heard him move in the bed, muttering something unintelligible. I stood in the doorway listening, trying not to breathe, trying not to wake him with the gasping sound of my breath.

"Oh, my God," said a woman's voice.

I shivered. It wasn't Consuela. It couldn't be Consuela, and this wasn't the way it had happened. I had been lying next to Jotham when he had turned toward me, half-asleep, half-awake. I had been lying warm and naked next to Jotham, and wanting me, loving me, he hadn't sent me away.

"What's the matter?" a man said.

It was a known voice, a beloved voice, but it wasn't Jotham. "It's here," the woman said.

I could smell the lilacs, the thick, sweet, sickening smell of lilacs.

"No," he said gently.

I left the door slightly ajar and backed away. I didn't dare to close it again. They would hear me if I closed it.

"Someone—something's in the room with us," she said. "I know it. I can feel it."

"There's nothing."

"Whatever there is in this house is here now," she said, her voice toneless. "Whatever horror—"

"Stop it. There is no horror."

"You haven't seen it. You haven't felt it. You just don't know."

Softly I moved back down the passageway. I didn't want to hear them. I wanted to clap my hands over my ears. I wanted to shut out the sound of their voices, but I couldn't move any faster and, oh, I could hear them so clearly.

"This is what I feel," he said. "Only this."

"No," she said. "Please, darling—"

"Come here," he said. And then, "There, that's better."

That's what Jotham had said to me. Those were his very words. "Come here," he had said, and I had gone to him, so that there had been no space between us anywhere, so that we had been linked together for all time until Consuela— I hadn't left his room this way in the night, fumbling and frightened.

"Gordon," Elizabeth cried.

"You'll wake everyone," he warned.

No, she won't, I thought. Just the way I won't. Not everyone.

We can't wake the living who sleep, but only the dead who cannot.

I moved faster now. Quickly, quietly through the dining room and the hall and the front parlor, and now I was in the back parlor. I couldn't hear them any more. Why had I come here? I wondered. There must be a reason. I could see the heavy, square outline of the piano. If there had been a moon, I could have played the piano by its light, the notes rippling silver and soft by moonlight, and the lovers, their bodies entwined, moving to the rhythm of my music. But, I reasoned, I could play in the dark if I wanted to. Did I want to?

I thought about it, leaning against the library table, considering. Did I want to? Did I want to do what?

My head hurt. I wanted to stroke it, my fingers moving back and forth across my forehead, my fingers knowing how to comfort my aching head, but there was something else I had to do. There was a drawer in the library table and I opened it and my clever fingers that knew how to smooth away pain and play the piano in the dark found it right away.

I held it tight in my hands, Elizabeth's notebook firm and hard in my hands and I walked through the front parlor and out into the hall, and there she stood, at the top of the stairs, looking down.

The rest of the house was dark, with shadows lying deep in the corners and running up and down the walls, but the hall upstairs was bright with light, and boldly, arrogantly, she sought the light, disdaining the safety of the dark. Her hair was fair and it tumbled loose about her shoulders, and my eyes, now accustomed to the dark, were blinded by the sight of her. She shimmered with light. She was everywhere. She was behind me, within me and in front of me, and there was no place I could hide from her.

"Who is it?" she whispered. "Who is there?"

It's Elizabeth, I thought, and I wanted to laugh. It's Elizabeth and she's afraid. She had a right to be afraid. She should be trembling with fear, standing with her back to Alarice's room, peering down the well of the staircase, searching the dark with terror, the blessed dark that a short while ago had sheltered her while she lay in Gordon's arms.

I was a wraith, a specter, a spirit, nothing she could see, nothing she could touch, but she knew I was there and there was a prickling between her shoulder blades. She wanted to run away, but she couldn't move.

Her terror was my joy. I held her notebook in my hands and I shook with silent laughter.

Scream, I thought. Why don't you scream? The dead are awake. Why not the living? Let the house echo with your screams. Let the house shake and vibrate with your screams and let the two old women, the snoring, sniffling, sleeping old women awake and let them listen to the sound of your screams and their own heartbeats. Let them count the beating of their hearts while they strain awake, each heartbeat ticking away their lives, the inexorable inner clock sounding an alarm that can never be turned off.

I put the notebook on the floor, part of the dark shadows that lay thick on the floor and, hands empty, I ran up the stairs.

"Elizabeth," I said. "You startled me."

She grabbed me. Her hands hurt my shoulders. She shook me back and forth and I went limp. "How could you?" she said. "How could you frighten me like that?"

"You're hurting me," I whimpered. "What's the matter with you? You frightened me, too, you know. I didn't do anything. I heard a sound and I went downstairs to see what it was. What's wrong with that? If you heard a noise, you'd want to know what it was, wouldn't you?"

She took her hands away. "Where were you?"

"I just told you," I said.

She sat down on the top step and rocked back and forth. "I'm sorry if I hurt you. I'd hurt myself before I'd hurt you. You know that, don't you, Gabrielle?"

"I love you, too, Elizabeth," I said serenely.

She looked at me, her eyes wet. "How long were you downstairs?"

"Long enough."

"Long enough for what?" Her eyes widened. She stood up.

"To turn off the faucet in the kitchen."

"And that was the sound you heard?"

"Of course."

She stepped back. "And there was nothing else?"

"What else could there be?" I said innocently.

"Nothing," she said, relieved.

Maggie's door opened. "Are you two going to stand there and talk all night?" she said hoarsely, fiercely. "If you are, just let me know and I won't even try to sleep."

"I'm tired," I said. "I'm going to bed." I smiled at Elizabeth. "And I suggest you do the same," I added, thinking, And in your own bed this time, my darling sister. Sleep soundly in your own bed for the rest of the night.

I leaned against my closed door until the hall was quiet again and then I stayed there a while longer, patiently waiting until I was sure they wouldn't hear me go down the stairs. It took only a moment to get Elizabeth's notebook. I opened the door to my room again and there was a light switch on the wall right next to the door. I turned it on and my room was as bright as the hall. I couldn't find an oil lamp anywhere and I could see that there were no candles on my dresser.

I put the wire-bound notebook on the table right next to the scattered sheets of paper I had been working on all afternoon. The notebook was real and solid with all the pages even, all the pages written upon, all the pages filled. Some were in ink, some in pencil, some typed, the unlined typing paper pasted in, Elizabeth fearful of losing some vagrant, valuable thought.

And what about my thoughts? What had I lost while I had sat at this table, filling page after page with unwritten words, day after day, each afternoon?

I sat very still. Each afternoon. I had wondered what time it was, when all along it had been the wrong time. Not afternoon for Alarice and me. Never afternoon for Alarice and me. I should have known better. Twilight, dusk, night was our time.

I would try again. I would sit at the table and hold the pencil in my hands and try again. But right now it was cold and I was tired and there was something else I must do.

I got into bed and pulled the quilt high around my shoulders. I tucked the pillow under my head, fussing, delaying the moment as long as possible, and then I propped Elizabeth's notebook across my raised knees. I flipped the pages, wanting to go backward, wanting to know the end before the beginning, and then, disciplining myself, I opened it properly and began to read.

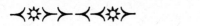 *Elizabeth*

✵

It seemed to me that i could hear the sound of the sea long before I went to Steppingstone, long before I even thought seriously of going there. As I walked the city streets, I pretended that the roar of the traffic was like that of the surf, and if I concentrated hard enough, I could imagine the waves frothing and foaming over the roofs of the cars.

It was only one of the subterfuges I used to keep myself from thinking. I kept a supply at hand the way Maggie hoarded groceries. "String beans?" I would say, frowning over the marketing list. "But Maggie, we have two cans in the cupboard."

"I'm going to use one of them for dinner and I like to keep one in reserve, just in case," said Maggie. "You never can tell when you'll run out of something."

Tricks to use and tricks to keep in reserve. A way to wake up in the morning without remembering and a way to fall asleep at night without thinking.

The mild sedative Gordon had prescribed didn't work, and I would lie there, counting backward. "One hundred," I said silently. "Ninety-nine." And I drew the numbers with an imaginary piece of chalk on the blackboard of my mind. Theoretically, according to the book I had read on self-hypnosis, I would be asleep before I reached eighty. "Forty-four," I said helplessly, furiously. "Forty-three."

Down to the beginning and up again, always going backward. Why backward? I thought idly, but I knew it took more of an effort that way. Like driving backward or walking backward or the going backward in time that was remembering. But there was no effort involved in remembering. Gabrielle was lucky. The difficulty for me was in forgetting.

The numbers written in a large, firm hand each night, and in the morning the physical effort of getting up, my eyes burning, my body aching as if I had been curled in the same position for far too long, immobilized in what sleep I had been able to find.

It was easier during the day, of course, except when I went to the hospital to see Gabrielle. During the day there were all sorts of things to be done and all sorts of tasks to be manufactured, which was the neatest trick of all.

But I hadn't cried. Not even at the funeral. "I can't," I told Maggie. "What's wrong with me?"

"It'll come in time," Maggie said. "It always does, and then it'll be worse because you held it back."

"But I'm not holding back," I said.

I was lying. If I ever let go—if, I told myself, I ever really let go, I will cry and never stop. I will cry until puddles form, until streams run, until the river overflows, until the sea inundates us all.

It was then that I would imagine the cars under water, the entire city buried in the sea but with everyone functioning normally, casually, the subways running and the sirens screeching and the people elbowing past.

"And with no one," I said to Gordon, "getting wet at all."

"Or even knowing they were drowning?"

"Not drowning," I said. "Just under water."

"All right. Under water then and no one knowing it."

"Of course not. If they knew, that would spoil everything."

"Wet newspapers," said Gordon, being practical. "Can't possibly start the day without the morning newspaper."

"You're not listening. I told you that nothing gets wet."

"Catastrophe, and no one gets hurt," said Gordon. "Is that it, Elizabeth?"

But it wasn't true. It was tragedy and we were all hurt. Even Maggie, who spent her time polishing silver that didn't need polishing and dusting furniture that didn't need dusting.

Maggie had always been with us. There hadn't been a time without Maggie. She was related to my mother. "A third cousin twice removed," my mother had said lightly. "I can never really understand complicated family relationships, but after your grandfather died, she lived with your grandmother, and then when your grandmother died, she came to us. She never married and frankly I don't know what I'd do without her."

"She's a servant," Gabrielle said.

"She's a cousin," I corrected.

"She does housework and she gets paid for it. That makes her a servant," said Gabrielle, her mouth thinning the way it always does when she intends to be stubborn. "I don't want Maggie to be my cousin. Any kind of cousin. Not twice removed or twenty times removed. As far as I'm concerned she can be just removed. She's stupid and provincial and she pokes her nose into everything."

Gabrielle was wrong. Maggie wasn't stupid. She just lived in a different era from the rest of us. She was a nineteenth-century woman pulled forward in time, a reluctant traveler moving along paths she was never meant to tread. And because of this she was content to stay in her tight, safe little circle within the larger one that was our home. She cleaned and cooked and scrubbed, and in her free time she sat in her room and read, wetting her index finger before she turned a page.

Her books were paperbacks, and the cover usually showed an open-mouthed young girl silently screaming in terror. Maggie read and dreamed of pointed arches, flying buttresses and the savagery of a barbaric horde. There in her room in the Gothic world in which she really belonged, she climbed a spiral staircase winding into darkness and she walked a wind-swept moor until she finally arrived at a castle with its turrets silhouetted against the sky.

She was our housekeeper, the keeper of our house, caring for possessions that didn't belong to her, loving children who weren't her own. She was in her late sixties now, but she belonged to me and I didn't know what I'd do without her.

I would come home from the hospital to find Maggie there, Maggie waiting to greet me, the lights burning and dinner on the table and Maggie's voice to break the silence.

"Eat your dinner, Elizabeth."

"I can't."

"Of course you can. That's the one thing you can do. That's the one thing you must do. Why do you think everyone brings and serves food after a funeral? It gives us something to do."

"Something the dead can't do," I said bitterly.

"There's nothing the dead can do. The dead are dead. But you are alive. Putting food in your mouth makes you know you are alive."

"I'm not hungry."

"It has nothing to do with hunger," Maggie snapped. "I'm not talking about hunger. I'm talking about food. You have to eat in order to live."

She fussed over me every day, but in all those months she went to the hospital only once to see Gabrielle.

"Gabrielle asked for you today," I said.

"No, she didn't," said Maggie, her voice matter-of-fact and without regret. "You're just saying that so I won't be hurt. It doesn't matter. Really it doesn't. I don't mind."

"Yes, she did, Maggie," I lied. "She did. She wanted to know why you didn't come to see her."

"And what did you tell her?"

"I said you were busy. I said you had so much to do and were so tired that the trip was too much for you."

"She doesn't want to see me," Maggie said quietly. "She told me so. She wanted me to go away. Don't tell me she's asking for me."

"She's been hurt, Maggie. Terribly hurt. She loves you. You know she does."

"Of course she does," Maggie agreed complacently. "I raised that child as if she was my own. Naturally she loves me, but right now all she wants is to be left alone."

"Gordon says she's still in shock. Not physically, not any more physically, but mentally and emotionally."

Maggie raised her eyebrows. "So it's Gordon now," she said dryly. "Since when has Doctor Inness become Gordon?"

He had become Gordon to me ever since we leaned over Gabrielle's bed together. Ever since we walked the sterile hospital corridors together. Ever since I sat in that waiting room, pretending to read a magazine, flipping the pages without seeing them, my knees shaking, praying soundlessly, praying without words that at least Gabrielle would live, that at least I would have Gabrielle left to love. Without words. Without even saying the words to myself, because if I had said them, my fear would become tangible. I didn't say, "God," and I didn't say, "Please," I just sent my longing winging away from me, not knowing where it was going but knowing somehow it was going somewhere, that it was touching something somewhere, because I knew hearing the sound of footsteps coming down the tiled hall that Gabrielle would live, knowing whose steps they were even before he came into the room, and knowing what he would say to me even before he said it.

"She'll need a good orthopedist," Doctor Henry had said after Gabrielle had been brought to the hospital, broken and bleeding. He looked at me, this old friend, this doctor, this thin little man with the graying mustache, his eyes still red-rimmed from weeping for my parents. "Inness is one of the best bone men in the country, Elizabeth."

Bone man! He was more than that. So much more than that. He used wires and splints and weights and plaster casts on Gabrielle, the bones snapped back in place, the legs drawn even and straight, the ribs taped and the skull bandaged, and then with all his skill, with all his compassion and tenderness, he healed me, too. He took the splintered pieces of my heart and wired them together, holding them tight with the sound of his voice and his deft, good hands.

When I was very, very young, much younger than Gabrielle is now, I used to dream about the man I would love. I imagined him tall and lean, moving arrogantly and with grace, the muscles hard under the smooth, always tanned flesh. His eyes would be gray, the gray of steel, his chin cleft and his mouth thin and firm.

Gordon is tall but he isn't lean. He enjoys good food. He butters his bread lavishly, and someday it is possible he will be fleshy, his waistline thickening. Right now there is the beginning of a double chin when he looks down the way he does when he's thinking or he's troubled. His eyes are brown and sometimes his glasses leave a red mark on the side of his nose. He flings back his head when he's amused and there are laugh lines around his eyes and his mouth and his forehead wrinkles when he's puzzled. His underlip juts out, his underlip a little too full, so that it's difficult for him to tighten his mouth.

And I love him. He doesn't know it. He is warmly protective, almost paternal, because he is ten years older than I.

"Middle-aged," said Maggie.

"Thirty-four?" I said defensively. "That's still young."

"Why hasn't he married?"

"He was in love with someone when he was an intern," I said. "He told me about it. She wouldn't marry him because he had no money. She didn't want to struggle with him."

Gordon interning, Gordon in a white coat with the stethoscope protruding from the pocket, Gordon young and eager and learning without me. All the things he learned without me. All the years he lived without me. Ten years ago, when he was twenty-four, I was fourteen and Gabrielle was nine, and, oh, I'm grateful to that girl who wouldn't marry him then. I'm so grateful.

"I'm so grateful," I said to Gordon the day Gabrielle first sat in a chair, the day Gabrielle was able to leave her bed for the first time. "I don't know how to thank you."

"What are you going to do now?" he said.

"I don't know what you mean."

124

"The day is coming when Gabrielle will be able to leave the hospital. Are you going to take her home?"

"Of course," I said, bewildered. "Where else would we go?"

"To Steppingstone," he said.

Steppingstone. I thought about the island, not able to picture it except as a gigantic rock. Something strong to rest upon, I told myself, remembering how Gabrielle and I, as children, would cross a brook, hopping from one stone to the other, careful not to get our feet wet.

I was glad not to have to take Gabrielle home. I had been there all along. Maggie and I had been there while Gabrielle was in the hospital because there was no other place for us to go. We had done all the necessary, all the painful, necessary, things that had to be done, and now the closets in my parents' room were empty and washed and clean. My father's papers were all in order and my mother's white leather jewel box with the pearl necklace and the emerald ring and the trinkets she had collected through the years was locked. The will had been probated, and all the time Maggie and I were erasing all trace of what had been, I was glad that Gabrielle wasn't there, and I was dreading the day when she would return.

She would walk through the front door ("She will walk again, Elizabeth, I promise you," Gordon had said), and she would turn to me and the tears would run so fast down her cheeks that I wouldn't be able to wipe them away.

But I hadn't told any of this to Gordon. I didn't have to tell him.

"Stay at Steppingstone for a while," he said.

"But your aunt—"

"I spoke to her. I told her all about you and Gabrielle. She wants you to go there, Elizabeth. The house is empty and has been empty for a long time. It's waiting to be lived in again."

"Why doesn't she use it?"

He hesitated. "It's haunted," he said.

Haunted. All those months while I wrote the numbers in the dark behind my closed eyelids, trying to concentrate on the numbers, another part of me, unreasoning, primitive and stubborn, had searched for what couldn't be found. How could my parents be dead? What was death? Was it nothing more than just the cessation of life?

Their coffins had been sealed, so I hadn't even seen their waxlike mannequins lying there, the art of the cosmetician simulating color in the colorless cheeks and mouth, my parents' images so alien to actuality that there was almost a horrible sort of comfort knowing that no semblance to reality could be buried in the earth. The flesh was hard and still and the grave was a fresh, raw mound. There must be something more, I screamed silently. I counted backward in the dark, not able to lie on my back with my arms quiet at my sides because that position belonged to the dead and I was alive. I thrashed and turned in the dark, hearing the sound of my own breath, my own heartbeat.

My father loved to laugh and my mother had a soft, serious way of speaking and one minute they were alive and the next they were dead and it was going to happen to all of us. We come from the dark into the light and we hold our faces upturned to the light and our hearts swell with joy because the air is sweet and good. One minute we are alive and the next we are dead and where was there any meaning in that? Why should we live only to die?

"Where are you?" I cried into the dark. "Where can I find you? Will I never see you again?"

"Haunted," I said. "Gordon—" My throat tightened.

"I'm sorry," he said. "That was stupid of me. Something happened there that my aunt can't forget, something she refuses to talk about and that's what I meant when I said the house was haunted. There are just too many painful memories. But surely that has nothing to do with you. To you it will be just another house and September is a good month on the island."

September, I thought with longing. September is like an island because it's a waiting month, a transition month, neither one season nor the other. September is a pendulum month, swinging back and forth between summer and fall, hot and hazy, cold and clear, and in between, all the days in between soft and warm.

126

"It will give you and Gabrielle a chance to be together again without having to make any decisions and without having to face everything Gabrielle's unable to right now," Gordon said.

"Gabrielle's face," I said, remembering, wanting to hide my own.

"I don't want to look," Gabrielle had said, turning that pitifully cropped head from side to side on the pillow. "You can't make me look if I don't want to."

"But there's nothing wrong."

"It's easy for you to talk," she said.

"It's not easy for me," I said. "Nothing is easy for me. I see you lying there and I feel your pain."

"How can you?" she said with contempt. "How can you say such a thing? Even a sentimental fool like you can't feel my pain. Don't even pretend you can. Just thinking about you pretending makes me nauseated. I might—I just might—throw up all over the bed again and I assure you the nurse will take a very dim view of it, especially when I tell her you made me. There's nothing wrong with you, Elizabeth, darling. No one took you apart and put you together again."

Only you, I thought. You took me apart and it was Gordon who put me back together again.

"I know," I said. I bent down. "Would you like me to crank up the bed? Are you comfortable?"

She laughed. "Comfy, cozy, that's me."

"If I could trade places with you, I would," I said quickly. "Please believe me when I tell you that your face is all right. I don't know why you insist that it has changed. It is exactly the same. I wouldn't lie to you. You must believe me. It was a miracle, but nothing happened to it."

"Plastic surgery," she said with conviction. "All done with very, very sharp knives and scissors, all the instruments *most* antiseptic and clean, and then snip, snip, snip."

"No," I said.

"You're lying," she said calmly. "I can always tell when you're lying. You get that silly, guilty look as if you're going to cry any minute."

"When you look in the mirror—if you'll just look in the mirror—"

"I don't want to."

"But you'll see then," I said desperately. "You'll really see yourself clearly then. You'll see that nothing has changed."

"Nothing has changed?" She laughed. "Are you now trying to convince me that nothing has changed? Thanks to you, my darling sister, everything has changed."

"What do you mean by that?" I said. "Gabrielle, what are you talking about?"

"I'm tired," she said fretfully, turning away.

"She won't do it," I told Gordon later.

"She doesn't have to. She already has."

"But she said—"

"I gave her a mirror this morning," Gordon said gently.

"Then why?" I said. "Why is she doing this?"

"She doesn't want to face the truth," he said. "Not any of it."

Gabrielle's face, the smooth oval of Gabrielle's face was still the same, still unmarred. She lay in the hospital bed, the sheets pulled taut, and I sat next to her, seeing Gabrielle's face with the eyes closed, watching over her while she slept. She slept quietly, the heavy, dark lashes resting, the curled fingers limp and resting, and I, sitting there without rest, brooding over the clear, clean sweep of my sister's brow, Gabrielle asleep, so young, so vulnerable, so hurt.

Haunted, I thought. We're all haunted, running from the past into the future, into the unknown. I will take Gabrielle to an island in September, to a crossing place in September, and there she will get well again.

September, I told myself. September and Steppingstone and a haunting as strong as memory.

☼

"MRS. SANDERS WON'T COME," I TOLD MAGGIE.

"Well, then," said Maggie calmly, "we'll just have to do for ourselves."

"It won't be so bad," I said. "Not with the two of us working together."

"I don't know what that woman did here anyway," Maggie said. "I don't know what Mrs. Bellingham paid her, but, whatever it was, it was too much. Considering that all the furniture was covered with dustcloths, I don't know what she found to do when she did come. While you were in town, I got the front parlor in shape. I polished all the furniture and I found a set of dishes in the kitchen cupboard that was coated with dirt and I washed those, too. If that's the way that woman cleaned, we can do just fine without her. Don't you worry about a thing, Elizabeth. We'll manage all right."

"You're wonderful," I said. I kissed her cheek. "Do you know how wonderful you are?"

"Now what's that for?" said Maggie suspiciously. "What did I do now?"

"Something special," I said lightly, beginning to unpack the groceries. I didn't tell Maggie it was because she hadn't asked any questions. If she had asked why Mrs. Sanders hadn't come, I would have had to lie, and I was much too tired to invent any stories.

Mrs. Sanders hadn't invited me in that afternoon. I had stood on the doorstep, feeling awkward and uneasy, shifting from one foot to the other.

"I can't understand why you won't help us," I told her. "It isn't as if you haven't been taking care of the house all along."

"I go once a month," said Mrs. Sanders stubbornly. She was thin and short, her head barely reaching the height of my shoulder, and her dark hair was fading as if a haze had been brushed over it. "For the last twenty years I've gone there faithfully. That's what I promised Constance Bellingham and I keep my word. I don't know why Constance told you to come to me. She knows I go there only once a month and no more than that. That was our agreement and no one can say I don't keep my word. I go once a month and it isn't time for me to go again."

"It was different before this," I said patiently. "Once a month was enough."

"That's exactly it, Miss—?"

"Thatcher," I said patiently. I had introduced myself to her only five minutes before. I had said I was Elizabeth Thatcher, and she had said, "How do you do, Miss Thatcher?," and now she didn't know who I was. "Elizabeth Thatcher," I said again, thinking of the packages I had left in the back seat of the car, the perishables left standing in the hot sun, the way I was standing in the hot sun. Only I wasn't perishable, I thought. I wasn't butter that could melt or lettuce that could wilt. I could see the cool, dim interior of Mrs. Sanders's house and I could feel the pain of fatigue moving between my shoulder blades. I took a deep breath. "Before this, the house wasn't being used, but now—"

"That's why I can't go," she said, her eyes narrowing. "That's why I won't help you. I'm not being mean. I know you think I am, but I'm not. There's those that won't do something just because they're mean and spiteful, but I'm not like that. You ask anyone what I'm like. I've lived in this town all my life and everyone knows me. I'd like to help you, but I can't. Before this the house wasn't being used, and when I went into it, I didn't stay in it long enough for the—" She hesitated.

"I don't understand," I said. "What is it?"

"I'm not sure if I should tell you. If Constance Bellingham didn't see fit to tell you, I don't know if I should."

"I wish you would," I said quietly. "You said you didn't stay in it long enough. Long enough for what?"

"For the thing to build up," she said quickly, seriously. "It takes time. Helen Warren says so and she ought to know. She has what they call psychic powers. Why, the night her mother died—and her mother lived over a hundred miles away on the mainland—Helen woke up and saw her mother standing at the foot of the bed just as plain as I see you now. Helen spoke to her and put out her hand and her mother disappeared, and the next day Helen learned her mother had died at that very moment."

"Who is Helen Warren and what has she to do with this?"

"She told Constance Bellingham what was going to happen in the first place, but Constance wouldn't listen to her. Constance should have listened. She knows Helen ever since they were girls together and she knows when it comes to things like this Helen is always right, but Constance only laughed then, and now she's laughing out of the other side of her mouth, I can tell you that. In the beginning she tried to rent it to summer people, but no one stayed longer than two weeks. It happened two summers in a row and then she just gave up. After that she couldn't sell it, either. Who would buy it—that's what I'd like to know."

"Look," I protested. I stepped back.

"It's perfectly safe if you're going to be there for just a few hours," said Mrs. Sanders, "but after that, I, for one, wouldn't stay. Not for a million dollars, and I'm not one to turn up my nose at money. You've been there for—" She pursed her lips. "How long did you say you've been there?"

I hadn't told her and now I didn't want to tell her.

I sighed. "We came last night," I said.

131

She raised her eyebrows. "That's much too long," she said complacently.

"Much too long for what?"

"It can't do it by itself," she said with authority. "When the house stands empty, it's perfectly quiet. There's never a light flickering or any nonsense like that. Why, there's young folk in this town who use that stretch of beach at night for all sort of shenanigans and no one's ever heard or seen a thing. There's never any trouble when it stands empty."

"I'll be going now," I said rapidly. "I'm sorry you won't come to us," I said politely, falsely, knowing I never wanted to see her again. "Thank you anyway." I started to walk toward the car.

"What's in that house needs people," she said loudly. "It's got to have people. Otherwise it can't *be*. Do you hear me?" she shouted. "It feeds on people!"

Feeds, I thought now, still unpacking the groceries, placing the cans in neat rows on the shelves. I was putting food away that would nurture, nourish and sustain us. It would feed us, Maggie preparing our meals painstakingly and with pride. Food and love, the two of them belonged together as far as I was concerned, and, I told myself as I shut the cupboard doors, there was nothing for me to fear in this house.

I was sure I knew it well by now. We had spent the night in it, Maggie and I, bringing our own fresh linens for the beds and giving it "a quick tidying," Maggie had said, frowning and looking around. "There's time enough for a good scrubbing after a good night's sleep."

I had slept in what had evidently been the master bedroom, for it had a fireplace, a large four-poster bed and a bright red rug on the floor. Maggie had insisted that I take that room.

"There's no point in telling me you want Gabrielle to sleep there," Maggie said. "Don't even bother to tell me Gabrielle would be more comfortable there. If I know Gabrielle, she'll choose for herself. If she wants it, she'll take it from you, and if she doesn't want it, there's nothing you can do about it. I'll take the bedroom across the hall, and if she makes us all move around again, that'll be all right with me, too, as long as I don't sleep in that one," said Maggie, pointing. "But I'm not too worried, because that's the room Gabrielle will take."

"How do you know?" I said, amused.

"Because I don't like it and Gabrielle likes everything I don't."

"There's nothing wrong with it," I said, standing in the doorway. "It just looks unfinished."

There really wasn't anything wrong with it then. Maggie and I were there a whole week before Gabrielle came, and the house was warm and good and quiet. I almost resented the normal, tedious routine in which Maggie and I lived and worked. We cleaned every inch of the house, the old wood floors glowing with polish, the shining mirrors reflecting our serious faces, the clock on the mantel in the parlor wound and ticking away time again, the house smelling of soap and sunlight, the telephone installed, the man from the phone company squatting on his heels, looking nervously over his shoulder and finding nothing.

The house was alive again, but it was just a house like any other, clean, well ordered, waiting to be filled. Doors that were left open, stayed open, and doors that were closed waited obediently for our hands to release them. The piano was played discordantly as Maggie's cleaning cloth gently rubbed the keys and I, missing Gordon and longing for Gabrielle, tried not to think of anything else.

For I wanted to believe. Oh, how I wanted to believe. If there was something in this house that needed me for its very sustenance, then I was willing to provide. I welcomed it. I opened my arms to it. I was willing to feed it. If I felt love, how could it be evil? If I felt no fear, how could there be horror? If I sought its memory, where then was the pain? If it existed—if it could exist—then my parents did, too, and we were all immortal.

But there was nothing. Day after day went by and there was nothing. It was a house like any other on this small island, shingled, scrubbed, flung open wide to the sea-smell and the autumn air.

And because there was nothing more I could do inside the

house, I turned to the garden, trying in those few days to undo the many years of neglect.

"You need green fingers," Maggie said.

I was kneeling at the edge of the flower bed, trowel in hand, fighting the weeds.

"You mean a green thumb," I said.

"Just a thumb won't do it," said Maggie thoughtfully. "Got a feeling this will take both your hands, Elizabeth."

I turned my head and looked at her. "Maybe it will," I said.

"And your prayers, too."

"Praying won't help," I said.

"I don't know about that," said Maggie. "I read once about a woman who prayed over flowers and how her roses grew twice as big and twice as beautiful, larger and more beautiful than any rose had a right to be. When I had a sick plant, I thought I'd try it. It was a geranium in one of those little clay pots and it was dying. The leaves were all curled and brown at the edges and I thought that maybe I could make it well again. I thought there was no harm in trying. I would take care of it in all the usual ways and I would try praying, too. It couldn't hurt anything and it might do a lot of good."

"What happened?"

"The plant died," said Maggie shortly, "but maybe I didn't know what I was doing, Elizabeth. Maybe it died because it was a geranium and not a rose. Maybe I didn't know the right way to take care of it and the right way to pray."

I sat back on the grass and stuck the trowel in the ground next to me. "What are you trying to say, Maggie?"

"Tomorrow you bring Gabrielle here. You told me Doctor Inness wanted her to stay in the hospital even longer than this. He didn't want you to take Gabrielle."

"That was in the beginning," I said impatiently. "That was before he knew how things would work out. Gordon agrees with me now that the best thing is for Gabrielle to be with us."

"She was always difficult. Even before all this happened, she was nothing but trouble. I saw the way she tormented your mother and I saw the things she did to you and I never said anything. It wasn't my place to interfere. But she's going to be worse now. You know it and I know it."

"No," I said. "She will get well."

"It will take both your hands and then some," said Maggie soberly.

She was right, of course. I knew it the next day when I watched Gabrielle walk toward me, leaning on a cane she didn't need. I knew it all through the long, tiring trip back to Steppingstone, a journey made more difficult because Gabrielle refused to drive with me and I couldn't use the car. I knew it as I watched Gabrielle choose her bedroom, Gabrielle going unerringly to the room next to Maggie's, Gabrielle gleefully planning how to finish her unfinished room.

"White organdy curtains at the windows," said Gabrielle.

"Are you sure you like this room?" I said.

"And a canopy for over the bed," said Gabrielle.

"If you don't like this room, you can have mine."

"But I want this one." She smiled at me.

I touched her arm. Green fingers, I thought. If I only had green fingers, healing, gentle, green fingers that would keep Gabrielle safe from harm.

"I want to talk to you," I said.

She yawned and shrugged away from me. "You always want to talk," she complained. "You'd like it if we sat together with maybe one light burning just for company and talked far into the night. You'd like me to confide in you, wouldn't you, Elizabeth?"

"Sometimes it helps just talking things out," I said.

"The confessional," she mocked. "The burden of guilt taken away in the confessional. Only instead of a priest I use your sympathetic, understanding ear. Oh, how you'd love to hear my secrets—that is, if I had any secrets from you. That is, if I dared to keep anything from you, Elizabeth. You'd put your arms around me and rock me back and forth and be very, very motherly and then you'd give me a sugar pill and tell me to go to sleep, for everything will be all right in the morning."

"Don't," I begged.

"You're shivering," she said softly. "Maybe you're getting old, Elizabeth. Maggie says your blood gets thin when you get old. When you get old, you get cold," Gabrielle chanted.

But I am young and I am cold, I thought. I am so cold.

"If you don't talk it out, it's going to get worse," I said. "Don't you see, Gabrielle? Don't you remember when you were little and you fell on skates and how I made you get up and try them again? It's the same thing with driving. I can understand why you're afraid to drive yourself right now, but surely you can trust someone else."

She opened her eyes wide. "Like you?"

"Yes," I said. "Like me."

She began to laugh. "You want me to put my life in your hands?"

"I will be very careful," I said gently.

"And you'll keep your eyes on the road? You'll never take your eyes off the road?"

"Yes," I said. "Yes."

"Keep your eyes on the road," she said thoughtfully. "Now that's something to consider, isn't it? You'd better watch the road very carefully from now on, Elizabeth."

"I will," I promised.

"Do you think I watch the road?" She wet her lips.

"It wasn't your fault," I said quickly. I blinked. I didn't want to cry. It wasn't time for me to cry. "Oh, darling," I said, "please stop torturing yourself. It was a terrible tragedy and I know how you must feel, but it wasn't your fault. The road was slippery and no one can blame you."

She clenched her fists. "How can anyone possibly blame me? What did I have to do with it?"

No, I thought. Don't say another word to her. Stop it now. This has gone far enough.

"Nothing," I said. "You're right, of course. You had nothing to do with it."

"And yet you want me to trust your driving." She shook her head in amazement.

"You have to get in a car with me sometime," I said miserably.

She sat down at the edge of the bed. "I am very tired," she said in a childish treble. "It's been a long trip and I'm absolutely exhausted. Maggie said I looked tired. Didn't you hear her? I have just come from the hospital and I really do think I should have some rest. I don't think it's kind of you to keep me up half the night talking. It's not like you to be unkind, Elizabeth."

"No," I said. I rubbed my arms and shivered.

"Where are you going?"

"I just want to close the windows," I said heavily. "It's chilly in here."

"Leave them open," she commanded, "but you can go now, and shut the door behind you."

"I'd like you to have it open just a little," I said. "If you should need me during the night, I'd be able to hear you if the door was open."

"Shut it."

"Gabrielle, darling—"

"The door," she said.

I shut it tight. The hall seemed very warm after the chill dampness of Gabrielle's room. Maggie's door was closed, too, and now all the doors that led to the hall were shut except mine. It stood wide open, my room and my bed waiting for me.

Gordon, I thought, knowing I was going to call him, knowing I was going to ask him to come to me.

I walked slowly down the stairs, keeping my back very straight. There was something unfinished in the unfinished room behind me, something evil and sick and filled with pain. There was a demanding hunger and I didn't know how it would be fed.

I walked down the stairs and I held onto the banister with one hand, the other limp at my side, and I could see that my fingers weren't green, a healing, soft, shimmering green. My fingers weren't green at all. They were cold and still and white.

I stared at my useless hands, and then I sat down on the bottom step and let them cover my face. The time had come for me to cry.

IN ORDER TO GET TO HELEN WARREN'S HOUSE I HAD TO drive along High Street, which bordered the water front. The ferry slip was empty, the ferry no longer in this off-season running every hour, but there were still boats in the water; the pleasure craft, buttoned-down and canvas-covered, straining futilely at their moorings, the fishing boats at the docks, and always the ever-present sea gulls and terns, wheeling and swooping, their cries mournful and demanding.

"Make a right turn on Front Street," Gordon had directed, "and then when you get to the top of the hill, turn right again. It's the second house from the corner."

I had driven him to the inn, which had been built when the town had started to change from an insular, self-contained community to a summer resort. Now, still standing on Merrymount Street, flanked by shops, it was an anachronism. It was an old-fashioned hotel, a relic of the nineteenth century, with its cupolas, circular, graveled driveway, large wooden veranda and porte-cochere. But Gordon said he preferred it to the new motel, which he called a phony colonial, with its huge white columns, shuttered windows and air conditioning.

"I used to come here summers with Aunt Constance when I was little," Gordon said, "and it's the same now as it was then; ice water in silver pitchers and napkins folded in rings and chairs to rock in. The plumbing has changed, of course, but in some areas even Steppingstone welcomes progress." He grinned at me. "Just the same, I won't mind leaving it. Much rather stay at the house. I have a feeling Maggie is a good cook."

"I won't be long," I said. "By the time you pack and check out, I'll be back."

He shut the car door and then turned and leaned on the open window. "Are you sure you want to see her alone? Don't you want me to go with you?"

"You know I do," I said. "I'd feel a lot better if you were with me, Gordon, but there's enough gossip now."

"Probably all started by Helen Warren," he said dryly. "Aunt Constance wouldn't have sent me down here if Helen hadn't written to her. You'd think Helen would fly over on her broomstick instead of sending something as prosaic as a letter." He smiled. "If she doesn't watch out, I'll go over there and break her crystal ball."

I laughed. "Don't be silly. She doesn't have a crystal ball." I stared at his suddenly serious face. "Or does she?" I said, amazed.

"I wouldn't put it past her. She probably dispenses herbs, prophecies and love potions." He started to open the door. "To hell with her," he said, frowning. "I don't like it. I'm going with you."

"No," I said, knowing it would be easier to talk to Helen Warren if I didn't have Gordon watching me, his eyebrows raised quizzically.

"All right," he said gravely.

I watched him walk up the steps. His hair was rumpled by the wind and his hands swung at his sides.

I had called him the night before, but he hadn't been there. Service had answered the phone, her voice metallic as she told me Doctor Inness had gone away. No, she didn't expect him back. She sounded bored and detached as if she had the phone tucked between her cheek and her hunched shoulder while she filed her nails. His associate, Doctor Palmer, was available, however, and, of course, in an emergency— But her voice, humorless and flat, told me she knew this wasn't an emergency.

And then only a few hours ago I had met him at the sea wall. The sky had been very blue and the bay had been dotted with whitecaps, and, seeing him, I felt sun-dazzled.

"If I had only known you were on your way here," I had said to Gordon, "I wouldn't have felt so lost. When you called me this morning and said you were at the inn, I had just finished turning off all the lights. I don't know why it's worse to have to turn off a light when the sun is shining, but it is." I thought about it for a moment. "Maybe because it seems so incongruous, so out of place. I couldn't believe it," I said, clasping my hands. "Wherever I went, in every room, I found a light burning. Why did she do it, Gordon?"

"Gabrielle? Something must have frightened her. She's like a child who finds comfort in a night light. It's an oasis in the dark. What can hurt you if there's a light burning?"

"Like a bad dream," I said. "Wake up and it goes away. Now I'm awake and you are here." I looked toward the house. There was a figure framed in the upstairs window. Gabrielle, I told myself with apprehension. Gabrielle is awake, too. I touched his arm, turning my whole body toward him. "Oh, Gordon, I'm so glad you came. I feel so much better now."

"Elizabeth—"

"It's so different with you here," I said rapidly. "I'm not afraid any more."

Gordon leaned against the sea wall and wouldn't look at me. "My aunt wants you to leave," he said abruptly.

"Leave?"

I thought of going home. I thought of packing our things and putting all the dustcloths back on the furniture and pleading with Gabrielle while she watched me, her eyes amused; Gabrielle saying over and over again, "You want me to drive with you, Elizabeth? You want me to put my life into your hands?" And then Maggie keeping Gabrielle company on the train, while I drove the empty car with the trunk filled with our suitcases. I thought of being at home again with Gabrielle and what it would be like for her there, and Steppingstone far behind us, the island and everything it stood for, behind us forever. I sighed and the wind blew my hair backward so that I had to cup my hands to keep it off my face.

Gordon turned and put his hands on my shoulders. "Don't," he said. "It can't be helped. Aunt Constance received a letter from an old friend of hers who said she didn't like to interfere, but she felt it was necessary in this case. She said she didn't want to approach you herself, that it wasn't her place to speak to you, but she did feel it wasn't wise of Aunt Constance to let you have the house."

I leaned against him and his fingers tightened. "Helen Warren," I said.

"What do you know of Helen Warren?" But his voice was suddenly disinterested, as if he didn't care. I looked up and his mouth was curved, the corners turning up, and his eyes were intent and tender.

"Gordon," I said, and then something, some instinct made me turn my head, and there was Gabrielle walking down the road and when I looked at Gordon again, it wasn't the same.

When Gabrielle was near us, nothing was the same. Just the way Gabrielle was never the same from one moment to the next. She changed like a scudded, cloud-flecked sky, the sun moving in and out, appearing and disappearing so that the day was neither one thing nor another. Her own private storm threatened and then cleared, and I didn't have a chance to be alone with Gordon again until we were on our way back to the inn.

"I wanted to see Helen Warren before this," I had said. "Now I must."

"To hell with her," Gordon had said, but bless Helen Warren, I thought now as I drove away. Bless Helen Warren for mumbo jumbo and spells and witchcraft and for sending Gordon to me.

She was waiting. Round of face, pink-cheeked, blue-eyed, white-haired, a little cherub of a lady, and she was waiting for me, walking up and down the red-bricked path that led to her house, her foot tapping impatiently.

I parked at the curb. She beckoned imperiously. She marched up the wooden steps of the porch. "I've been expecting you," she said briskly, holding open the door.

Oh, no, you don't, I thought grimly. You didn't know I was coming and you're not going to convince me that you did.

"You must be thinking of someone else," I said politely. I took off my gloves and put them on again.

"You're Elizabeth Thatcher, aren't you?"

"But—"

"You either are or you are not," she said firmly. "There is no *but*. I dislike that word intensely. It is totally redundant and I prefer that it not be used around me. And since you *are* Elizabeth, you'd better come in."

"Yes," I said meekly.

She moved ahead of me, trotting swiftly down the long, cluttered hall with its rococo mirror and elaborately framed pictures, and I followed, both of us hurrying as if we were on our way to some definite, most urgent appointment.

"We will use the back parlor," she said. "The cats are in the front one. Right now Matilda is nursing her kittens and *really* can't be disturbed. In a little while she will join us for tea."

She was smiling and bustling about the sun-flooded room. There was a blue-brocaded couch near the fireplace and a battered black leather easy chair with a hassock, and the bookcases were untidy and overflowing, books tucked in every available space, some standing upright, and some lying on their sides, the very book ends consisting of the books themselves. The blue curtains were faded but crisp and starched, and the heavy, dark coffee table was highly polished.

Maggie would approve of her, I thought, dazed.

"I do hope you like tea." She motioned me to the chair. "Nowadays this is the cocktail hour, but I find it necessary to keep my wits about me and alcohol always makes me sleepy. Spirits don't mix well with spirits." She beamed and glanced at me sideways. "Just a bit of a joke, my dear."

"Yes," I said, sitting down.

"I don't mind a sip of wine before I retire at night. I take ordinary table wine and mix it with water, half and half, you might say, and it does make for a rather pleasant drink. Ordinarily I prefer tea, except for the one cup of coffee I allow myself in the morning." She smiled at me. "I usually rattle on like this deliberately," she admitted candidly. "It helps put my visitors at their ease. You're quite comfortable now, aren't you, Elizabeth?" She nodded her head, satisfied, and then placed the back of her hand against the china teapot. "Still good and hot," she informed me complacently. "It's all in the timing, you know. Boil the water too soon and it would be lukewarm by now. You'll have lemon, of course."

It wasn't a question. She had known I was coming, and she knew how I liked my tea, and what, I thought, staring at her, what else does she know?

"Don't look so somber," she said, still smiling. "It really isn't mysterious at all."

"You can't read my mind," I said defiantly.

"I never said I could."

"How did you know when I would be here?"

"How do you know the sun is shining?"

"I can see it," I said.

"I see things, too, Elizabeth."

I forced myself to take a sip of the tea. It was very strong, very hot and very good. "It's delicious," I said.

"I'm glad you like it," said Helen Warren.

I took another sip. "Absolutely delicious," I said. "You must tell me how you brew it. I—"

"Elizabeth," said Helen Warren, "please listen to me. I'm old now. I'm only two years younger than Constance Bellingham and the things I know I have known since I was younger than you." She put her teacup in the saucer and set both carefully on the table. She stood up and opened the folding doors that divided the front parlor from the back one. "Come in, Matilda," she said.

The cat moved slowly into the room. She was dark gray, but her ears and her front paws were white. Her eyes were yellow in the sunlight. She looked at me and then brushed against my legs.

"She likes you," said Helen Warren, pleased. She poured

cream in a dish and placed it in front of the cat. Matilda lapped it, flicked a drop from her whiskers and then sat back on her haunches, bored. She began to wash her face, purring so that the room seemed to vibrate with contentment.

"She's beautiful," I said. I leaned back, suddenly relaxed. "I had a kitten once."

"You can have another now," said Helen Warren. "It's about time Matilda weaned them. They're old enough. I want you to take one home with you. There's a male, larger and stronger than the others, and he would be perfect. No house can be completely bad if there's a cat in it, and I know you're not going to leave the Lysander place."

"How do you know?" I said loudly.

The cat was staring, her eyes, wide and intent, fixed on a point just beyond my left shoulder, and automatically I turned my head. There was nothing there.

"How do you know?" I said again.

"Gordon is here because Constance sent him, and if you were going to leave, you'd have made your decision by now. You wouldn't have bothered to come to see me."

"That's how you knew I was coming," I said, relieved. "Because of the letter and because Gordon is here."

"Sometimes I know who is calling me even before I pick up the phone," she said gently. "Not always—but sometimes. Hasn't that ever happened to you, Elizabeth?"

"That's just coincidence," I said scornfully.

"Or you're in a strange place and you look around you and you suddenly feel detached, knowing you've been there before, knowing what is going to happen next, the words that will be spoken, the very gestures that will be used."

The cat, crouched low, still stared into the distance. Bemused, she purred, her claws kneading the rug in ecstasy.

"What is it?" Helen Warren watched me. "You've remembered something, Elizabeth."

"Yes," I said.

And then I told her about the phone call that came the night after my parents' funeral. It was after midnight when the phone rang. The line was open, but when I spoke, no one answered.

"Hello?" I had said, over and over again. "Hello? Who is this?" Frustrated, annoyed, I hung up.

The phone rang again.

"I can't get through," a woman's voice said desperately. "Why can't I get through?"

"Who is this?" I said again.

"She can't hear me," the woman said, her voice breaking.

"But I can hear you," I said. "You can't hear me. Why can't you hear me?"

"When can I try again?" She was crying. "Will I ever be able to try again?"

"Please," I said thickly. "Please tell me who you are."

"And then," I said now to Helen Warren, "the line went dead."

"The line went dead," said Helen Warren quietly. "The line of communication was cut. You recognized the voice, didn't you, Elizabeth?"

"It was my mother's voice," I said dully. "I could swear it was my mother's voice. I know it's impossible and yet—"

"Our eyes are like slits," Helen Warren said. "They are open just a fraction, just enough so that we can see where we are going without stumbling. Our ears are stuffed so that we are not deafened by all the sounds that are to be heard. We take a little box and turn a switch and move from one channel to another, tuning into a broadcast emanating from others just like ourselves, the blind and the deaf. When we turn off that switch, the room becomes very quiet. We hear nothing, and yet, just the same, on all channels, on all stations, the programs continue and the airwaves are filled with sound. For us, because we cannot hear, the line is dead."

"It was my mother's voice," I said. "It couldn't have been, and yet it was my mother's voice." I put my empty teacup on the table. My hands were shaking. "I never read the obituary page," I whispered. "I don't want to know the daily list of the dead. I don't want to know how old they were and who the mourners are and where the services will be held and where the interment will take place. I don't want to know those things, but the day before my parents were killed, I found myself scanning the obituaries searching for their names. I knew they were in the house. I knew they were alive and well and safe in our house and yet, appalled, I sat there looking for their names. Why did I do that?"

"Why?" said Helen Warren gently. "I don't know why. I don't know why I was born with my eyes wide open and my ears unplugged. It's the sixth sense, the most indefinable and therefore the most valuable of all our senses—the one we dismiss as intuition or, worse, mere coincidence. It's the one we refuse to admit we possess, the one that will really show us where we are going so that we can proceed without stumbling."

In the next room one of the kittens mewed. Matilda raised her head.

"I was afraid last night," I said. "I was afraid this morning, too, but when Gordon told me his aunt wanted us to leave, I couldn't bear it. I'm more afraid of going home than staying."

"Come here," she said, patting the couch.

Obediently I stood up. I skirted the coffee table and sat next to her. She reached for my hand.

"What—?"

"Be quiet," she ordered. "The vibrations—" Her fingers were surprisingly strong, the old flesh cool, dry and papery. "Yes," she said. "I thought so." She drew back. "Be more afraid of staying," said Helen Warren harshly.

"I can't go home," I said. "Not yet."

She picked up a napkin and, absorbed, began to pleat it. "What you are searching for exists," she said slowly. "I give you my word that it exists. Nothing is wasted. Time as we measure it has no importance. If the answer to all this is what you hope to find by staying, then I'm telling you to go. What lingers in the Lysander house is evil, otherwise it would have left long ago. What clings to that house remains only because of hate and despair, and if you stay, I don't know if I can help you."

"I must stay," I said stubbornly.

The cat yawned and stretched. She stood, back humped, stiff-legged for a moment and then she left us, her tail held high.

"Jotham Bellingham died in that house because he wouldn't listen to me. Gordon's mother, Ruth, was only a child then, but

146

she remembers it well. There must be times when she still wakes in the night and remembers. She came back to Steppingstone once when Gordon was a child. She opened the house and announced she was going to live in it, but she couldn't, just the way no one else could, and she will never come back again. She promised me and I know she will never return. What has happened in that house has nothing to do with you and you must leave it immediately."

"I have seen nothing," I said. "I have been there for a week and I have seen nothing and I have felt nothing."

"Last night you were afraid."

"It was my sister," I said defensively. "My sister made me afraid."

Helen Warren sighed. "You will take the kitten," she said wearily. "An animal is an enormous help, and for this sort of thing a cat is indispensable."

"I can't. Gabrielle is allergic to cats. She hates them."

She raised her eyebrows and the blue eyes widened. "So," she said thoughtfully. "Gabrielle hates cats, does she? What a strong word to use, Elizabeth. What else does Gabrielle hate? Surely if she hates one thing, she hates another. Can you make a list? Is she good at hating? Does she have a talent for it?"

"No," I said firmly. "No."

"Last night she frightened you. Have you ever been afraid of Gabrielle before?" She leaned forward. "Please answer me, Elizabeth. This is important."

"I'm not afraid of Gabrielle."

"You said you were."

"I said she made me afraid. There is a difference."

"Is there?"

"Gabrielle has been sick." I stood up. "It has nothing to do with the house. She was in an accident. She was driving and she was in a terrible accident. Both my parents were killed. Gabrielle was hurt, badly hurt, both physically and emotionally. She's been in shock. Gordon says so and he ought to know. It will take time—lots of time—but she will heal."

" 'But,' " she said softly. "Always that word." She looked at me. "And there will be no scars?"

"There are no scars," I said stupidly. I bit my lip. "At least none that I can see, and the ones I can't see will go away. It'll take time, but they will go away. If we go home, there will be too many memories and—"

She turned her head as if she were listening, but not to me. "And there is hate waiting," said Helen Warren, her voice low, murmuring to herself. "Hate patiently waiting, not caring how long it waits or for whom. Hate, incarnate, waiting and calling. What am I going to do?" she whispered. She shook her head and stood up. She walked across the room, her back toward me. "I have to think," she said. "I have a lot of thinking to do, Elizabeth. I wonder if you will excuse me now." And then she walked out of the room.

"Please—" I said foolishly, standing still. The cat scampered back and began to weave about my ankles. "Please," I said, hurrying after her, "there are so many things I haven't asked you. There are so many things I want to know."

She didn't turn around. She continued down the hall with her quick steps and I followed her, the cat padding silently next to me. I caught a glimpse of my reflection in the mirror as I went past, and I saw myself again in the glass-enclosed water colors, each like a smaller mirror with my image momentarily superimposed across the seascapes filled with the immensity of water and sky, and I had an odd sense of unreality, as if this had happened before, as if in some distant dream I had rushed down a long, dark hall after a retreating figure I could never grasp.

She held open the front door. "We will see each other again," she said. "We will talk again."

"But—" I said awkwardly.

She looked at me, frowning.

"But," I said again, emphasizing it. "*But!* The word has to be used. I have to use it. You can't ignore it. Nothing is unqualified. Nothing is sure."

"Perhaps you're right," she said. "I really don't know."

I stared at her. She looked exhausted. What did I want from her? I wondered. What did I expect to get from Helen Warren?

Belief without proof, I told myself bitterly. That was what I wanted, and wasn't that exactly what she had given me? And now, seeking, unsatisfied, I wanted the proof. If I probed further, would I turn into an open-mouthed creature, part of a credulous, avid group sitting around a table with the lights dimmed and fingers touching? Would I sit there praying for the coming message, the table-tapping, the bells ringing, the tambourines shaking and the spirits dancing on demand? Was that the proof I sought?

She doesn't know, just the way I don't know, I thought as I drove along the cobblestoned streets, as I turned back to the inn, back to Gordon and back to the house that waited for me. She gave me her word, but her promise is only her own faith and her own belief. She is no different from the rest of us. She doesn't know. She really doesn't know at all.

G ABRIELLE WOULDN'T LEAVE THE CAR. SHE SAID SHE wasn't hungry and she would wait right where she was for Gordon. No, she didn't want Elizabeth. She wanted Gordon. She folded her hands and smiled, the slow, satisfied smile Gabrielle uses when she intends to have her way, and I had to go back into the house without her.

"Aren't you going to have your breakfast?" Maggie said irritably. She set a saucepan on the stove with a thump. "Isn't anyone around here going to eat this morning?"

"I'll have breakfast in town with Gabrielle," said Gordon, coming into the kitchen. He had shaved and changed his clothes. His blue slacks were sharply creased and he was wearing a white knit sport shirt. He smiled at me. "But Elizabeth will eat, Maggie. She'll have bacon and eggs and toast and—"

"Just coffee," I said dully.

"Stop fretting so much, Elizabeth," Gordon said.

The coffee was too hot. I burned my tongue and the back of my throat felt seared and tight. "Are you going to tell me I'm nagging, too?"

He looked at me, his eyes thoughtful. "You can't keep at her all the time. You have to give her a chance to work things out for herself. Just be glad Gabrielle's becoming interested in something. Her desire to decorate the room is a good sign."

"I'm glad something around here is a good sign," said Maggie dryly as Gordon closed the front door behind him.

I poured too much milk into the coffee. "I don't know what you're talking about," I said.

"Oh, yes, you do. She wants him. He's yours and she wants him."

"He's not mine," I snapped. Now the coffee was lukewarm and tasteless. I pushed it away.

"When she was little, she screamed for your toys and, like a fool, you gave them to her."

"Why must you exaggerate? It was just one doll."

"Your favorite doll, and then later on it was your gold bracelet and then—"

"One doll and one bracelet," I said coldly.

"And one man," said Maggie shortly. "I know Gabrielle. Are you going to give everything to her? Is that what you intend to do with your life?"

"I thought you loved her."

"Of course I love her," said Maggie. "How many times do I have to tell you that? Why do I even have to tell you that at all? If I didn't love her, I'd have washed my hands of the whole situation long ago, but just because I love her doesn't mean I can't see what she's like."

"I don't know what you're getting so excited about," I said with dignity. I stood up and the coffee spilled on the table. "It's all very simple, really. Gabrielle wanted to go shopping and Gordon was kind enough to take her."

"And why didn't you go, too?"

Because Gabrielle didn't want me, I answered silently.

Maggie reached for the sponge and began to wipe the table. "I know why you didn't go," she said fiercely. "Just don't come crying to me when this is all over. You'll get no sympathy from me." She walked over to the sink and let the water run. "Or maybe," she added sarcastically, "you just decided to stay home and help. Gabrielle got on her knees to you, just begging you to go with them, and you said you had to stay here and help me."

"Maggie—"

She turned off the water. "I don't know what I'm yelling about," she said, leaning on the sink. "I'm glad you're here. I don't like staying in this house alone. I didn't feel that way in the beginning, but now I'm just as glad to have company. Some houses are friendly and some are just places made of wood or brick or stone and have no feelings at all. Here I find myself looking over my shoulder." She wiped her hands on her apron. "Anyway, as long as you're here you can help. You can make Gabrielle's bed. I don't like that room. It gives me the creeps and, what's more, there's something wrong with that door. It just won't stay open."

"Something must be broken," I said. "It was all right before—"

"Before what?" she prodded.

I didn't answer her. I didn't want to answer her. She was still leaning against the sink, using the blue porcelain sink for support. She's getting old, I thought, startled. She's younger than Helen Warren, but she looks much older standing there like that with the sunlight streaming through the window, the morning sun harshly outlining the bent shoulders, the gray hair, the ugly brown spots on her hands.

"I'll be upstairs if you want me," I said because I couldn't stay there any longer, shaken with pity, watching Maggie age before my eyes.

Gabrielle's door was closed, of course. I turned the knob. It opened easily at my touch.

It was all right before Gabrielle came. There was nothing wrong with it before Gabrielle came.

The room was still cold. Gabrielle's warm, living presence hadn't changed that. The windows were open wide and the sunlight danced on the ceiling and on the floor, and yet the room was without light, the sunlight just a mechanical flickering image that had no reality here. I watched the door close behind me, slowly, silently, as though guided by an unseen hand.

152

It had closed last night in the same controlled way and I had stood there as I stood now with that same prickling sensation between my shoulder blades, but last night I had left the room quickly, not able to bear it without even the shadow of the sun to sustain me. I had left the room to lean over the banister, to call to Gabrielle, to tell her I couldn't find her cane.

She had been standing at the foot of the stairs, pretending to speak to me, her mouth opening and closing soundlessly.

"I can't find your cane," I said, not wanting to admit that I hadn't looked for it, that I couldn't bear to stay in her room one moment longer.

Looking down, leaning on the banister and looking down at her, she seemed distorted. I felt as if I were viewing her through a flawed pane of glass, the glass murky and mottled with hair-line cracks, and Gabrielle standing behind it, caught behind it, trapped behind it, out of my reach forever.

"What is it?" I whispered "What is wrong?" And then I could hear my own voice ringing in my ears, my own voice reverberating, the sound of my own voice crashing against that barrier to my sight, a boomerang heading straight for me. What had been a whisper was a shriek. The hall echoed, and each echo created another in an endless chain of sound, the echoes multiplying, magnifying and monstrous. The words flowed together. The words fused together, and yet each was clear and distinct. "What is it? What is wrong? What is it? What is wrong? *What is it?*" Up and down the hall, around and around my words raced until I wanted to crouch right there on the landing, lie right there on the floor with my knees drawn high and my head bent so that it touched my knees, my body returning to the fetal position, returning to the safety and the quiet of the womb. Only, the womb that had created and cradled me was destroyed, and all I could do was listen to my own words, part of the sound of my own words.

And there was Gordon. The glass shivered and dissolved, and there was Gabrielle in Gordon's arms, Gabrielle held safe and quiet in Gordon's arms, and I walked slowly down the stairs, holding onto the banister, and I said the only thing I could say, the only thing left for me to say.

"What is it?" I said. "What is wrong?"

"Something frightened Gabrielle," Gordon said, not looking at me, his concern, his tenderness only for Gabrielle.

And I had to stand there and watch while he carried her up the stairs. She could walk. Gordon knew she could walk, but just the same he carried her. She put her arms tight around his neck and her hair brushed his cheek, and when they reached the top of the stairs, she turned her head and smiled, that same lip-licking smile she had used just a little while ago.

Then when the door to Gabrielle's room had closed behind them, and Gordon had stayed away so long that I couldn't bear it, I had knocked on the door, a stranger knocking on the door to my sister's room.

Now I had to make her bed.

One doll and one bracelet, I thought, as I pulled the top sheet tight, as I smoothed out the patchwork quilt. Gabrielle would lie between these clean, ironed sheets, lie wrapped in the softness of this quilt, those dark lashes quiet, that satisfied smile on her lips as she remembered how she had stepped back at the sight of me.

"Oh, Elizabeth," she had said, her hands against her cheeks, her eyes mocking. "Elizabeth, darling, how you startled me."

And then Gordon babbling nonsense about Gabrielle sleeping with me that night as if Gabrielle needed protection, as if there were some force she had to be guarded against. It would have been far better if Gordon had left Gabrielle's bones crooked and had probed into her brain instead, poking and prying into the convoluted gray mass that was Gabrielle's brain, saying "Yes, this is a badly twisted thought that needs straightening and here is an emotion all broken and bent," and then the splints put on so neatly and cleverly, and Gabrielle limping physically because Gordon had no time left for her body, Gabrielle still limping and yet standing whole and straight.

"Aunt Constance will come," Gordon had said, cradling the phone. He looked at me. "What is it, Elizabeth?"

"There was something on the stairs," I said. "I lied to you before. I don't know why. Maybe I didn't want to admit it in front of Gabrielle. Gabrielle called it a wall. To me it was—" I hesitated. "I don't know how to describe it except that it was real and it was there. It was like some sort of barrier, only it was transparent and it was between us." I went toward him. "Gordon, we mustn't let your aunt come here."

"We have already decided—"

"We were wrong," I said miserably. "Besides, I didn't think she would come. I should have listened to Helen Warren."

"Elizabeth." He put his arm across my shoulders. He stroked my cheek with the back of his hand. I leaned against him for a moment and then I moved away.

"It's dangerous for your aunt," I said angrily. "Who are we to say she's old and therefore it's time she faced things? What things? What is she supposed to face? Your own mother won't come back. Helen Warren said so. She said your mother promised her and she has kept her word."

"Come," said Gordon gently. He held out his hand.

We walked through the dining room. He held my fingers lightly in his. He opened the front door.

"Let's go out for a while," he said. "There's a whole world outside this house."

A whole world of sky and sea and sand, with a lopsided moon cutting a path across the water, and the house behind us; Gordon and I walking away from it, walking hand in hand.

Away from it, I thought with longing. If I could only walk away from it, away from this house and all houses, all man-made enclosures, away from responsibility and routine and regret.

"Elizabeth," said Gordon, "listen to me. I don't know what it was that you and Gabrielle felt tonight. I don't know what you thought was on those stairs. It wasn't a wall or a transparent barrier. You know it and I know it. When I came in, the two of you were shouting at each other and there was nothing standing between you. Absolutely nothing. For the past few months each of you in a different way has been through hell. Perhaps this was a sort of translation of the agony, making your lack of communication almost a tangible thing. What you felt was all in your mind. What my aunt feels about this house is all in her mind." His fingers tightened. "It's the power of suggestion. Say a thing, repeat it often enough, and it's believed."

"No," I said. "Gordon—"

"Let me finish," he said. "My grandfather, Jotham Bellingham, died in this house. After that, Aunt Constance closed the place and went away. My mother was a little girl then. She saw my grandfather die. He had a heart attack. It must have been traumatic for a child and heartbreaking for Aunt Constance, but there was nothing mysterious about it." He was holding my hand so tightly that my fingers ached.

"Where did he die?" I said.

"In the house."

"Gordon." I stood still. I could hear the water lapping at the small beach. "Gordon, don't be obtuse. Don't pretend you don't know what I mean. Where in the house?"

"In my grandmother's room," he admitted reluctantly.

"In the room Gabrielle has now?"

"Yes," he said. "In Alarice's room."

"Then—"

"No," he said harshly. "There is nothing in that room except some painful memories. And that is exactly what I want Aunt Constance to face. Her own memories. Just the way you and Gabrielle have to face what has happened to your lives. There has been tragedy. Gabrielle runs away from it in one direction and you in another."

"I'm not running away," I said defensively.

"Aren't you? Then why don't you want to go home? If you leave your own house closed up long enough, if you don't return, won't the rumors begin? Children will run past its darkness at night, taunting each other, daring each other, until finally one braver than the others will run up the steps and peer in a window, and then, all courage gone, he'll tear away shrieking that he saw something in the shadows. Then people will talk about the Thatcher place. They will detour around it. The grass will grow tall and it will be unkempt and neglected and—"

"Please stop," I said.

156

"My mother opened the house again many years ago when I was too young to remember, just before my father died. She couldn't stay in it for the summer because my father was transferred and we had to move."

"But Helen Warren said—"

"I don't care what Helen Warren said," he interrupted. "I'm not trying to hurt you. I want to show you how these things begin. And that's why I want Aunt Constance to come back. If Helen Warren convinced you of one thing, she managed to convince me of another. This house has to be lived in again."

We had reached the end of the driveway. We crossed the road. There was sand in my shoes. I balanced, leaning on Gordon's arm, and took them off, glad that my legs were bare, glad that I wasn't wearing stockings. The sand was cold and damp and my toes curled against it.

This is reality, I thought. This moment right here and now. This moment to grasp, to hold onto, and to know for what it is. There was the wind cool against my face, and Gordon's hand was pressed to mine, and I could feel the gritty, damp sand and hear the sound of the sea and see the arch of star-blazed sky. Eyes like slits and ears that were stuffed, perhaps, but I could see and I could hear all I wanted to see and hear. Why did I have to look for anything else?

We leaned against the sea wall, and once more I faced the house. We had left the lights burning downstairs, but the bedrooms were dark.

It is lived in again, I told myself. This house, once useless, cold and untenanted, is lived in again. There Maggie and Gabrielle sleep and dream and there Gordon and I will sleep this night, and tomorrow and all the days after, we will love and laugh and fill it with new memories.

"You're right," I said. "You were right to ask your aunt to come. This is a good time for her to return while we're all here to help her, and after this month, Gabrielle and I will go back to our own house. And we'll both go in the same direction from then on, Gordon, I promise you that."

He turned to me then the way he had once before. It had been morning then and it was night now and yet it happened the way it had happened once before. He drew me close, bending toward me, and why wasn't I facing another way? Why with the panorama of sky and sea did I have to find that one dancing pinpoint of light, find the figure framed in the upstairs window, the figure of a woman watching us now as she had then?

"Don't," I said.

I put on my shoes. I began to walk away from him, back toward the house.

He caught up with me. "What's wrong?"

"Gabrielle's awake. I must go in."

"If she needed you, she'd call. Besides, Maggie's there." He looked up. "How do you know she's awake? Her room is dark."

"I saw her. She was standing next to the window. There was a small light as if she held a candle and she was just standing there."

"Why should she light a candle?" said Gordon, puzzled.

"I could see her," I said. "I could see the moving light and the outline of her body. She had long hair and—" I stopped. I stood very still. My heart lurched. "Long hair," I babbled. "She had long hair. Gordon, I could see her and she had long hair. Gordon, we left Gabrielle alone in that room. Gabrielle is alone in that room with— Gordon, what are we going to do? Please tell me what to do."

"Stop it," he said. "For God's sake, Elizabeth, stop it. It was an illusion, a trick of the moonlight. You saw nothing."

His fingers closed around mine again, but this time we weren't holding hands for the sake of the warm, human touch. This time he pulled me along, and then we were inside the house again, running up the steps, pausing only for a second outside of Gabrielle's closed door.

"Be quiet," said Gordon, and then he opened the door.

There was the pattern of moonlight on the floor and the sound of Gabrielle's deep, even breaths as she slept serenely, the quilt pulled up to her chin. And there was nothing else. Nothing inside the room and nothing outside it as Gordon and I quietly closed the door behind us, as we stood there in the hall,

Gordon avoiding my eyes as he said good night, Gordon going to his room and I to mine.

He didn't believe me. Gabrielle was asleep and he didn't believe I had seen a woman standing at the window. First I had said that it was Gabrielle and then I had said it was someone else and he didn't believe me. Because he didn't believe me, I didn't believe in myself.

It was Gabrielle, I thought. It had to be Gabrielle and what I thought was long, flowing hair was just a trick of the light. Knowing we were coming, she got back into bed, pretending to be asleep, laughing softly to herself because once again she had separated Gordon and me. If it weren't for Gabrielle, I would be in his arms.

And now I was making Gabrielle's bed for her to sleep in with the pillow plumped high and the bedspread placed just so, making her bed smooth and clean and fresh for her to wrinkle and soil.

One doll and one bracelet and one man, I told myself. One doll smashed and one bracelet lost, and would she love Gordon? How would she love Gordon? Would she know when he was tired? Would she know when he needed to be alone? Would she wait for him patiently? Would she take care of him or would she lean back smiling and let him carry her in his arms?

Each time he turned to me, she appeared. Reality or illusion, in spirit or in the flesh, she stepped between us, claiming him for herself.

I don't love her, I thought, startled. How can I say I love her? I was shaking with the cold and with something else—a kind of excitement I had never felt before.

"How can I love her?" I said aloud. "After all," I added slyly, "she killed my parents."

I looked at the bed and then I tore it apart, flinging bed-spread, quilt and sheets to the floor. The bed was Gabrielle and I was destroying her before she destroyed me. I was twenty-four. Soon I would be twenty-five. The years would go by and some-day I would be like Maggie, leaning against a kitchen sink, aging before another's eyes. I had found the man I wanted. I

159

would sleep with him, live with him, live for him, love him and have his children.

I walked across the room. I stood next to the dresser. I touched her hairbrush. There were some strands of her hair wound in the white bristles, dark threads of Gabrielle coming loose in my fingers. I took a deep breath. With this and a few nail clippings and some cloth, I could make a puppet, a simulacrum, and every night and every morning it would be I who would stick in the needles, piercing first her eyes and then her mouth and finally her heart.

Her heart, I thought, gripping the edge of the dresser, and then I saw the Bible lying there, a limp, black leather book, a different book, and yet the same one I had held in my hands so many times.

I picked it up. It opened. The passage was underlined and I read it, and I saw it while I read it, and even though I didn't understand it, just the same I knew what it meant.

"The place of sapphires," I whispered, knowing it for what it was, the quiet place, the good place, that of the seeking and the sought, the lost and the found, that of the search never-ending, everlasting, and always beginning.

I held the Bible in my hands as my sister had held it in her hands, and I knew how Gabrielle had looked standing there with that cropped dark head and within her the pain that was greater than mine, within her the guilt that was also mine, within her the fear and the love.

The love, I thought. She is my sister and what has happened to my love?

I forced myself to walk back across the room. I remade her bed, doing it very slowly and very carefully, concentrating on Gabrielle and my love for her, weaving the two together so that each reinforced the other, so that each gathered strength from the other.

"I love Gabrielle," I said.

I turned and faced the room. "Do you hear me?" I said. "You tried, but it won't work. You've failed. I love Gabrielle."

The room was very quiet. It was getting colder.

"I'm not afraid," I said defiantly.

160

But I was. There was ice, an ice-hood around my head, an ice-noose about my neck, an ice-chain girding my waist. There was nothing but ice sealing my lips, closing my eyes and stopping my breath.

I'm not afraid, I said silently, not able to speak, not able to scream because my vocal chords were frozen. I ran across the room. I tried to open the door, but I couldn't turn the knob. My fingers were numb and I couldn't turn the knob.

I could feel the room quiver. Some switch had been thrown, the current turned on, the electricity alive and humming. The room began to spin. I held onto the door, but it wasn't enough. I had to find something else.

The vibration grew stronger and it was like the sound the cat had made purring and I thought of Matilda and her kittens, picturing the small, live things wriggling and squirming, mouths open and the milk flowing. They were in a basket and the basket was lined with old towels and a soft blanket because young things, tender things, have to be kept warm.

Warm, I told myself, wrapping the warmth around my fingers, feeling them tingle, the flesh warm because it was alive and I, holding onto the thought of all the good things that were warm and all the warm things that were good, and the warmth now all the way through me so that the knob turned in my hand.

"I'm not afraid," I whispered. "I'm not afraid to love," and the door opened, and I let it close behind me without once looking back.

It was all within me. Everything that had happened had happened within me, the hate, the love and the battle that had to be fought over and over again.

The room was cold and the door to the room was always closed, but there was nothing else.

"Nothing else?" said Helen Warren quietly. She sat on the blue-brocaded couch with the cat next to her. "Are you sure, Elizabeth?"

"Just those two things," I said.

"I see." She stroked the cat. "Will you have dinner with me?"

"No, thank you," I said. "I must be getting back. They will be expecting me."

"It gets dark earlier now," she said. "Does anyone know you're here?"

I shook my head. "I told them I was going for a drive. I said I wanted to get away from the house for a while."

"And you came to me." She scratched the cat behind the ears. "You came straight to me because you were worried about only two things. Just two things," she said, her hand moving under the chin where the fur was soft and thick.

"Yes," I said.

"A door that won't stay open and a room that is much too cold and that is why you came to me. No other reason. Have you imagined all the rest, Elizabeth?"

"I didn't say that."

"Didn't you? In that case, perhaps I misunderstood. Now suppose you tell me why the barrier on the stairs, the figure at the window and the vibration of the room are so different."

"Because the door is a fact." I stood up and walked over to the fireplace. There, on the mantel, were yellow marigolds in a low black bowl. I touched them. They were real. The petals were soft and I could smell their bittersweet aroma. I turned around. "The door is solid. It can be touched. It's something that everyone sees, and the room, too, is a fact. Everyone who goes in there feels the cold."

"I see." She was smiling. "So it's only the facts that trouble you—not the so-called illusions. Well, like all facts, they can be explained very easily. We can assume that the room isn't insulated and the door isn't balanced properly, and then everything becomes so simple. All your problems are solved just by the hiring of a competent carpenter."

"Is that what you believe?"

"It isn't important what I believe. It's what you believe that counts, Elizabeth."

"I don't know what I believe," I said. I leaned against the mantel.

"You believe in what you call the facts. You refuse to commit yourself. You're afraid to take the leap across the chasm that lies between science and pure faith. Do you believe in God?"

I hesitated. "I pray," I said.

"I didn't ask you that," she said blandly. "I asked if you believed."

"Yes," I said uncertainly. A tendril of hair fell across my forehead. I pushed at it with the back of my hand. "Yes," I said again, my voice stronger. "I have to."

She nodded, satisfied. "So do we all. In one way or another, so do we all. Isn't the Bible truly a record of what we now call parapsychology? Man talked with God. Man expected miracles, looked for miracles and received miracles. The paranormal—precognition, clairvoyance, psychokinesis, extrasensory perception, apparitions, levitation—is all there and is taken for granted."

"It's an allegory, a parable," I said.

"And not to be taken seriously?"

"What do you want me to say?" I sat down on the hassock, leaning forward so that my elbows rested on my knees. "You asked me if I believed and I said I did. Isn't that enough?"

"You said you believed in God because you had to. That's not very logical of you, is it, Elizabeth? Is God a fact? Can He be touched? Can anyone see Him?"

"I'd better go," I said. I stood up again. "It's getting late and they'll be wondering where I am."

She made no move to rise. She was unperturbed, her voice even. "How can you believe in God? Your parents died suddenly, horribly. Even without your own personal tragedy, how can you believe in a just, merciful and compassionate God? A baby is born deformed and a plane filled with people crashes, and men spend their nights and their days in laboratories thinking up new ways to kill each other. They deal only with facts. Their evidence is all very scientific and they can show you step by step how they arrived at each conclusion. We live in a world filled with pain and disease and famine and heartbreak, and yet you tell me you believe in God. It doesn't make sense."

"I never said it did."

She laughed. "So facts really aren't enough for you, are they? Let us say that you bring in an expert and he tells you that the room is insulated and there is nothing wrong with the door. Will you be satisfied then or will you know as I know that there is some other agency at work?"

"You said you didn't know."

"What are you talking about?"

"When I saw you last. You said you really didn't know."

She sighed. "There is a mass of evidence," she said, "much of it introspective and unprovable. This is an empirical age and psychic research deals with the intangible. No, I don't really *know* in the sense that I can show you step by step in a laboratory filled with test tubes how I arrived at my conclusions. I can only tell you that too many things have happened to me personally that cannot be explained any other way."

"The supernatural," I said with contempt.

"No," she said quietly. "The natural. There is only the natural. There's no such thing as the supernatural. One hundred years ago most of the things we now take for granted didn't exist. Anyone who claimed he could fly through the air or transmit sound around the world would have been burned at the stake. A hundred years from now man may use his mind naturally in ways we now can't understand. Telepathy might be commonplace and we might move from one place to another without mechanical means, and when someone leaves this earth through the process we call death, continued communication might be established without fear."

Communication, I thought. Mind speaking to mind without the barriers of speech and language, mind to mind transcending the flesh, and all locked-in loneliness ended forever.

The cat yawned. She looked at me, her eyes glowing, and then leaped from the couch. She moved toward me, gracefully, sinuously. Almost standing on her head, she rubbed against my foot. I lifted her and carried her back to the couch.

"If what is happening in that house is what you call natural," I said, sitting next to Helen Warren with Matilda supine and content in my arms, "why did you tell me it was dangerous? If this is an attempt at communication, why did you say it was evil?"

"Because," said Helen Warren simply, "I knew Alarice."

I buried my fingers in the cat's fur. "No," I said. "I won't believe. I can't."

Helen Warren leaned back. She kept her hands folded in her lap. She didn't answer me. She just watched me, her eyes soft.

"Gordon was right," I said vehemently. "I should have listened to him. What nonsense. Herbs and prophecies and crystal balls."

She was laughing at me. "No herbs," she said, amused, "although I must admit they may be beneficial in some cases, and the prophecies and the crystal ball are one and the same, Elizabeth. The crystal ball is only used to help me concentrate. There are times when I manage quite well without it."

I put the cat on the floor. "I really have to go home," I said.

"Of course you do," she agreed. She was still smiling. "Why did you come to me, Elizabeth?" she said amiably.

"I wanted you to tell me you didn't know," I said loudly. "I wanted you to tell me that there's nothing there."

"And now you're angry."

"No," I said soberly, knowing the truth. "No. Now I'm afraid."

"Of course you are," she said. "How can I help you? If I could only help you—" She frowned and then rubbed her fingers between her eyes as if in that way she could erase the deep lines. "Come with me," she said.

I followed her into the front parlor. There was the basket as I had imagined it, the wicker basket lined with the soft blanket and the old towels; gray and white and gray-white were the three kittens playing. Their eyes were wide and round with wonder and they attacked their own lashing tails.

In front of the window was a small round table covered by a white cloth and on it was what looked like an enormous paperweight, a glass ball reflecting the light, a ball of glass and nothing more.

"Sit down," said Helen Warren, pointing to the chair opposite hers.

"I don't want to," I said stiffly. "I don't want you to look into that thing. I don't want to know what's there."

"Then you believe," she said flatly. "You have finally answered my question, Elizabeth. You believe that with this object I can move through time, that I can show you scenes from the future."

"You can look through that without me," I said. "I don't want to be here when you look through that."

"You are afraid of the past. Are you going to be afraid of the future, too?"

Glass, I told myself. Hard, smooth and clear and as real as the marigolds in the black bowl and Helen Warren at the table and the kittens tumbling in the basket. It is real and reality reveals only what is here and now, what is open to our senses here and now.

I sat opposite her. Under the table our knees touched and I remembered what it had been like when Gabrielle and I as children had crouched over the Ouija board, knees touching and the letters spelling out the message without our conscious volition.

It's a game, I thought. A game for children, charlatans and the credulous. Look into the crystal ball, I mocked. Look deep, Helen Warren, I commanded her silently, and tell me what you see.

I reached out and touched the glass, and under my fingers it went opaque.

Helen Warren's body was rigid. Her lips were white. "It's too cloudy," she said.

She's frightened, I thought. I could feel the beating of my heart.

"We will try again some other time." Her hands were trembling.

"You saw something," I said. "I know you did. You saw something dreadful and you don't want to tell me about it."

She shook her head. "The scenes were blurred. There's nothing I can tell you. Doing this is a strain and," she added wryly, "I'm not as young as I used to be." She stood up, her chair scraping, and walked across the room.

She's always leading the way, I told myself, and I follow obediently.

I stopped, relaxing at the sight of the kittens. "This must be the one you wanted to give me," I said, scooping up the gray.

"No," she said sharply. She turned around. "I don't want to give you a kitten. I've changed my mind. Put it down. Do you hear me, Elizabeth? Put it down immediately."

"But you said—"

"You told me your sister hates cats. Don't you bring a cat into that house. You must give me your word." Her voice rose.

"You must promise that you will never bring a cat into that house."

I stared at her in amazement. "But—"

"Always that 'but.' Don't argue with me, Elizabeth. This is one time you must listen."

I put the kitten back in the basket. "Oh," I said, straightening.

She came toward me. "Why did you do that?"

"What did I do?" I said, puzzled.

"You touched your throat."

"Did I? It's a habit," I said. "I do it automatically, I guess, without thinking." I took a step toward her. "You did see something, didn't you?"

"No," she said, turning away. "Go home now, Elizabeth."

"And then she sent me away," I told Gordon later, when the others were in bed, when we stood together in the hall downstairs, I using every pretext so that I could be alone with him for a moment. "But first she made me promise I wouldn't bring a cat into this house."

Gordon raised his eyebrows. "A cat?"

"She saw something," I said stubbornly. "She was frightened and it's something to do with cats."

"I don't think you have anything to worry about," he said dryly. He touched the banister. "Please don't go there again, Elizabeth."

"Why?"

"Because she's not to be trusted. I know Helen Warren. She took care of her widowed mother, who was a chronic invalid, and then when it was much too late for Helen to live her own life, she was forced to put her mother in a nursing home. I don't think Helen ever forgave herself. She was always interested in spiritualism. After her mother died, she became obsessed. This is a dangerous business, Elizabeth, and the danger doesn't lie in this house or in any prophecy Helen will invent."

"That's just it. She refused to tell me what she saw in the crystal ball. She said it was blurred."

"The future usually is. The day you are in mortal peril from a cat," said Gordon quietly, "will be the day I apologize to Helen. And I have no intention of apologizing to her."

"Gordon—"

"Good night, Elizabeth."

He was annoyed with me, therefore I was dismissed.

"Good night," I said angrily.

I ran up the stairs. I could hear his footsteps as he went to his room. The house was dark now except for the light burning in the upstairs hall. I left the door to my room slightly ajar in case Gabrielle needed me during the night.

That's why I heard the music. It was so soft that if my door had been closed, I don't think I would have heard it at all.

At first it was part of my dream. I was at home in our living room listening to Gabrielle play the piano. She was twelve years old and she hated to practice and I had never heard her play like that before. The piano, for some reason, was out of tune, but the singing tenderness infolded the discordant notes, harmonizing all disharmony, Gabrielle finally understanding Schumann, finally loving Schumann, Gabrielle playing the *Kinderscenen.*

I sat up in bed, humming. "About Strange Lands and People," I thought, smiling, how I love that, and then I was wide awake, seeing my room by moonlight, knowing where I was, and knowing, too, that Gabrielle was no longer a twelve-year-old child carelessly leaning on the loud pedal.

I turned on the light. It was two o'clock in the morning. I didn't stop for robe or slippers. All the doors to the hall were closed except mine. I leaned over the banister. There was no light downstairs. The music stopped and then began again.

In the dark, I told myself, going down the steps. She is sitting there in the dark playing the piano, remembering her childhood with a melody that is the essence of childhood, remembering what it was like when we were very young. My sister has to get up in the night, walk the house in the night, looking for music and memory.

I stood in the downstairs hall. "Gabrielle," I whispered.

169

If I turned on the light, I would startle her. She would blink in the sudden glare, exposed, vulnerable, resentful, and I would lose my chance to be close to her again.

My eyes were accustomed to the dark by now, and there was a path of moonlight for me to follow. Just as I reached the archway that led to the back parlor, the music stopped.

The windows in this room were small, set high, and the room itself was shadowed and quiet. I could see the outline of the library table and the large, heavy square that was the piano, but it seemed to me, standing there, that the piano stool was empty.

"Gabrielle?" I said.

I waited. All I could hear was the sound of my own breath. "Gabrielle," I said again, fumbling for the light switch, "where are you?" And then because I couldn't bear the silence, because I couldn't face the shadows and the silence, I said in a conversational tone, "I can't find the light switch. Please tell me where you are. Please tell me you're here. Don't hide from me, Gabrielle. I heard the music and I loved it. I came down to be with you," and all the time my fingers were moving up and down the wall, moving clumsily, ineffectually because my hands were shaking. "Oh, here it is," I said, relieved.

I heard the little click, but I still stood in the dark. I had turned on the light, but I still stood in the dark.

I backed away. I walked backward with my hands outstretched, my hands not in front of me to lead the way, but stretched out to fend off whatever might follow.

There was something behind me, something hard and unyielding pressing against me. I turned and ran.

It was the couch, I thought, running blindly, heedlessly. Where are you going? What is the matter with you?

It was the only way I could stay sane, concentrating on something as mundane as a couch, pretending I was frightened because I had bumped into a piece of furniture in the dark. I heard the tinkle of the dining-room chandelier and then I felt the linoleum, the kitchen floor smooth and cold under my bare feet.

"Gordon." I leaned against his door. "Gordon, Gordon, Gordon," I said when the door opened, when he pulled me toward him, when I was safe in his arms. "Gordon," I said, able only to say his name, repeating his name over and over again while he held me close.

I shivered against him. I wept against him. I trembled against him. I could feel his touch, his hands holding my head close to his chest, his fingers stroking my hair, my cheek. I knew he was speaking to me, but if he asked any questions, I didn't know what they were, and the only answer I had for him was the sound of his own name.

He carried me to the bed. He bundled me under the blankets, holding me under the blankets, and then his touch was different and my trembling was different and there was no fear anywhere, wrapped in this warm, good place that Gordon had made for me, and there was no search for anything but the flesh, and for me, for this moment, that was enough.

I COULD HEAR GORDON AND GABRIELLE UPSTAIRS, GOR-
don insisting that he could fix her door and Gabrielle prattling
in that high-pitched voice she uses when she wants to annoy
me. The sound of her voice and the sound of the door opening and closing seemed louder than the clicking keys of my
typewriter. It was impossible for me to concentrate. I spent
most of my time threading a new ribbon, not caring that my
fingers were smudged, thinking only of Gordon.

"Hello, darling," Gordon had said last night.

"Hello, darling," I said softly to myself now. "Hello, my
darling, my love."

My darling, my love, and the necessity of inventing words
new-minted for this, our exchange. At first we were incoherent,
no words good enough, right enough, splendid enough. My
darling, my love, we said, and there was nothing new to be
found, and yet when we finally spoke, it was with the startled
realization that, because we sought, in our seeking the old became new, the shopworn, unhandled, the dull, shining. Oh,
how our words gleamed there in the dark, and what did it
matter if man and woman had loved this way before? For us

together it was new and fresh and clean. There was no such thing as fear and no such thing as evil, and when I left Gordon and went upstairs, I looked at Gabrielle's closed door without a tremor of apprehension.

My darling, my love, but we met at the breakfast table as though we were still strangers; we passed and repassed each other on the stairs, in the hall. We went from room to room in our usual fashion, and no one looking at us could see that we were different.

He was my love, but he knew none of the things I knew. He heard no music in the night. For him no piano keys played without human touch and there was no darkness that a light couldn't dispel. When he pressed the switch, the light went on obediently, as it should.

"It works perfectly," Gordon said.

"Then why didn't it go on last night?"

"Perhaps you didn't touch it. Perhaps you only imagined that you did."

"And I imagined the music, too?"

"I didn't say that."

"Gordon, I heard it."

"It was Gabrielle."

"She wasn't there. The room was empty."

"She might have slipped past you in the dark."

"That's impossible. I would have seen her. There was enough light so that I could have seen her."

"Then she heard you coming," Gordon said, considering. "She could have hidden, crouching next to the piano or behind a chair."

"Gabrielle wouldn't frighten me like that. She wouldn't do that to me," I said without conviction.

"Wouldn't she?" said Gordon.

And now he was upstairs, working on the door, swinging it to and fro, Gordon concerned only with the facts. Was I just a fact to him, something to touch, see and hold, or was I more intangible, moving beyond all the senses so that he had to reach inside of himself to find me?

My darling, my love, I thought as I sat at the breakfast table.

I avoided looking at him and I talked to Gabrielle and to Maggie so that they would see that I wasn't looking at Gordon at all.

Gabrielle was sullen and abstracted, pushing her food around her plate and paying no attention to any of us. Maggie was her usual morning self, insisting that there was going to be a change in the weather and making mental notes for the marketing list she would be sure to give me.

"This is it," she said when we were alone in the kitchen. "I want to have plenty of food in the house when Mrs. Bellingham comes."

"I'll shop when we go to meet the ferry," I said.

"It'll be too late then. The stores will be closed."

"All right," I said, capitulating. "I'll go into town later this morning." I folded the list. "Why did you put down butter? We have plenty of butter."

"There's nothing in reserve," Maggie said. "I'd like to have another pound in the house just in case—"

"In case of what?" I teased. "In case it snows?"

"That's not as funny as it sounds," said Maggie. "There was frost last night. The leaves are turning." She frowned and untied her apron. "Talking about last night—where were you?"

Where was I last night? I thought. Into what strange land had I wandered? But I was home again and there was no way for Maggie to know that I had been away.

"We weren't talking about last night," I said, "and I don't know what you mean."

"Gabrielle woke me," said Maggie. "It was two o'clock in the morning."

Two o'clock, I thought. At two o'clock I had heard the music. At two o'clock I had tiptoed down the stairs, moving in rhythm to the tender strains of Schumann, and at two o'clock Gabrielle had awakened Maggie too.

"Are you sure it was two?" I asked.

"Of course I'm sure," said Maggie impatiently. "I know what time it was because I turned on the light and looked at my clock. Gabrielle was crying. I could hear her. It was like she was in the same room with me. I could hear every time she stopped just to catch her breath and I could hear every time she started up again. I couldn't just lie there listening to her. That poor child—when I think I ever said a word against her, and there she was sobbing like it was the end of the world, although," said Maggie, pleating her apron thoughtfully, "I guess what had happened was really the end of the world for Gabrielle. I didn't think so at the time, but I was wrong. I'm always willing to admit when I'm wrong. I've never heard her cry like that before, not even when she was little. This wasn't like a tantrum. This was the kind of grief no one should feel." She stopped. "Why are you looking at me like that, Elizabeth?"

Because I'm frightened, I answered her silently. It's morning and I hold a marketing list in my hand and I shudder because last night at the same hour, at the same moment, there was music and weeping in this house. Who was it who played the piano and who was it who wept?

"You said you heard Gabrielle crying," I said. "Then what?"

"I got up, of course," said Maggie, surprised. "Naturally, I got up. I just wanted to be with her. I couldn't let her cry like that in the night without any comfort, could I? That's when I saw that your door was open and your light was on. I looked into your room, but you weren't there and when I called your name, you didn't answer."

The two of us, I thought. Maggie and I looking for someone, for something that wasn't there when we called.

"I was downstairs," I said.

"Of course you were downstairs. Where else could you be? Anyway I opened Gabrielle's door and looked in. I could see her very clearly because the hall light was on just the way you always leave it and I could see that she was sound asleep. She must have cried herself to sleep and I was glad to shut her door again, I can tell you that. No wonder she huddles in that quilt all night long. If I slept in that room, I'd get one of those little electric heaters and—" She unpleated her apron. "I didn't want to call you again. I didn't want to wake up Gabrielle and I felt I had no right—" Her mouth twisted. "What were you doing downstairs at that hour?"

"I thought I heard a noise," I said.

"Maybe you heard Gabrielle cry, too."

"Maybe," I said.

"In any case," said Maggie, becoming very busy at the sink, "I didn't hear you come up again. I was awake for a long time, waiting and listening and I didn't hear you come up again."

"I was very quiet," I said evasively. "I didn't want to disturb you."

"Elizabeth—" She let the water run and then turned it off. "Elizabeth," she said again, her voice uncertain, "I don't know how to say this to you."

I touched her arm. "Then don't say it, Maggie."

"I have to. I'm not a fool. I know I'm old-fashioned, but that doesn't make me a fool. Things were different in my day. There was love and permanence. Today people go to bed together like they were shaking hands." She wiped her eyes. "I want more than that for you."

Oh, Maggie darling, I thought. It is so much more than that.

"Let's tell everyone," Gordon had said.

"No," I said. "I don't want Gabrielle to know. It's too soon for her."

"She'll have to know sometime."

"Not yet," I said.

Not yet, I told myself now. Not even to Maggie. Not yet. I put my cheek against Maggie's. "It's all right," I said.

"Is it really?" she said wistfully.

"Yes," I said.

"It's just because I love you," she said.

"I know."

"That's why I worry about you."

That's what I had said to Gabrielle. "It's because I love you," I had said. "That's why I worry about you." Over and over again, time after time, I had moved toward Gabrielle and never once reached her.

Was it like that for Maggie, too? I wondered now as I wiped my smudged fingers, as I listened to the door upstairs opening and closing as Gordon tried to make it behave. Maggie had gone to Gabrielle last night only to find that Gabrielle had retreated into sleep, and last night when I had gone to Gabrielle, she wasn't there at all.

I went upstairs. The door was propped open with a large porcelain figurine and Gabrielle stood in the doorway, glaring at it. "It won't work," she said. "Nothing can keep that door open."

It's a cat, I thought, startled. What would Helen Warren say if she knew there was a cat in this house? I was almost amused, picturing myself running down the stairs with the cat smooth and heavy in my hands, running out the front door because no longer was it safe to have a cat in this house. But, surely, I told myself, even Helen Warren would have no objection to such a ridiculous, elongated, misshapen version of a cat, with painted eyes and whiskers, this inanimate object used to hold Gabrielle's door open.

"Gabrielle hates cats," I said lightly.

"That's because I'm allergic to them," she said. "I start sneezing."

"I had a kitten once." I looked at Gordon, but he was watching the door.

"It scratched me," said Gabrielle.

It had been such a small kitten, with minute, sheathed claws, and the scratch had been invisible, like the hurt I had felt when I had lost him forever.

"It doesn't matter," I said. "It was such a long time ago."

"But it does matter. What a good memory I have," said Gabrielle in a singsong voice.

What sort of memory does she have? I thought. If our clocks had been wrong, if there had been a difference of even ten minutes between Maggie's time and mine, Gabrielle could have played the piano and still have been back in bed when Maggie had looked into her room.

I stood shivering in the doorway and prayed that our clocks had been wrong. I had reached into the cold and the dark and I didn't know if I had the strength to go beyond it. Wasn't this life, this moment that belonged to me, enough? I longed to be immersed once again in the reality of day-by-day existence. I wanted to be part of all the things we take for granted, sheltered behind the walls we build, the walls we all hope will be high enough, safe enough, so that we cannot see eternity.

"Gabrielle," I said quickly, "do you remember the *Kinderscenen?*"

"What are you talking about?" She was bewildered.

"You used to play it all the time."

She began to laugh. "But of course," she said, amused. *"Scenes from Childhood.* How appropriate. I haven't thought of it for years."

"Last night—"

"It moved," said Gordon, staring at the door.

"Of course it did," said Gabrielle smugly.

"Did you play it last night?" I asked Gabrielle.

She didn't answer me. She turned to Gordon. They were talking. I knew Gordon and Gabrielle were talking, but I wasn't listening. It seemed to me that the porcelain cat was studying me, its eyes intent.

"If I only had a desk," Gabrielle said loudly.

I blinked. "What do you want a desk for?"

"To write on, of course," said Gabrielle, smiling, "and I want your red rug, too, Elizabeth. It doesn't belong in your room, you know."

How does she know where it belongs? I thought resentfully. Does she want the rug because it's mine? I looked at her, but her face was impassive. So cold, I told myself as Gordon brought in the small table for Gabrielle. It's so cold in here and red is a bright color, a gay color. Would a red rug be enough to warm this room?

We put the rug in the middle of the floor, but she still wasn't satisfied.

"It doesn't belong there," she said crossly. "It goes near the wall, Gordon. Originally it was in front of the fireplace, and right there," she said, gesturing, "is where the fireplace would be if I had one. Don't look at me like that, Elizabeth. I know there's nothing there, but if I had a fireplace, isn't that *exactly* where it would be?"

"If we're going to meet the six o'clock ferry—" Gordon looked at his watch.

"I won't be long," I said. I walked toward Gabrielle, forcing myself to walk toward the center of the room where Gabrielle stood at the heart of the ice, the cold swirling about her.

"You didn't answer me," I said.

"Did you ask me a question?"

"I wanted to know if you played the piano last night."

She flung back her head. Her eyes widened. "Music in the night," said Gabrielle dramatically. "How romantic. Is that what you heard, Elizabeth? Did you hear music? Did strange strains and ghostly fingers tapping waken you?"

"Oh," I said. I was determined not to cry. I stood very still for a moment, feeling almost lightheaded. There was a bright red rug on the floor now, but it couldn't stop this gathering of cold darkness long before twilight was due. Gabrielle closed her eyes, her face contorted, and, standing there, I felt that all this had happened before. But when? I thought. Where and when?

"Why did you do that?" Helen Warren had said.

"What did I do?"

"You touched your throat," she had said, and her eyes were bleak.

I had touched my throat then. I had touched my throat now. It was nothing more than that, nothing more than *déjà vu*, an interruption in the memory time-sequence prompted by a small, hesitant habit.

"Gabrielle, please tell me," I said.

"Elizabeth," said Gordon, his voice warning me.

"I must know," I said, ignoring him. "Gabrielle, it's important. Were you downstairs last night?"

She shrugged. "I could ask you the same thing," she said insolently. She was peering over my shoulder, concentrating on something behind me. "You'll be late," she said, giving me a push.

I turned, wanting to see what she had seen. She pushed me again and I swayed, momentarily off balance. The door swung forward. The cat, I thought. Oh, my God, it's the cat. I was transfixed, impaled on a spear of ice. Gordon leaped toward me. He shoved me aside.

Gabrielle bent double, holding her stomach.

"She's been hurt," I said. I ran toward her.

"I can't bear it," Gabrielle screamed. She straightened. She put her hands against her cheeks and I could see that her eyelashes were wet.

She's all right, I thought. She was only afraid for me. Her tears are tears shed for me, and what do I do? Helpless, I stand beside her. That's what I do. I stand beside my sister and I shed no tears because I am afraid for myself.

"Don't cry." I put my arms around her. "There's no need to cry." I rocked her back and forth, holding her tight. "I'm not hurt, darling. There isn't a scratch on me."

"I was frightened," she whispered.

"This damn door," Gordon said.

He was right. The door was damned and the room was accursed, and hell itself wasn't aflame but lay trapped under ice piled high, layers of ice lying one on top of another, and beneath, far beneath, were the frozen souls of men crying for the sun.

The cat, I told myself. Helen Warren looked into crystal, looked into the depths of crystal, and saw this moment when the door was damned and the cat crashed and I touched my throat. This is what she saw in the quiet depths of a ball of crystal.

Gabrielle was trembling. I took a deep breath. "Gabrielle didn't like that thing anyway," I said easily, trying to reassure her. If I hadn't cried for my sister, at least now let me smile. "Did you, darling?" I said.

"You've got to find the head," Gabrielle told Gordon. "It must be in the room."

Maggie opened the door. She had the cat's head in her left hand and a dustpan and brush in her right. "I just got the house cleaned," she complained.

I wanted to laugh. There had been an icy abyss at her feet, but she hadn't seen it. Impervious, Maggie had marched into hell carrying a dustpan.

I put out my hand and then let it fall by my side. "I can't touch that door," I said.

"Why do you blame the door?" Gabrielle said, surprised. "You kicked the cat and knocked it over."

"Did I?"

"Of course you did. I saw you."

Maggie saw nothing and Gabrielle saw only what she wanted to see. And what about Gordon? He was my darling, my love, but what did he see? What did he feel?

"I'll only be a minute," I told Gordon.

I heard the door close behind me, locking them all in that hell together and I walked down the hall. I went into the bathroom and I bathed my face. I went into my bedroom and I put on fresh make-up. I changed my dress and I heard Maggie go downstairs. I heard Gordon go downstairs. Now Gabrielle was alone in that room and the ice was piling around her and would I hear her if she called to me?

The clock in my room said it was five-fifteen and the clock in Maggie's room ticked away in agreement and last night in two different parts of this house there had been music and tears at the same moment.

I stood outside Gabrielle's door and told myself that I didn't have to open it. I didn't have to stand there. I could run downstairs and find Gordon waiting for me. We could get in the car and drive to the ferry to meet Mrs. Bellingham. The autumn air would be crisp and clean, and the leaves would be changing to bronze and yellow and gold. But Gabrielle was caught fast, and even the warm tears she had shed for me wouldn't be enough to melt the ice that had held her.

"Gabrielle," I said. I knocked lightly. "It's Elizabeth," I said, rapping again. The third time is magic, I told myself, but it wasn't. The door remained closed and there was no answer for me.

I turned the knob. There had been time for the ice to barricade the door, because it didn't want to open. I had to use all my strength, leaning on it, and then I saw her, with her back to me, standing in front of the dresser. She was slim and young and she was brushing her hair, using long, smooth strokes. She bent her head forward, flinging her hair forward so that it covered her face, and then she flung her head back so that her hair cascaded over her shoulders and it was yellow silk shimmering about her. I could see my reflection in the mirror, my own face wavering as though I searched for myself in a wind-ruffled pool of water, but she hid herself from me, the mirror revealing nothing, and from the back she could be me, an Elizabeth split down the middle so that I could view myself without any artificial aid. This was the color of my hair. This was the length of my hair. This was the texture of my hair, and this, too, was the way I brushed it morning and night, only I stood straining, wedged in this doorway, and what was in front of me was not me.

It was not Gabrielle and it was not me.

Let the door close, I thought. I will not hold it open any longer. Let it close quickly. I pray that as I step back the door slams. I pray that I may leave this place before this creature turns, before I see her face.

I was in the hall now, but the door didn't close. For once the door didn't close. It moved slowly, deliberately, inching its way shut, and, rooted there, I watched as she turned.

IT WAS GABRIELLE. SHE HAD TURNED AND IT WAS GA-brielle. She looked at me. She spoke to me. I saw her and I heard her. She was solid. She was real. She was Gabrielle. Her hair was dark and cropped short and there was a hairbrush in her hand.

There was a hairbrush in her hand because she had been standing in front of the mirror brushing her hair.

The fault was mine. The flaw lay within me. It had been Gabrielle. All along it had been Gabrielle, only I couldn't see her. I refused to see her. I changed her, turning the figure of Gabrielle standing at the window into a woman with long, flowing hair, turning the figure of Gabrielle standing at her dresser into the same apparition, my eyes tricking me, my eyes deceiving me, just as my ears had deceived me, hearing music that had been played years ago and was played no longer.

Had I seen my own *Doppelgänger*, my own etheric double, an Elizabeth projected out of my own desire? If there could be two Elizabeths, then there was no Gabrielle at all in that room. Eliminate Gabrielle, and the cause of my parents' death was eliminated. Take away the cause of my parents' death, my unconscious mind urged, and they still would be alive.

Which must be why I had never seen the face of the woman with the long, yellow hair. Not even as spirit did she exist. She emanated from me.

"And the cold and the door?" Gordon reminded me gently.

My darling, my love, I thought. Why do you question me now? If I cannot bring you to my way of thinking, then I must bring myself to yours, seeing only what you see, knowing only what you know.

"The two incontrovertible facts?" I shrugged. "Both of them can be remedied by the hiring of a competent carpenter."

"What about the strange prophecy of the cat?"

"It was a doorstop," I said. "An inanimate object molded into a likeness. Actually, you know, it could have represented almost anything. It could have been a lion or a tiger or even a man. As a matter of fact," I said, leaning against him, "if I remember correctly, aren't most doorstops elephants?" I relaxed, amused. "Wouldn't it have been funny if it had been an elephant, Gordon? Then I could say that an elephant attacked me."

His arm tightened. "You wanted to believe," he said. "It was heartbreaking the way you wanted to believe."

"That was before I knew you loved me." I kissed his cheek, his mouth. "This is enough," I said. "This has to be enough."

"So now we're back in our own world again," he said, smiling at me, "and I have to admit that I'm glad. Not only for your sake and for mine but also for Aunt Constance. She's here to dispel ghosts, not discover them."

To dispel ghosts, I thought. To wave a magic wand over this house, exorcising all that was evil. Why did the gentle souls, the loved ones, the dear ones, leave us behind without a backward glance? If something had to remain behind, if something had to linger so that we could sense its presence, why did it have to be the tormented, the anguished, the damned?

She had turned, her image dissolving, melting into Gabrielle so that it was Gabrielle's face I had seen. That much of the truth I had told Gordon. I had gone forward step after step with eternity beckoning, the prize gleaming in the distance, but the crossing here was too dangerous and the place of sapphires had been seen but dimly. The stones shone at the bottom of a chasm, but evil guarded the way, evil strong enough to bridge two worlds, and if I didn't know how to fight Alarice, if I didn't know how to conquer Alarice, now, at least, I could deny that she existed.

I could deny her to Gordon. I could deny her to myself. She was dead, and I had to bury her over and over again because she was dead.

To dispel ghosts, and Constance Bellingham home again and I, the coward, pretending to be happy in her house, pretending that this was a house like any other. No more music in the night for me. If the piano played, I would clap my hands over my ears and lie rigid in my bed, waiting for it to stop. No more tears in the night for me. Whoever wept behind the closed door to Gabrielle's room would weep without comfort, for I had gone as far as I dared to go.

"This far and no further," Constance Bellingham said to me.

I stood very still. It was late afternoon and we had walked together as far as the sea wall.

"That's because I'm tired," she added apologetically. "Jotham always said that as a joke. We would walk to the water's edge, and we'd stand there looking toward the horizon and he'd say, 'This far and no further.'"

"We can go back to the house," I said.

She shook her head. "I like it here. I have always loved it here. Jotham and I would lean on this wall and watch the sun set, and yet, even then, even with my back to the house, I used to feel Alarice watching me."

Standing at the window, I thought, with her hair tumbling about her shoulders, standing there, watching.

"It's all right now," I said slowly, "isn't it?"

She looked at me, her eyes brooding. "I should be the one to ask you that, but I'm not going to. I don't want to know your answer. I prefer to believe what you told me the first night I came home. I prefer to believe that you're happy in my house, that it has brought you some measure of contentment and peace of mind. I don't think I want to know anything else."

The stones of the wall were rough under my fingers. "I'm not going to tell you anything else," I said.

"I know you're not." She turned and looked toward the house. "Perhaps we should start back. It's getting late, but I think I have time for a nap before dinner." She hesitated. "Would you mind holding my arm, Elizabeth? I remember when I used to run along this strip of sand, but that was a long time ago."

She wore a heavy sweater, but it seemed to me that I could feel her bones, brittle against mine.

"I say it was a long time ago, but I don't really mean it. It was yesterday, Elizabeth. I see it so clearly and to me it was yesterday, and yet, to you, to someone like you, it was so long ago." She stopped walking and I stopped, too, and we stood facing the house, not looking at each other. "How can I tell you about it? I think I'd like to tell you about it. You listen so intently and you have a way of putting your head to one side—" She sighed. "It's not like a progression or layers like waves rolling onto the shore. I used to think it was like that, but it isn't really."

"What isn't?" I said, thinking, So delicate, so fine, those flesh-sheathed bones and the high arch of her forehead and the lids heavy over the deep, dark eyes. Yesterday the young girl running across the sand, and today the old woman resting against me.

"I don't know how to explain," she said. "It's not time. I'm not talking about time at all. I'm not even talking about the generations. When my grandparents died, my mother wept and I had to stand by helpless. She wouldn't let me touch her. I tried to put my arms around her, but she wouldn't let me. I can still see her the way she was, lying across her bed, her eyes wide open, staring at the ceiling, and the tears running down her cheeks. She made no attempt to wipe them away. She said she was ashamed that she was crying because only part of her grief was for her parents. She said that the rest of it was all for herself because she had seen the older generation disappear and she was now taking their place."

Step after step, I thought. Blindly we take one after another, moving closer and closer to the edge.

She gripped my arm. "I was very young then. I saw her cry, and when she told me why, all I could feel was relief. I was young, and because I was young, what had I to do with death? I was a generation removed from it. The older generation was my shield against it and I was still safe. But that was when I believed in time. Death has nothing to do with time. Jotham died before our child died and the baby died before it was born. There are layers. I don't say there aren't, but death digs deep, finding what it wants to find, and where is anyone going to hide?"

"I didn't know you had a child," I said.

"The doctor said it wasn't a child. I remember that well. Doctor Kirk. Oliver Kirk. He's still living, the old fool. He called it an embryo. Not even a baby. A fetus, a three-month-old beginning without even a heartbeat. He wouldn't tell me what it was. All my life I have to think of it as an 'it' because he wouldn't tell me what it was. He said it didn't die because it hadn't felt life. What was it then, just a formation of flesh?"

"Don't," I said.

"I wanted Jotham's baby. Why should his only child be Alarice's child? That is, if Alarice told the truth and Ruth was Jotham's child. Alarice could have tricked him. She could have been pregnant before she went to him. He was drunk. I don't blame him. I've never blamed him. She hated me more than she loved him, otherwise she would have wanted him to be happy." Her fingers dug into my flesh. "It was yesterday," she said. She bent her head. "Everything was yesterday. There are never days of the week or months or years in the past. At least not for me. I can't tell you when things happened. I can just tell you what happened."

It was long ago and yet it was yesterday. They had returned to Steppingstone. The house had been closed since Alarice died, but "It belongs to me now," said Constance, "and I'd like to

187

bring Ruth there for the summer. It's a place for a child to spend the summer, isn't it, Jotham?"

"Are you sure you want to go back?" he said.

She turned in bed, moving close so that the length of her body pressed against him, wishing that the child within had distended her so that he could feel the swelling, so that he could feel the strong thrust and kick of his growing child, but her baby was too small to make itself known, and in the next room Alarice's child slept, her breathing deep and even, her arms flung over her head.

"No," she said. "I'm not sure of anything, but we do have to make a decision. We either live in the house again or we sell it. We have to be practical, darling."

Practical? she thought, scoffing at herself. Practical, when her heart leaped as they boarded the ferry, the salt smell, the churning wake, the vibration of the engines so much a part of her that standing there on the deck she felt whole again, and then there was Steppingstone, the island on the horizon, Jotham's fingers closing hard over hers, the ferry docking, the old wharfs still there, everything still there where it was supposed to be, the pilings, the swirling green water, the cobblestoned streets, the whitewashed houses, the blinding blue of the sky, the tall elms, and her house, silver-shingled, her house waiting for her.

Practical? Who was going to be practical when the child danced up and down, the six-year-old Ruth, Alarice's child dancing with excitement as she ran up and down the stairs, exploring, exclaiming, ecstatic.

And unerringly, drawn to it without question, she went to Alarice's room. "I want to sleep in here," said Ruth.

"We want you next to us," Jotham said, putting his arms around her.

"This is the room I slept in when I was a little girl," said Constance, flinging open the door. "It has a big four-poster bed and it's on the same side of the hall as we are. Wouldn't you like this room?"

"No," said Ruth.

"You will obey your mother," Jotham said.

188

"She's not my mother," Ruth said in a high, sweet voice. "She's my aunt. My mother wants me to sleep in her room."

"She's always called me 'Mommy,'" Constance said that first night when the child was tucked into bed. "She knows I'm her aunt. We both agreed that she should be told the truth, but she's always called me 'Mommy.'" She looked up the stairs and shivered. "How did she know which room was Alarice's?"

"It doesn't matter," said Jotham. "At least she obeyed me."

"That's because you bribed her," said Constance wisely. "You promised to take her sailing."

"If you behave," said Jotham, smiling at her, "I'll take you sailing, too."

Then there was the sun and the sea and the water slapping against the side of the boat and the child between them, the child with Alarice's long, fair hair and green-blue eyes, and the days and the nights serenely slipping by, and "Now I'm sure," said Constance. "Now I know that what happened here is truly gone. People make a house. Once there was sadness here, but now we're happy and the house feels it, the house knows it, the house reflects it. Oh, Jotham," she said joyfully, "it's so good to be home again."

And there were the old friends to see, Oliver and Susan Kirk, the Hansoms, the Loughlins, Helen Warren and her querulous, aging mother.

"Helen, how can you stand it?" asked the young Constance. "It's ninety degrees and she sits there with a shawl over her shoulders and she doesn't stop nagging you, not for a moment. All she talks about is food. She only lives from one meal to the next. Her breakfast wasn't good. The eggs were hard and the toast was cold, but she's looking forward to lunch because," said Constance, mimicking, "'Helen does broil a *lovely* chicken.'"

Helen laughed. "I'm used to it," she said. "Besides, what do you want me to do? There's no one breaking down my door, begging my hand in marriage, and someone does have to take care of Mother."

"I don't want to get old," said Constance. "I want to stay just the way I am."

"With the baby only half-done?"

"Not even half," said Constance. "Only one-third done. Helen, I'm so happy. Did you think you'd ever hear me say those words again?"

Helen sighed. "Move Alarice's grave," she said abruptly.

Constance stepped back. "What are you saying?"

"Move Alarice's grave into the family plot and then close your house and leave Steppingstone."

"How can you talk to me like this? How can you stand there and do this to me?"

"Because I must," said Helen Warren.

"You are my friend. You have always been my friend—not Alarice's, never Alarice's—mine."

"Because I am your friend."

"No," said Constance. "Alarice will not lie next to my mother and my father. She will stay where she is." She stepped back. "Your mother is calling you, Helen. Don't you hear her?"

"I hear her," said Helen, not moving, still standing on the steps.

"Then why don't you go to her? She's your excuse for backing away from life, isn't she? You can't get married, you can't leave Steppingstone, you can't do anything for yourself because you have your mother to take care of. Then why," said Constance spitefully, "don't you do a good job of it? Why don't you take care of her?"

"It's no good, Constance," said Helen quietly. "I'm not going to quarrel with you. I'm not asking you to move Alarice because I want to hurt you. I didn't bring up the subject because you said you were happy and I couldn't bear your happiness. It's because I want you to be happy that I'm telling you this. I went to a séance the other night and—"

"A séance? You actually went to a séance?" Constance began to laugh. "And Alarice spoke to you? Alarice told you she wasn't resting easy where she was in the cemetery so far from her loved ones? Alarice asked you to speak to me, to intervene on her behalf? Was there a trumpet suspended from the ceiling? Did the medium go into a trance and did you see ectoplasm come from her mouth and her fingers? Did you see ectoplasm turning itself into another hand and did that hand tap you on the shoulder so that you knew it was Alarice?"

"No," said Helen calmly. "It wasn't Alarice. I spoke to the control. But there was a plea and a warning and I want you to heed it."

"She can lie where she is," said Constance, thinking, I'm going to be sick. I'm going to make a spectacle of myself and throw up right in front of Helen. "She can lie there and rot in hell for all I care," said Constance, speaking very softly because she wanted to scream.

"She can rot," said Constance that night, her head on Jotham's shoulder, her arms tight around him. "When she died, I didn't cry for her. I cried because I couldn't cry for her. I hated not being able to cry. Someone should have shed a tear, Jotham. Someone should have been able to cry for Alarice."

"Be quiet," Jotham said.

"I've been quiet long enough. May she rot forever for what she did to you and to me. May her flesh fall away and her bones dissolve and—"

"No more," said Jotham, putting his hand over her mouth. "No more. Never again," said Jotham angrily. "I never want to hear you talk like that ever again."

His fingers had bruised her lips. Her mouth felt swollen as she lay in the dark, her eyes, wide open, staring in the dark of the room that had once been her parents' room, she and Jotham lying together in the bed that had once been their bed.

Jotham had his back toward her. He was asleep with his back toward her, and that, too, was Alarice's fault.

"Move her grave," Helen Warren had said.

Move her grave, thought Constance. Get out the shovels and dig down deep. Turn over the earth, the black, wet earth falling to one side and lift the casket high out of the earth, lift the remains of Alarice into the sunlight, move it from one deep hole to another, move it next to the gentle people who had been her parents, who had been together in love and in passion, who had created the flesh that had become Alarice, and who now lay together without love and without passion, lay quietly together with the entwining ivy and the stones that spelled out their names.

The family plot, Constance told herself, only Alarice had died a Bellingham, not a Lysander. Would Jotham's parents have minded if Alarice had been placed next to them?

"She doesn't belong there either," Constance had wanted to tell Jotham after Alarice died. "She doesn't belong with your family. She doesn't belong anywhere. Alive or dead she has no place on this earth."

But she didn't have to say the words. Jotham, white-lipped, stony-eyed, holding the day-old baby in his arms, had let her do as she wished. He had looked at her bandaged hands and at his unmarked child and he had let her make all the funeral arrangements for Alarice because "She's my sister," Constance had said.

My sister, she said now, speaking silently into the dark, and she will lie where she is forever, alone and among strangers, where the cemetery ends and the wild fields begin. When I die, I will be next to Jotham and she will be far away from both of us. And if Alarice wants to send me some message, let her do it for herself, not through some medium's control, not through a squeaky puppet's voice speaking through the slack lips of a woman in a trance.

"I don't understand how it could have happened," Jotham had said.

"She almost burned the house down once before this. She had an obsession about that fireplace. Mama put a screen in front of it and Alarice moved it away. She said she couldn't see the fire dance with anything in between. She said she wanted to lie in bed and see the flames leap high."

"But there was time for her to get out."

"She asked me to take the baby. She stood up and almost fainted and asked me to take the baby. I went back for her, but the smoke and the flames—" Constance held up her bandaged hands. "I tried," she said simply.

"I know you did," said Jotham.

She had tried. She had started up the steps. The hall was filled with smoke. It spilled over the landing and ran down the stairs. She had walked through the smoke, her hands outstretched, but Alarice's door was closed.

"Why do you shut your door?" Mama always said.

"To keep everyone out," Alarice had answered pleasantly.

To keep me out, thought Constance, and Alarice burning there behind that closed door, Alarice's lungs seared, Alarice's body wedged behind the door so that it wouldn't open.

And then when Alarice was buried and when it no longer mattered whether the room had a fireplace or not, the whole side of the house had been rebuilt, the kitchen modernized, the chimney removed from the dining room and Alarice's room, the scorched wall replaced, the charred mattress gone, the white organdy curtains gone, the room refinished and the house closed because "I can't live in it," said Constance to Jotham. "How can I ever live in it alone?"

"You can't live anywhere alone," said Jotham. "I won't let you."

And now she was home again, lying next to him, and she was alone because he had turned his back toward her.

But I am alive, she thought. I am alive, and curled in my womb is Jotham's child. I am alive. I have both children. I have Jotham's child and Alarice's child. I am alive and Alarice is dead. Alarice, who had returned home for her mother's funeral and who had remained to give birth to her child, is dead.

Damn you, Alarice, she said silently. You loved fire. You loved the crackling warmth, the searing heat of a fire, and if you send me a message, may it come from the flames that consume you, may it come from the everlasting flames that leap about you, and may you burn forever wherever you are.

Damn you, Alarice, she said softly into the dark, and then fell asleep.

✼

"Ruth woke me," she said dully. "She was screaming. At first I didn't know it was Ruth. I thought it was Alarice. Against all logic I thought it was Alarice. I had been
dreaming of her and in my dreams she was screaming. I
stretched out my hand, but Jotham wasn't there. I ran into
the hall, calling his name. Alarice's door was closed and I
could hear Ruth on the other side of that closed door, Ruth
in Alarice's room pounding on the closed door, and she
wouldn't stop screaming. Not even when I turned the knob
and got the door open. Not even when I took her in my arms.
The room was dark and very cold. I remember being amazed
that it should be so cold on such a warm night. I called
Jotham's name, but he didn't answer me. I tried to take the
child out of the room, but she wouldn't let me. She kept
screaming, 'No. Please don't. I want my mother.' I managed
to turn on the light and then I saw Jotham stretched out on
the floor of that room. I knelt next to him. I touched him and
he didn't move. It was yesterday," she said, and the thin, old
hands trembled, fumbling with the buttons of her sweater.

194

It was yesterday, I thought, and the child, Ruth, had shouted to Constance, "You're not my mother. You're my aunt," and yesterday, in the cold and in the dark, she had cried out for someone she called her mother. It was yesterday and there had been a fireplace in that room, a fireplace on the far wall of that room, and today Gabrielle knew just where the red rug should go, Gabrielle knowing exactly where that fireplace had been.

"Let's go back to the house," I said. "You're so tired, Aunt Constance. You'll take a nap, and then when you get up, you'll feel better."

"Doctor Kirk said Jotham had a heart attack. Jotham was young. He never had anything wrong with his heart, but the old fool called it a heart attack." She looked up. "And she did it," she said, pointing.

Something inside me leaped. "Oh," I said. I touched my throat. I could feel my fingers touching my throat. "That's Gabrielle," I said quickly. "That's only Gabrielle standing at the window."

"Gabrielle?" She swayed. "Of course. It's your sister, Gabrielle. She sleeps in that room. Why does she sleep in that room, Elizabeth?"

"She likes it," I said.

"Likes it?" said Constance Bellingham, incredulous.

"She chose it."

"Gabrielle," she said slowly.

"What is it?"

She looked at me, bewildered.

"You said my sister's name and then you didn't say anything else."

"She's tall and dark, isn't she?"

"Yes," I said.

"Alarice was fair like you. The woman at the window—" She put her hand back, leaning heavily on my arm. "You're right, Elizabeth. We'll go back to the house." She sighed. "It's getting chilly. I used to love autumn. I used to love the colors of autumn. Why is such a sad season so beautiful?"

I could see that Gabrielle was still watching us, her hand holding back the curtain.

"You'll have a nap," I said. "I'll take you upstairs if you like, and I'll stay with you until you fall asleep."

"Yes," she said obediently.

"It's because she's old," Maggie said later when I helped her do the dishes.

"She said it had nothing to do with time."

"Then she's lying. It has everything to do with time. I'm in my sixties now. When I was your age, I thought anyone over thirty was old, and now I'm sixty-five. The thing to do," said Maggie briskly, "is to keep busy and not think. The trouble with Mrs. Bellingham is that she thinks too much. Maybe she's depressed because she's going to have a birthday soon. The worst birthdays are when you start a new decade. I had a fit on my sixtieth birthday, but when I was sixty-one, I felt quite young again."

"Who's going to have a birthday?" said Gabrielle, coming into the kitchen.

"Mrs. Bellingham," said Maggie. "It's a special occasion. She's going to be eighty."

"No great accomplishment," said Gabrielle carelessly. "All you have to do is live long enough."

I put down the dish towel. "Why were you standing at the window this afternoon?"

"Is there any reason why I shouldn't?" She began to laugh. "It's my room and I think I'm entitled to look out the window if I want to."

"Yes, of course," I said.

"Did it bother you, Elizabeth? Did something about it upset you?"

"It was Aunt Constance. I guess seeing you standing there brought back too many memories for her."

"Why should it?"

"Her sister used to stand at that window looking out."

"I know," said Gabrielle calmly.

"Then if you knew, why did you ask?"

"Just to hear it from you," said Gabrielle.

I began to stack the dishes into the cupboards. "We'll invite some people and have a party for Aunt Constance," I said. "We'll have a wonderful party."

"The gathering of the ghouls," said Gabrielle gleefully.

I dropped a dish.

"Now see what you've done," said Maggie crossly, but I didn't know whether she was speaking to me or to Gabrielle.

"What are you going to do—invite half the cemetery?" said Gabrielle, smiling. "How many friends do you think she has left?"

To watch your contemporaries go, I thought. To watch them go one by one and to live on.

I took my time picking up the pieces. "Gordon will know," I said, my back to Gabrielle, not wanting to look at her.

"Aunt Constance mentioned the Hansoms and the Loughlins," I told him when we were alone, "and there's Doctor Kirk and Helen Warren and maybe Julie Sanders. Do you know of any others?"

"I'll give you a list," he said, "but I don't know how many will come. It's been a long time since there was a party in this house."

"It was yesterday," I said.

He frowned. "Not yesterday," he said. "We're not dealing with subjective time, Elizabeth. Aunt Constance can be very persuasive when she wants to be."

"She wasn't trying to convince me of anything. She just told me how it was and what happened. She told me how Jotham died and how Alarice died. I can just see her trying to reach Alarice and Alarice upstairs trapped behind that closed door."

"What are you talking about?"

"The fire," I said.

"The fire?"

"It happened the day after your mother was born," I said. "You must have been told about it. I can't understand why you didn't remember that there was a fireplace in that room. I don't know how Gabrielle could have known about it, but she was right."

"I don't know anything about a fireplace," he said impatiently. "What difference does it make if the room had one or not?"

"It means that there is communication," I said. "It means that we do not end with death."

"Elizabeth—"

"Darling, don't you see?"

"Alarice died in childbirth," he said quietly.

"I don't understand," I said. "That's not what Aunt Constance told me."

"She's always been clear-minded," he said. "But she's getting very old. It's possible she's becoming senile." He hesitated. "I wonder when she had her last checkup? A series of small strokes, perhaps," he said thoughtfully.

The physician, I thought. The practitioner of the physical exploring the intricate network of blood vessels and veins and muscle, seeing the miracle of the body and accepting it as the commonplace.

"Perhaps," I said, yielding.

"Her eightieth birthday," he said. "You're right. It is an occasion. I'm going to call my mother. She should be here, too."

I closed my eyes for a moment. "Ruth promised me," Helen Warren had said. "She promised me she would never return."

It's all right, I told myself. Gordon will ask her and she will make some excuse, find some pretext for not coming back.

His fingers traced the curve of my cheek. "Are you sure you want to do this, Elizabeth? I won't even be here to help you. I'm going to have to leave for a few days, although I should be back in time for Aunt Constance's birthday."

We'll be all alone here, I thought. I drew back. Five women together. There was Maggie, Aunt Constance, Gabrielle and me. What had made me say five? There were only four of us. Would Gordon be going away if he knew that I was still afraid? I had minimized, rationalized and skirted my own fear for so long now that I had finally convinced Gordon he could leave me. What would he do if I asked him to stay?

"Gordon—"

"What is it?"

Alone, I reminded myself. Constance Bellingham had been lying next to Jotham, but she had felt alone.

"Nothing," I said. "It's nothing."

"There's a limit to the amount of time I can stay away from my office," he said reasonably.

"I know."

"Lord knows I don't want to leave you."

"It's all right," I said. "Really it is."

"It's just for a few days."

"I didn't ask you to stay, Gordon."

"I know you didn't."

"By the time I get things ready, you'll be back," I said briskly. "Helen Warren will help me."

But she wouldn't.

"No," she said firmly. "I won't go from house to house with you, Elizabeth. It's nonsense to think of having a party for Constance. Do you think Alarice is going to permit it?"

I stood on her front steps and stared at her. There was a gust of wind. An October wind, I thought. The leaves on a maple made a dry, hissing sound and one drifted down, landing at my feet.

"What can she do to stop it?" I said with some acerbity. "Come down the stairs wrapped in a winding sheet, wailing like a banshee?"

"You know better than that, Elizabeth."

"I suppose I do." I looked at the list of names I held in my hand. "It's Aunt Constance's eightieth birthday," I said. "Children and old people should have parties. I want her to know that she's loved. I want there to be happiness in that house again."

"Love and happiness." Helen Warren laughed. "Do you think they go together?"

"Don't they?"

"Are you happy, Elizabeth?"

"Sometimes," I said, thinking of Gordon, feeling guilty.

"Don't reproach yourself," she said shrewdly.

"It's too soon for me to be happy," I said rapidly. "I loved my parents. When they died—"

"I'll come to the party," she said. "I won't go with you when you invite the others, but I'll come and I'll help you in any way I can."

It will be all right, I reassured myself as I drove away. It has to be. Fill the house with enough people, with enough noise and love and laughter and even Alarice won't be able to get through.

Enough people. But there weren't enough people. I lied to Gabrielle when I told her everyone was glad to be invited to Aunt Constance's party. How could I tell her the truth? How could I tell her the way the Hansoms had looked at me, two frightened old people looking at me and shaking their heads.

"Oh, no," they chorused. "It's impossible. We wish Constance well, of course, but we go nowhere nowadays, my dear. Absolutely nowhere."

"It's a previous engagement," said Mrs. Loughlin, her voice quavering. "I wrote it right on my calendar so that I would be sure to remember. I've become a little forgetful lately, but this is one thing I remember very well. We have a very important previous engagement."

"A party for Mrs. Bellingham?" said Julie Sanders, twisting her hands together. "You want me to come to a party for Mrs. Bellingham?"

"We'd love to have you," I said.

"I don't know, Miss—"

"Thatcher," I said patiently. "Elizabeth Thatcher."

"Well, I don't know, Miss Thatcher. You've been in the house quite a while now, haven't you?"

"Yes," I said.

"And everything's—"

"Everything is fine," I said.

She unclasped her hands. "And you're giving Constance Bellingham a party?"

"Helen Warren is coming," I said persuasively.

"I'll think about it," said Julie Sanders. "I don't have to let you know right now, do I? Can't I think about it?"

"Constance Bellingham," said Doctor Kirk, rocking back on his heels. "To think that Constance is going to be eighty. Not," he added, smiling at me, "that I'm any youngster myself, but still—" He stopped smiling. "That was a bad business. I remember it well." His eyes were thoughtful. "I'll speak to Mrs. Kirk. It's up to her, of course. For myself, I should be delighted to attend, but after forty-some-odd years of marriage, I've become a very well-trained husband." He smiled again. "I shall have to ask Mrs. Kirk, young lady, but I do thank you for inviting us."

"You should have been with me," I said to Gabrielle, speaking quickly, glibly, knowing how she would have laughed if I had told her the truth. "There were so many old friends still living and so many people in town who have known her through the years."

"You had Gordon," she said spitefully. "That should have been enough for you."

"You know Gordon left early this morning," I said.

"You're a liar." She spun around on the piano stool. Deliberately she began to play the *Kinderscenen.* "'About Strange Lands and People,'" said Gabrielle gently. "It's been years, but there are some things you just don't forget. Isn't that true, Elizabeth?"

"I suppose so," I said helplessly.

"I really shouldn't play the first one," she said, lifting her fingers from the keys, "when the second piece is so much more appropriate."

I walked over to the library table and leaned on it. "I don't remember the second one."

"Now don't tell me you're getting forgetful." She raised her eyebrows. "It's called 'Curious Story.'"

"I told you about Gordon and you forgot," I said. "I told you at breakfast."

She rocked back and forth on the stool, considering. "I don't think I feel like playing the piano after all," she said. "It's time for my nap."

"You stay in that room too much," I said.

"What would you rather I do? Do you want me to go marketing for Maggie? Do you want me to take a walk along the beach or a drive with you? Do you want me to go fishing with

Gordon? Isn't it better if I stay out of your sight? That way," said Gabrielle, smiling, "you can forget about me. Even with your *perfectly* marvelous memory, Elizabeth, there are some things you obviously prefer to forget."

I knew what she was going to do. I watched her leave the room. I heard the sound of her footsteps going up the stairs and I knew exactly what she was going to do. She wasn't going to take a nap. She was going to sit at that small table that Gordon had put in her room. She was going to sit there for hours with a pencil in her hand. Maggie had told me about it.

"She just stares into space," Maggie had said. "She holds the pencil in her hand, but she isn't writing. I wouldn't have known about it, but I looked into her room. When she first said she wanted to take a nap, I worried about her. I thought she wasn't feeling well. I knocked on her door, and when she didn't answer, I looked into that room. There she was, just sitting there, and when I spoke to her, she didn't answer me. She acted as if she didn't hear me and I couldn't just stand there with that door pushing me out."

Every afternoon, I thought, sitting up straight with the pencil in her hand and the blank sheets of paper before her. Every afternoon she sits there in that cold room until finally the cramped fingers open and the pencil rolls to one side. She stretches and walks over to the window, pulling back the curtains. She looks out the window, scanning that deserted strip of beach, seeing the sea wall and the waters of the bay.

She's so lonely, I told myself. How did she become so lonely? How did I let it happen?

I knew the answer. I walked through the front parlor and into the hall, and all the time I knew the answer. Gabrielle was right. I had let her stay in that room because it was convenient for me. How pleasant to have Gabrielle tucked out of sight while I ran off with Gordon. How convenient to pretend that Gabrielle was contentedly napping while I went my own way.

I ran up the stairs and opened her door. She wasn't seated at the table. She wasn't standing at the window. She was leaning back in the rocking chair, her hands flat on the arms, her eyes closed.

"Gabrielle," I said.

She didn't answer me. The door closed soundlessly. The room was very cold. I rubbed my arms. "Gabrielle," I said again.

She began to rock. "I didn't hear you knock."

"That's because I didn't."

"When you leave, close the door behind you," she said pleasantly.

"The door is closed," I said, surprised. She knew the door wouldn't stay open. I opened my mouth. I wanted to say, "It's impossible to keep it open. Don't you remember?" I looked at her and I didn't say anything.

She stood up. "We've talked like this before," she said fretfully. She walked over to the far wall. She bent, adjusting the red rug, and then she stood on it with her legs apart. She reached forward, her right hand grasping the air, her fingers curved, and then she thrust out her arm.

She was pantomiming, each gesture timed, each movement so real that for a moment I expected to see the fireplace materialize, the fireplace in this room where it used to be, the coals glowing, the licking flames dissipating the cold, and Gabrielle standing in front of it, the poker in her hand.

"You were right," I said in a conversational tone. "I don't know how you could have known, but you were right. There was a fireplace in this room. Aunt Constance told me about it. There was a fire, and when they repaired the wall, they took the fireplace away."

She put the imaginary poker down and held out her hands, fingers spread wide as if she were warming them. "No, they didn't," she said serenely.

"There's nothing there," I said. I walked over to her. I touched her shoulder. I was shaking. "Please stop pretending, Gabrielle. You know there's nothing there."

She turned around. She looked at me for a moment, puzzled, and then her face cleared. She licked her lips and smiled. "Who are you to tell me what I know?"

I stepped back. "Let's go downstairs. I can't talk to you in this room. You mustn't shut yourself away like this. I want you to spend your time with me."

"With you?" She began to laugh. "With Gordon and you?"

"Yes," I said. "With Gordon and me."

"You and Gordon," she said. She moved toward me. "Are you so sure that it's *you* and Gordon?"

"No one can be sure of anything," I said carefully.

"I want you to remember that, Elizabeth. You're the one who is supposed to be so good at remembering things. Just remember that no one can be sure of anything and you'll be all right."

"Gabrielle, darling—" I stepped back and felt the knob of the door pressing into me.

" 'Gabrielle, darling,' " she mocked. "Don't bother to finish, Elizabeth, *darling*, because I know just what you're going to say. You're going to tell me you love me, that you're concerned about me, and I'm sick and tired of hearing about your love and your concern. You didn't come to this house for my sake. Why not be honest for a change and admit it? You came here because you knew in that way you could see more of Gordon. What could be more delightful than having Gordon in the same house with you? Proximity is half the battle, isn't it, Elizabeth, darling?"

The room was so cold. Everything was so cold. I leaned against the cold door and shook with the cold. I longed for the fireplace to be real again, to reappear on that white wall, the flames leaping high, the room warm again, and I warm again.

"Gordon came after we arrived," I said, knowing that Gabrielle chose to ignore the truth, knowing that Gabrielle wouldn't believe me no matter what I said. "I didn't know he would come here."

"It would serve you right if I wanted to leave," said Gabrielle, still smiling. "If I went away from here, you'd have to go, too, wouldn't you, Elizabeth? And it's much too soon for you. You won't be ready to go until he asks you to marry him. Do you really think he's going to ask you to marry him?"

I stood very still. "I've never seen you like this," I said.

She compressed her lips, confused. "You said that once

before. You stood there just like that and said exactly those same words to me, only then you were wearing a black dress. As a matter of fact," said Gabrielle, frowning, "you were all black. Your hair, your eyes."

"I don't know what you're talking about," I said, appalled. I reached behind me. My fingers closed on the doorknob.

"It doesn't stop," she said. "You think you live through something and it's all behind you and then you have to do it all over again. Over and over again. It doesn't seem fair. How many times do you have to go through it before it's finished?"

I let go of the doorknob. I ran toward her. I put my hands on her shoulders and shook her. "Stop it," I said.

She flung back her head and laughed. "Can't you see that's just what I'm trying to do?" She pushed me away. "Do you think I'm hysterical, Elizabeth? Why don't you slap my face? Isn't that the approved method?"

"I don't want to slap you," I said, my throat aching. "I don't want to hurt you in any way."

"Don't you?"

"Do I have to answer that?"

"Then why don't you tell me the truth?"

"But I do tell you the truth."

"About you and Gordon," said Gabrielle. "Isn't that what we're thinking about? We discuss everything else, but there's really only one thing we're both thinking about. Let's sit down together and talk the way sisters should. You can sit on the rocking chair and I'll sit on the straight chair because I'm the hostess and you are my honored guest. We'll make ourselves comfortable and we'll be very confidential and bare our souls. Wouldn't you like that, Elizabeth? You always wanted me to tell you things. How many times have you begged me to confide in you? Now it's my turn. I want you to talk to me. Now," said Gabrielle with satisfaction, "that's something new, isn't it?"

"I want to talk to you," I said. "There's nothing more I want than to be close to you, Gabrielle, but I can't sit and talk in this room. I can't bear it in here."

"You'll get used to it," said Gabrielle casually. "I have."

Used to it? I thought. There on the floor near the bed

Jotham had lain, body limp, fingers inert, and here, at the door, Ruth had pounded on the unyielding wood, and here, too, Alarice had slumped, gasping for air, each of them alone, each caught in a separate moment of time, alone.

"Come with me," I said persuasively. "We'll go downstairs. We'll talk to each other the way we should have talked long ago. We'll look ahead. We'll make plans." I took a deep breath. "We'll go home again," I said quietly. "Right after Aunt Constance's birthday party, we'll leave here."

"But I don't want to."

"You said—"

"I gave you all the good reasons why you came here and why you didn't want to leave. I didn't tell you mine, did I?"

"No," I said slowly. "You didn't."

It's impossible, I thought. I can stand right next to her, but I can't reach her.

"I'll be downstairs if you want me," I said bleakly.

I opened the door. I waited for a moment, standing in the hall, hoping she would call to me, but the only sound I heard was the click of the latch as the door closed behind me.

I stood there, knowing that I should open that door again and stay with her, and I left, knowing that I couldn't do it. I went down the stairs, turning my back to Gabrielle closed up in that room with the cold and the memories of others, Gabrielle shut up in that room, locked up in herself, trapped by her own fears, her own guilt, Gabrielle alone and getting used to it.

"THAT SHOULD DO IT," SAID MAGGIE. SHE STEPPED BACK and then looked at me, uncertain. "Is it all right, Elizabeth?"

"It's a beautiful cake," I said.

It was late afternoon. Maggie and I were in the kitchen. Aunt Constance was upstairs changing her clothes because Maggie had told her she was going to have a party.

"There's no point in trying to keep it a surprise," Maggie had said wisely. "It's more fun to think about a thing ahead of time anyway."

Surprise, I thought wryly, wishing that Gordon hadn't told me that his mother was coming, wishing that I hadn't known, so I wouldn't have to walk around with this tight knot of apprehension inside me. And yet I didn't know why I felt the way I did. If Ruth Inness wasn't afraid, why should I be? She was arriving on the four o'clock ferry and Gordon had asked me not to tell anyone.

"It's a surprise," he had said.

And now Aunt Constance was in her room, the thin, tremulous hand moving the dresses back and forth on the rack, picking, choosing, the tired, worn hands busy because Constance Bellingham was once again hostess in her own house.

And Gabrielle—what was Gabrielle doing? Was she, too, dressing for the party or was she seated at the table, the pencil in her hand? Was she in the rocking chair or was she standing at the window? Was it possible that she slept while the day chilled, while the shadows lengthened, while Maggie and I got everything ready?

Gordon had left to pick up his mother and Helen Warren, and "On the way stop by for Doctor Kirk," I told him. "His wife won't come, but he wants to, and he's much too old to drive himself."

"No Julie Sanders?" said Gordon.

"No Julie Sanders," I said. "She refuses to step foot in this house while we're all here. Did you ever hear of such nonsense? She prefers the house empty."

And we're busy filling it, I thought now, walking back and forth between the kitchen and the dining room, setting the table. Would more people appease the hunger in this house? Would there come a time when the longing was sated, when the search was ended?

The crystal chandelier swayed, reflecting the light, the prisms tinkling softly. Whose footsteps set it in motion? I wondered. Gabrielle's or mine?

I walked back into the kitchen. Maggie was sitting at the table and my coffee was waiting for me.

She looked at me. "This house is afflicted," Maggie said abruptly.

I sat down. "What do you mean by that?" I said.

"I don't know what I mean," said Maggie, troubled. "I was just sitting here and all of a sudden it came to me and I said the words out loud. Maybe I wanted to say it. Maybe I wanted you to hear me, otherwise I would have kept it to myself. I can't stand it much longer, Elizabeth." She stood up and carried her cup and saucer to the sink. She poured the remains of her coffee down the drain and then she turned around. "Lord knows I need help," she said. "The Lord knows I do. I prayed in church yesterday, but it didn't do any good."

I put down my cup. "Maggie, darling, what is it?"

"Don't get up," she said. "Just sit there. I don't want your arms around me. I love you, but you're not my child. I should have had a child of my own. I should have made another creature of flesh and blood so that I could know when I die that a bit of me still walked this earth. I've spent most of my life pretending that you and Gabrielle were my children, just the way I pretended that what I was doing was useful and meaningful. It was useful, I suppose. I cooked three meals a day and I cleaned house, but what I did one day had to be done all over again the next, and meaningful it wasn't and isn't. I was afraid to live and now I'm afraid to die."

"We're going to have a party," I said inanely. "You know you love parties."

"It means Mrs. Bellingham is a year older. That's all a birthday means. Another year gone. Another year gone for her, and another year going by for me, and, Elizabeth," she said, her voice rising, "I don't want to see the things I have seen."

You, too? I thought, appalled. Oh, Maggie, darling, not you, too!

I pushed back my chair. "Maggie—"

"Sit down," she commanded.

My throat tightened. "We're so far apart," I said. "The length of the whole room is between us."

"We're not far apart," said Maggie. She rinsed her cup and put it neatly to one side. Then she turned around again. She leaned against the sink. "I wouldn't be talking to you like this if I didn't feel we were close, Elizabeth. When I said I had been afraid to live, I meant I stayed on the outside of your lives, living in your mother's house and helping her raise her children. That way I could have a family and at the same time keep myself safe. That's all I wanted to do. If terrible things happened, they happened to other people, not to me, and if I saw things I didn't want to see, I could keep quiet about them."

"What things?"

"It doesn't happen often," said Maggie. "If it happened often, I wouldn't know what to do. It happened just twice before this. I knew when your grandmother was going to die. I dreamt about it the week before. I saw her lying in the bed and I saw myself bending over her and calling her name."

"Lots of people dream," I said.

"Not like that."

"Yes," I said. "Like that."

"Then there was going to be another baby," she said. "When you were ten and Gabrielle was five, there was going to be another baby. Your mother was so happy. I said to her, I said, 'Maybe this time it'll be a boy,' and she said in that quick, gay way of hers (you remember the way she spoke), 'Maggie, I'll probably have another girl,' and then she crossed her fingers and we both laughed. She was wearing a white robe, a long, white hostess gown that your father had given her for her birthday, and while I was looking at her, the front of it began to change color. One minute it was white and the next it was red. From her waist down her robe dripped blood. I wanted to scream, but I couldn't make a sound. Your father walked into the room and he wanted to know what was wrong with me. He said I was as white as your mother's robe. He hadn't seen a thing. He had looked at her and he hadn't seen a thing. She kept on standing there with the blood streaming and I was the only one who could see it. Neither of them knew anything except that dinner was supposed to be ready and I was behaving like I was going to faint. They kept fussing over me, insisting that I lie down, and because I couldn't look at her any longer, I was glad to leave the room." She held onto the sink. "And that night," said Maggie, "your mother had a miscarriage."

"You never told me," I said.

"I never told anyone. Who would believe me? I didn't want to believe it of myself. I was almost relieved when your parents died and I hadn't known it was going to happen. That's a terrible thing to say, isn't it?"

"No," I said quickly. "I understand."

She let go of the sink. She walked toward me. "I think you do," she said. "I really think you do."

I didn't want to ask her, but I had to. "Why are you telling me all this now?" I said.

"Because of last night," Maggie said simply. "I've been

thinking about it all day, but I didn't have a chance to be alone with you. Maybe if I tell you about it, that will change something. I don't know. I only know I have to tell you."

Because of last night and Maggie lying awake in the dark. Deliberately she had taken her time getting ready for bed, emphasizing the routine, trying to dull her mind and her senses so that she could sleep. Her legs ached and she had let the water run slowly into the tub and then she had soaked in the hot bath until the water cooled and the skin on her fingers was puckered. When she finally got into bed, there was a cramp in her left foot, and, resentful, hating her own pain, hating her own fragile, aging flesh, she sat up and rubbed the foot, massaging it until the tense muscles relaxed.

Then she turned out the light, closing her eyes against the darkness, trying not to think because "The trouble with Constance Bellingham," Maggie had said, "is that she thinks too much."

Trouble, thought Maggie now, lying there in the dark, trouble and sorrow and worry, and I have spent my whole life trying to avoid thinking. At night I try not to think because that will keep me from falling asleep, and I know if I don't go to sleep, I'll be tired in the morning, and in the morning there is no time to think and I'm glad. I keep myself busy doing things over and over again, cleaning and cooking, the two things that are never finished, the two things that go on day after day without end. One minute I clean a floor and the next it's dirty again, and if my work never ends, then how can I? Because I kept on feeling the same inside myself, I pretended that the outside remained the same, too, but it's not true. I know it's not true and the time has come for me to think.

About what? asked Maggie silently. About my life running by? About the cake I'll bake tomorrow for Mrs. Bellingham's birthday party? About the way Elizabeth looks at Doctor Inness when she thinks no one is watching her? About the headlines in the newspaper? About war and death and unhappiness and disease? About the minister's sermon yesterday and the search for God? About putting on the marketing list the polish I need for the library table in the back parlor? About Mrs. Bellingham and how she walks past the closed door of Gabrielle's room and the way she won't go into that room, even though Gabrielle has asked her to? About the tone in Gabrielle's voice when she speaks to Mrs. Bellingham? About Doctor Inness coming back a day earlier as if he couldn't wait and Elizabeth going down the stairs in the middle of the night? Dear God, said Maggie to herself, the time has come for me to think and I don't know what to think.

She could feel a tear slide down her cheek. "No, you don't," said Maggie fiercely, sitting up in bed. "Don't you dare cry."

As if in answer, defiantly, bitterly, the sobs began, but her own throat was quiet and her own cheeks were dry.

Gabrielle, thought Maggie, still sitting in the dark, turned to stone. It's Gabrielle.

She switched on the light. Her clock said it was two. The same hour as last time, Maggie told herself, listening. Will it be the same as last time? Will I open her door only to find her asleep, the weeping stopped as if it never began?

She put on her flannel bathrobe and fumbled for her slippers. The light in the hall was on and she was grateful for it. All the other doors were closed. Even Elizabeth's.

But Elizabeth never closes her door, thought Maggie. She always leaves it open. Why should she close it now? Because she isn't in her room, Maggie told herself savagely. Because she's downstairs with him and she doesn't want anyone to know her room is empty.

She stood there for a moment, hesitant, irresolute. Gabrielle's room was quiet now. She didn't want to go in by herself. Standing there she knew she didn't want to go into Gabrielle's room. She had hoped to wake Elizabeth. She had hoped that Elizabeth would sit up in bed, saying, "What's the matter, Maggie? You want me to go with you? Of course I will. We can't let Gabrielle cry in the middle of the night, can we?" And Elizabeth's light now burning, too, her soft, flecked eyes tender and concerned in the light, and Elizabeth holding Maggie's hand while she did what had to be done, while Maggie opened Gabrielle's door.

"I can't do it," said Maggie softly. "I just can't do it," said

Maggie, feeling sorry for herself, and then she put out her hand and turned the knob.

The door wouldn't open. There was a weight pushing against it, wedged against it, and although she used all her strength, the door wouldn't budge. She took her hand away.

It's locked, thought Maggie, knowing it wasn't. Everything is quiet now. Why should I disturb Gabrielle? Why should I push against this door as long as everything is quiet? The sensible thing, Maggie argued, is to go right back to bed. I have a million and one things to do tomorrow with all those people coming for dinner and the cake to bake and there is no reason for me to stand here. No one else cares. Why should I? Mrs. Bellingham is sound asleep and Elizabeth is downstairs doing God knows what, and why should I stand here any longer?

But there was sobbing again on the other side of that door, there was weeping again, the choking, tearing cry of overwhelming grief, and "I'm coming, darling," said Maggie, and as if she had been invited, the door opened easily at her touch.

The room glowed with light. The room flickered and shimmered and throbbed with light. It ran up and down the walls and danced on the ceiling, and in the middle of it, in the very center of the vortex, was Gabrielle. She was seated at the small table, writing, the pencil in her hand, the pencil moving rapidly across the paper. Her eyes were closed and her cheeks were dry.

There was weeping, but it was not Gabrielle who wept. The cries came from the corners of the room, started in all the empty corners simultaneously and climbed the walls, the sounds and the sights blending together so that Maggie, dazzled, stunned, found herself unable to distinguish one from the other. The room was ablaze with grief, and Maggie, her heart thudding, stepping into it.

"Gabrielle," she said, and the door closed behind her.

The light, thought Maggie foolishly, fumbling for the switch not because she needed to see any better, but because she had to touch something of reality. She felt it move under her fingers, but the overhead fixture remained dark.

She stood next to the door, not knowing whether she could

walk across the room, not knowing if she could walk through the cold and the crying and the dancing lights.

"Gabrielle," she said again, but the figure at the table was a mannequin, white and quiet and lifeless, the eyes still closed, the lashes dark against the pale cheeks, the mouth bloodless. Its fingers curved about the pencil, the hand moving because the pencil moved, the pencil writing rapidly, automatically.

Maggie began to shiver. She leaned against the wall and shook with fear and the cold. Gabrielle sat at the table in her thin, white nightgown, her arms bare, and Maggie, wrapped in her flannel bathrobe, shook until her teeth chattered.

"Gabrielle," she said again because there was no other name she could call. Who was she going to turn to for help? Elizabeth? Doctor Inness? Mrs. Bellingham?

Trapped in this vibrating, trembling room with her was another human being, entranced, but made of warm pulsating flesh, and it was Gabrielle's name that Maggie said, Gabrielle's name that Maggie repeated, but Gabrielle didn't answer. Gabrielle, unhearing, turned inward, lost in some strange place where Maggie couldn't follow, didn't answer. Who will help me? thought Maggie desperately. Oh, my God, who will help us?

Maggie could walk. Amazed, she knew she could walk. Carefully she put one foot in front of the other. She moved toward Gabrielle, step by step she moved toward the center of the room, toward Gabrielle, toward the whirling, whimpering lights.

She could touch Gabrielle. All she had to do was reach out and she could touch her. She put her hand on Gabrielle's shoulder.

Gabrielle's head rolled forward and Maggie stood in the center of the whirlpool, the lights circling, swinging around her until dizzy, panic-stricken, she shouted to Gabrielle, "Wake up. You're dreaming!," saying to Gabrielle what she wanted to say to herself.

Gabrielle's eyes opened. Her mouth smiled but her eyes were without expression and her hand didn't stop moving, her hand obediently following the pencil.

214

"You must wake up," said Maggie. "Dear God, you must," and Gabrielle looked at her and really saw her. Gabrielle said, surprised, "Why, Maggie, what are you doing here?" And as Gabrielle spoke, with the sound of her voice, the crying stopped, the room steadied, the shimmering lights faded, and with the switch still in position the way Maggie had left it, the overhead light went on, an ordinary light bulb shining normally.

Now Maggie's hand rested on my shoulder, her fingers gripping me. "But even then," she said, "the pencil kept on writing as if it had nothing to do with her. She spoke to me. She saw me. She knew I was there, but her hand kept on writing and she paid no attention to it."

I rested my cheek against Maggie's hand. "I don't know what to say," I whispered. "Are you sure you didn't dream it?"

"I made her get into bed," said Maggie. "I stayed in that room shivering and arguing with her until she saw she couldn't get rid of me any other way, and all the time she kept on writing. I think that frightened me more than anything else, the way she kept on writing. She spoke to me, paying no attention to what she was doing, but she was writing. Then she saw I wasn't watching her, that I was watching the pile of papers in front of her and she looked down and her hand stopped moving. Her fingers opened and the pencil fell down. It rolled across the table and she smiled at me with that little smile she puts on when she's pleased and then she stacked the papers neatly together and got into bed. I asked her if she wanted to sleep with me and she said, 'Oh no, Maggie, this is my room,' in a self-satisfied voice that went with the smile, and I tucked her in and left."

Maggie going down the hall, I thought, her head bent, the old flannel bathrobe wrapped around her, Maggie going back to her own room, all the other doors closed to her, even mine.

"Don't put your arms around me," she had said. "You are not my child." But now her arms were around me, and I was her child, and Gabrielle and I were her family and she was not alone and even closed doors could open.

"Oh, Maggie, darling," I said. "I'm so sorry."

"There's nothing for you to be sorry about," she said.

"My door was closed," I said. "When you needed me, I wasn't there."

She didn't fall asleep until she heard Elizabeth come up the stairs. Elizabeth moved quietly, but the third step from the bottom creaked and Maggie could hear the click of the latch as Elizabeth opened and closed her door again.

And then she turned on her side and slept, knowing that she was asleep, some part of her still awake and alert so that in her sleep she knew when she turned in the bed, she knew when her legs began to ache again, she knew when the morning began.

The morning began.

"Happy birthday, Mrs. Bellingham," Maggie said, and "Gabrielle, I do wish you'd eat your eggs and stop pushing them around your plate," and "Would you like some more coffee, Doctor Inness?," and "If you're going marketing, Elizabeth, I'll make a list," and Maggie bustling back and forth, doing all the things that had to be done and saying all the things that had to be said, and all the while thinking about the pile of papers that had been on the table in Gabrielle's room, thinking about the pencil that seemed to move by itself, thinking about the way Gabrielle had stacked the papers together before she had let Maggie persuade her it was time she went to bed.

"I'll do the upstairs," said Maggie quickly as they all sat at the breakfast table, and then she almost ran up the steps, her legs without pain, her legs almost young again, her heart not so young, her heart pounding from exertion and excitement. She opened the door to Gabrielle's room and let it close behind her before she allowed herself to slow down.

But the small table had been cleared. The papers were gone.

"Where could they be?" said Maggie, turning toward the dresser. She had just opened the top drawer when a little sound made her look up and there, in the mirror, next to her own reflection was the reflection of Gabrielle, and "Are you looking for something?" said Gabrielle.

Maggie straightened. She cleared her throat. "I just thought I'd tidy up a bit," she said.

"But I always do my own room now," Gabrielle said sweetly. "You told me you didn't like it in here. You said it was much too cold in here and that's why I offered to take care of my own room. I must say you did seem relieved, Maggie, and although it's very considerate of you to come in here this morning, I do think it's a bit unnecessary, don't you? You have so much to keep you busy today that I wouldn't dream of allowing you to take on any more work," said Gabrielle, smiling at Maggie.

"I just wanted—" Maggie hesitated.

"You just wanted to snoop," said Gabrielle without rancor. "I'm not annoyed with you, Maggie. Really I'm not. I think it's almost funny."

"You were writing," said Maggie. "In the middle of the night. I saw you. You didn't even know you were writing. I saw that, too."

"When I was little, I kept a diary," Gabrielle said. "My mother couldn't understand why I locked it, but that's because I never told her about you."

"I wanted to help," said Maggie. "You seemed in trouble. I just wanted to help."

"Mind your own business," said Gabrielle, her voice low, her tone almost amused. "That's the best advice I can give you, Maggie. Stop trying to take care of us and start thinking of yourself. Pretty soon you won't have us to take care of and then you'll *have* to think of yourself, and it would be very wise," said Gabrielle calmly, "very, very prudent, Maggie, darling, to start making provision for your future."

My future, thought Maggie, going through the day as if she had a future. Elizabeth will marry and she won't need me any more, and Gabrielle has never needed me and has never wanted me, and what am I going to do?

Now she held onto Elizabeth. She stood in the kitchen holding onto Elizabeth, rocking back and forth with Elizabeth's head cradled in her arms and she had told Elizabeth what had happened and what she had felt and what she had thought, and she still didn't know what she was going to do.

She heard the sound of the car turning into the driveway and she knew that the moment with Elizabeth was over. And more

217

than this moment, she told herself, going to the door with Elizabeth. Much more than this moment is over, she thought, watching Elizabeth open the front door, knowing that the guests were arriving and the party was beginning.

✻

AUNT CONSTANCE KEPT REPEATING IT. SHE SAID IT WHEN they first arrived and she said it again when they had finished the roast beef, when they all leaned back in their chairs for a moment, waiting for dessert.

"I can't believe it," Aunt Constance said. "I can't believe you're all here," and she dabbed at her eyes with a handkerchief, smiling while she wiped her eyes.

I helped Maggie clear the table, watching Helen Warren as she spoke to Doctor Kirk, watching Ruth Inness as she sipped her water, seeing the way she turned her head, the way she set down the goblet, her long, white fingers playing with the stem. She was almost sixty, but the line of her jaw was firm, her eyes were blue-green and her hair was still fair, the gray blending, the white streaks only enhancing the soft, pale yellow.

She is Gordon's mother, I told myself, and then I looked at Helen Warren. Our eyes met. She is Alarice's daughter, said Helen Warren's eyes, her mouth a thin line.

She is Alarice's daughter, I agreed, walking back and forth between the kitchen and the dining room with my laden tray,

219

and each time I took a step, the chandelier swayed and the prisms tinkled.

"It's so good to be with you, Mother," Ruth Inness had said, kissing Aunt Constance, the grown-up Ruth denying the existence of the child who had pounded with clenched fists on that closed door, who had called to another woman in the cold and in the dark. "I want my mother," the child Ruth had screamed, and then once before this the grown-up Ruth had returned and once before the grown-up Ruth had left, even Alarice's own daughter unable to live in this house.

Why? I wondered, scraping the plates. Why would Alarice send her own daughter away? Why had Alarice allowed her sister to stay this time, showing herself only to strangers, only to Maggie and Gabrielle and me?

Now Constance Suellen Lysander Bellingham sat in her own dining room celebrating her eightieth birthday, Constance Bellingham alive and well with her friends around her, with her family around her, with the presents in the front parlor waiting to be opened, and the decorated cake with its candles in the kitchen waiting to be served, and Alarice, who sucked at human warmth so that all in her presence felt cold, Alarice, who could spin a room, become a dancing light and guide another's hand across paper, was trapped, impotent, helpless and—

Dead, I thought, lighting the candles, watching the years of Constance Bellingham's life leap into flame before my eyes. Alarice has done all that she could do. She has approached each of us in turn, and each of us, each in his own way, has defeated her. She has closed the door to that room, closed it against the world and closed it against herself. What happens happens only in that room. It had to be Gabrielle who had played the *Kinderscenen* that night, Gabrielle proving that she still knew it, and although Gabrielle lives in that room, too, she thrives, her cheeks pink, her limbs supple, her walk quick and easy. Soon I will take Gabrielle out of that room, take Gabrielle back into our own lives, back where we both belong, and the room instead of being a tomb will have been a healing place, the grief in there superseding even Gabrielle's own grief, so she can walk away from it, shutting the door behind her forever.

And we surround Constance Bellingham, I told myself, lifting the cake high. We protect her with our love and our laughter. She is called mother and aunt and friend and we are as a shield around her.

"Turn out the lights," said Doctor Kirk.

I held the tray in front of me, the cake with its candles in front of me, and thought of crossing the room in the dark with only these small, blazing candles to light my way and I shivered.

She's upstairs, I reminded myself impatiently. Nowhere else in this house have I found her. Not really. It was Gabrielle at the piano while Alarice wept in her room, and if it were not Gabrielle, if it were reversed and Alarice played while Gabrielle wept, she has never done it again. Certainly by now we have her penned, imprisoned upstairs while we laugh and talk and break bread together.

"No," said Helen Warren quickly. "We are not children. We don't have to sit in the dark. Constance knows she's having a birthday cake," and then, relieved, I put the cake in front of Aunt Constance, and we all sat around the dining-room table and watched as she tried to blow out the candles.

"Happy birthday, Aunt Constance," said Gordon, and "Happy birthday, Mrs. Bellingham," said Maggie, and "Happy birthday, Mother, darling," said Ruth Inness, and "Happy birthday, Constance," said Doctor Kirk and Helen Warren, and "Happy birthday," I said happily, and only Gabrielle was silent.

"Make a wish," said Maggie, and Aunt Constance leaned back and closed her eyes for a moment.

The prisms tinkled and I looked up, startled. The chandelier was swaying slightly, as though someone had walked across the room, but we were all sitting quietly at the table.

The tiny flames bent and then stood straight again, each still lit, each defiant against such fragile human breath.

"Need any help?" said Gordon.

"Nonsense," said Aunt Constance. "I was blowing out candles before you were born."

"There are just too many," said Ruth Inness. "Do stop, Mother, you'll strain yourself. How many candles are on that cake, Elizabeth?"

"Not eighty," I admitted. "I just put on as many as I could. I didn't count them."

"Give me the cake," said Helen Warren.

"It's mine," said Aunt Constance.

"Don't be a silly old woman," Helen Warren snapped. "I know it's your cake, but you'll never blow out those candles that way."

Aunt Constance pushed the cake over to her and Helen Warren clapped her hands. "There," she said. "There and there and *there*," and the candles went out, little puffs of smoke drifting up, and Aunt Constance said, "Does that mean I won't get my wish?" Doctor Kirk said gallantly that of course she would get her wish, and if she would tell him what it was, he personally would see to it that it came true, and she said, laughing, "Oliver, you're an old fool," and all the time the chandelier was swaying, its movement almost imperceptible, the chandelier vibrating, and no one was walking, all of us were sitting there, surrounding Constance Bellingham, guarding her, all of us with a slice of cake in front of us, all of us gathered together.

The prisms tinkled, and now Helen Warren was watching, too, her eyes wary. Ruth Inness stopped eating and Gordon's fork was held in mid-air.

The chandelier moved faster, as if it had been set in motion, as if, now that it had our complete attention, it was ready to perform.

"Someone must be walking around upstairs," said Doctor Kirk matter-of-factly.

"But we're all here," said Ruth Inness.

"Are we?" said Gabrielle, smiling. She was sitting next to Maggie. She filled her mouth with cake, enjoying it. "Are you sure we're all here?"

"The ceiling must be uneven," Gordon said. "This is an old house. It's been built and rebuilt. Something is off kilter."

Helen Warren nodded her head. "The carpenter theory," she said softly.

"She's done this before," said Constance Bellingham. She pushed her plate away. She was white. Her hair was white and her dress was white and her cheeks and her mouth were drained of all color. "I thought it had stopped," she said. "I thought there had to come a time when it would stop. I thought this house could be lived in again. Elizabeth said she was happy here, and since I've been home, nothing has happened, has it, Elizabeth?"

"Why don't you answer her, Elizabeth?" said Gabrielle, still smiling. "Why do you just sit there?"

"Who has done this before?" said Doctor Kirk loudly. "What are you talking about, Constance?"

"Alarice," said Constance Bellingham.

"Alarice? But she's dead," said Oliver Kirk. "She's been dead for a long time."

"What difference does time make?" said Gabrielle reasonably. "You're just as dead in one minute as in one year."

Helen Warren looked at Gabrielle and Gabrielle stopped smiling.

"Oliver," said Helen Warren, "don't be obtuse. You know why your wife wouldn't come here and you know all the stories that have been circulating and you know exactly what we're talking about."

"I know all the stories," said Doctor Kirk, "and I know they're exactly that—just stories. I made out the death certificate for Alarice myself."

Gabrielle leaned forward. "How did she die?"

"Gabrielle," I said, appalled.

"Oh, I know the answer," Gabrielle said airily. "I just wanted to see if the rest of you did."

The chandelier trembled and Helen Warren stood up. "I think we ought to get out of here," she said.

"We'll go in the front parlor," said Aunt Constance.

"We should leave this house," said Helen Warren.

"She's upstairs," I said inanely. "How can she affect us if she isn't here?"

"Like this," said Gabrielle, and one of the crystal pendants fell off the chandelier, the heavy glass landing on the table.

"I shouldn't have come back," said Ruth Inness, her voice thin and shrill. "I promised Helen and I didn't keep my word. I came back once before searching for her, thinking that because she was my mother I could reach her, that I could find out what she wanted, what held her here, but she never loved me, and if she wanted something in this house, it wasn't me."

Another prism rolled across the table.

"I cleaned it yesterday," said Maggie, dazed. "The wires are old and worn. Maybe I loosened some of them. Maybe that's why they're falling down."

Gordon pushed back his chair. "I'm going upstairs," he said.

"No," I said.

He looked at me and his eyes were questioning.

My darling, my love, I thought. What will you do if something happens now that you can't explain?

"I don't want to leave," said Aunt Constance. "I've been running all my life. I'm tired of running away. I'm not afraid of her. I'm not afraid of anything she can do." She flung back her head, shouting, "Do you hear me, Alarice? I'm not afraid of you. What will you do to me now? What is there left for you to do to me? Will you kill me? Is that what you want? I'm not afraid to die. You've taught me that much. Isn't that ironic? By remaining here, by refusing to leave this house, you've given me what you never wanted to give me. You've taken away my fear of death. You've given me comfort, Alarice."

The chandelier shuddered and then was still.

"It's all right now," said Maggie. She looked at me, pleading. "Isn't it all right now, Elizabeth?"

"Please," I said to Gordon, "don't go upstairs."

"What's wrong with everyone?" he said harshly. "What kind of nonsense is this?"

"Let him go," said Helen Warren quietly. "He won't find anything. He's looking for nothing and that is exactly what he will find."

We could hear his footsteps on the stairs and then the sounds he made as he moved in the room above. The chandelier trembled, but this time we knew it was Gordon. He came down the steps and walked into the dining room.

"Nothing," he said firmly.

"Of course," said Helen Warren. "Sit down again, Gordon. I

want you at the table. There are eight of us, a good even number, and we can sit comfortably with our hands linked."

"No," said Aunt Constance. "Not a séance, Helen. I won't be a party to it."

"Not a séance in the technical sense," said Helen Warren. "We don't have a medium with us, but if we hold onto each other, perhaps we can generate enough force so that Alarice can break through. That's the only reason I came tonight. To be useful. Not to celebrate your birthday, Constance, because I knew your birthday could never be celebrated properly in this house. I knew there could be no peace, no joy, no laughter in this house for you. Not the way things were and not the way things are."

"She always hated you," said Aunt Constance. "You were my friend and because of that she always hated you. Aren't you afraid?"

"I'm going to clear the table," said Maggie quickly, standing up. "I can't just sit here with all these dirty dishes."

I made no offer to help her. I sat there with my hands clasped.

"She hated everyone," said Helen Warren. "She hated then and she hates now. Not only me. Not only those who are dead. Not only those who died in this house, but also those who have lived here and who try to live here now. The time has come for her to tell us why she hates. The time has come for her to communicate with us, to tell us what she wants, and the time has come for her to leave here because if she won't, you must."

Maggie walked back and forth, her steps heavy, and the chandelier swayed musically.

"I won't be a party to this," said Doctor Kirk.

"Party," said Gabrielle scornfully. She began to laugh. "That's funny. Don't you see how funny it is? Isn't this supposed to be a party?"

"Just take the cloth off the table, if you will, Maggie," said Helen Warren, "and please sit down."

"I've got to get home," said Doctor Kirk.

"I'll drive you," said Gordon.

"I'll go to the inn," said Ruth Inness. "I'll sleep at the inn tonight."

"You will go nowhere," said Helen Warren sharply. She looked at Doctor Kirk. "You'll stay right where you are, too, Oliver. You're a skeptic and having a skeptic— No," she corrected herself, smiling at Gordon, "having two skeptics here will be a healthy thing. All I ask is that you form part of the circle, that you stay with us and that you watch us all carefully."

"All right," said Doctor Kirk. "It should be interesting, if nothing else."

"It will be boring," said Gordon. "We'll sit here like idiots waiting for what?"

"She gave birth to me," said Ruth Inness, "but she wasn't my mother. She never was my mother. She didn't raise me. She didn't take care of me. I saw her, you know," she said, talking to Aunt Constance. "I never told you, but I saw her the night my father died. She called to me and I went to her. I went into her room and she was there, all soft and beautiful and smiling, and I cried out because I was so happy to see her and my father heard us and he came there, too, and when he came into the room, she changed."

"What did you see?" said Helen Warren.

"My mother," said Ruth Inness. "I was a little girl, but I remember it very well. She had long fair hair and she was standing next to the window and there was a candle in her hand, and when I came into the room, she smiled at me and I thought that she loved me, I thought that was why she was smiling at me, and I ran toward her, but when my father came, she disappeared. I had my arms outstretched to her and she just disappeared. I couldn't find her anywhere. I kept looking all around the room, but she wasn't there."

"You said she changed when Jotham came into the room. How did she change?"

"I don't know. I can't explain it. She stopped smiling and then she just faded away."

"Did he see her?"

"I don't think so because he tried to take me out of there. He said there was nothing in the room. He said I was having a dream. He said I must go back to bed."

"Then what did you do?"

"I began to cry. I told him I wanted him to go away. I kicked at him. I yelled that I hated him because he had married Aunt Constance. I told him he had no right to marry her. And then he bent over and fell on the floor. I could feel the hate inside me, but it wasn't my hate. It couldn't have been my hate. I always loved him and I loved Aunt Constance, too, so how could it have been mine?"

"It wasn't yours," said Helen Warren softly. "I've told you this before, Ruth, and I'll tell it to you again. And I'm glad you're here. It's your place to be here right now."

Doctor Kirk reached out and took my hand. His fingers were dry and firm.

We sat around the table, linked to each other, Gordon between Aunt Constance and his mother, and next to Ruth Inness, Doctor Kirk, and on the other side of me, Gabrielle, her hand clasped in Maggie's, and Helen Warren was between Maggie and Aunt Constance.

"Isn't this usually done in darkness?" said Gordon dryly.

"The light won't make any difference," said Helen Warren, "but our talking will. I want us to sit here and concentrate."

"Concentrate on what?" said Gordon fiercely. "Concentrate on old sorrow, on bygone agony? Does my mother have to go through with this? Does my mother have to subject herself to this, and what about my aunt?"

"Old agony," said Aunt Constance. "That's exactly what it is, Gordon. You're right. I don't have to take any part in this. Whatever remains in this house can stay here as far as I'm concerned. I can leave. I've lived without this house all these years and I can live without it again."

"I'll go home in the morning," said Ruth Inness eagerly. "Tonight I'll sleep at the inn and tomorrow I'll go home and I'll pick up my life again just where I left it."

"Both of you came back," said Helen Warren. "I begged you not to and neither of you would listen. Now you must stay for a

227

while longer. When you were away from here, you always wondered what would happen if you returned, and now if you go, you'll always wonder what would have happened if you stayed."

"I suppose you're right," said Ruth Inness, resigned.

Aunt Constance said nothing.

Gabrielle's fingers lay passive in mine. I held onto Doctor Kirk and Gabrielle. Our linked hands rested on the table, which was bare now, its polished surface reflecting the light. The chandelier was still. The room was very quiet.

Alarice, I thought. If there is something you want, something you need that will give you release, tell us what it is. They say you are filled with hate. They say you are evil, but it wasn't always that way for you, was it? You were young, young as Gabrielle and I are young, and your hair was fair and your eyes were blue-green and surely you loved as I love. You wept in the night, and does evil shed tears? Come to us. I beg you, Alarice, come to us. Tell us what it is that keeps you here, that keeps you earthbound, haunted and haunting, barred from the place where you belong.

Aunt Constance stirred restlessly. "How long are we going to sit like this?" she said.

"Until something happens," said Helen Warren.

"And just what do you think is going to happen?" asked Gabrielle. Her fingers twitched in mine.

"I don't know," said Helen Warren softly. "Suppose you tell me."

"You're the expert," said Gabrielle rudely. "You always have been a nuisance, do you know that, Helen?"

"Gabrielle, stop it," I said rapidly.

"Let her talk," said Helen Warren.

"But I thought we were supposed to be quiet," said Ruth Inness.

"I'm going to be sick," Maggie said. "There's something wrong with me. I keep feeling that the table is moving. I know it can't be, but it seems to be rising in the air. If I sit here any longer, I'm going to be very sick."

"She's right. The table is moving," said Doctor Kirk, amazed.

"Don't be a fool, Oliver," said Aunt Constance.

I held onto Gabrielle and Doctor Kirk and watched our hands rise in the air, our hands on the surface of the table, rising with the table.

Gabrielle's fingers were ice-sticks lying within mine. It's cold in here, I thought, shivering. How can it be cold in here? It's never been cold in the dining room before.

"Is that you, Alarice?" said Helen Warren eagerly. "Are you trying to reach us? Rap once for yes and twice for no."

Gabrielle's hand moved in mine. I looked at her. Her eyes were closed. Her mouth fell open and a little saliva dripped down her chin.

"Gabrielle," I said. "Gabrielle, darling, what is it?"

She shuddered. She opened her eyes. "I don't have to stay here," she whispered. "You can all sit here if you want to, but I don't have to, and no one can make me." She pulled her hand away. The table rocked violently for a moment and then straightened, its legs resting on the floor. Gabrielle pushed her chair back. She stood up and walked across the room.

"Gabrielle," I cried.

"Let her go," said Helen Warren.

"Let her talk. Let her go," mocked Gabrielle, pausing in the archway to the hall. "What good advice you give, Helen. Now it's my turn to give some advice. Why don't you all pretend this is a party like any other? Why don't you all go into the front parlor and sit around and watch while the presents are opened? Who ever heard of a birthday party without presents? And while you're doing that, I'll go upstairs and get my gift, and then when she has opened all her other presents, I'll give her mine because," chanted Gabrielle, running up the stairs, "the last is best and we always save the best for last."

"I'm an old woman," said Constance Bellingham, blowing her nose. "I can't go through a scene like this again. It was cruel of you to do this to me, Helen. I'm an old woman," she repeated, wiping her eyes, her chin trembling, "and all I want to do is just wake up in the morning and get through the day without pain. That isn't too much to ask, is it?"

"Gabrielle is right," I said, my throat closing. "We'll go inside. Aunt Constance will open her presents. Maggie will bring in the coffee, won't you, Maggie?"

"I'm not going in that kitchen alone," Maggie said. "If you'll stay with me, Elizabeth—"

"There's nothing wrong with the kitchen," I said, following her.

"Before this there was nothing wrong with the dining room either," said Maggie, lifting the percolator, "and now there's something wrong with every part of this house." She looked at me and her eyes were bleak. "We're going to have to leave, Elizabeth."

"Yes," I said. "I know."

"Right away," she said.

"Soon," I said.

"How soon?"

"As soon as we can get ready."

"How long will that take?"

I swallowed hard. "I don't know, Maggie. We'll be out of here as soon as we can."

"And we'll go home?"

"Yes," I agreed. "We'll go home."

"And what about Doctor Inness?"

"He will come with us," I said.

"Will you marry him?"

"Yes," I said.

She touched my hand. "I'm glad." She turned away. "And what about Gabrielle?" said Maggie, leaving the other question unasked, Maggie averting her head so that I couldn't see the look in her eyes.

"It will be all right, Maggie," I said quickly. "You'll see. We'll go home and Gabrielle will be well and when Gordon and I are married, you can live with us and—"

"And bring up your children?" said Maggie dryly.

"Maggie—"

She shook her head. "I don't know what's going to be, but someone's going to have to take care of Gabrielle. It seems to me that I'd better finish with this generation before I start on the next." She smiled. "You carry the tray," she said briskly, "and I'll take the coffeepot."

Maggie sharing the burden, I thought as I lifted the tray, the tray light without the load of the heavy pot. Maggie making things easy for me.

We walked through the dining room, past the corner cupboard where the flowered cups and saucers decorated the shelves, past the swaying chandelier and into the hall.

"I'd like to leave tonight," said Maggie.

"I'm not going before Aunt Constance does," I said quickly. "I can't do that to her."

"If we go, she'll have to," said Maggie. "Hold that tray straight, Elizabeth."

"I am," I said obediently.

She walked ahead of me. There was a crash. My heart jumped and Maggie whirled around.

"I told you to hold the tray straight," she said. "It isn't as if I didn't warn you and—" Her eyes opened wide as she saw me standing there, the tray safe in my hands. "What happened?" She looked beyond me, her gaze fixed and staring over my shoulder. "Oh, my God," she said.

I put down the tray. Very carefully, very slowly, I walked over to the dining-room table and put down the tray. Then I looked at the empty corner cabinet and at the far corner of the dining room, the broken pieces of china lying in a heap in the corner of the dining room as if they had been thrown there in a burst of savage temper.

"Across the room," said Maggie, trembling. "How could they fall right across the room?"

Helen Warren came out of the front parlor. "Constance is like a child," she said. "I can't believe she's in her dotage. She has always been so clear-minded, yet she sits there exclaiming over her presents as if nothing has happened."

"Look," I said, pointing.

Helen Warren compressed her lips. "I didn't hear a sound," she said.

"It was an awful crash," said Maggie.

"I should have known," Helen Warren said softly, "and yet

when you deal with things like this, there is so much to look out for that sometimes you forget."

"They were thrown," I said, shivering.

"And we tried to communicate with her," said Helen Warren. "We asked her to speak to us and this is how she answered."

"Alarice?" I said.

"She has broken through," said Helen Warren.

There were footsteps on the stairs, footsteps coming down. I could hear the voices in the front parlor and the measured steps on the stairs. Helen Warren walked back into the hall. She looked up and I touched my throat.

"It's Gabrielle," said Helen Warren.

Gabrielle stood in the hall. There was a package in her hand, the small box wrapped in white paper and tied with a red ribbon.

"Are you waiting for me?" she asked.

"Yes," said Helen Warren, "we're waiting for you."

We all went into the front parlor. Aunt Constance sat on the love seat, the discarded wrappings scattered about, and there was color in her cheeks again.

"What a beautiful scarf, Elizabeth," she cried out in delight at the sight of me. "I must thank you for a most thoughtful gift."

"Wait until you see mine," said Gabrielle, putting the small box on Aunt Constance's lap. "This is something special and it's for you."

"How kind you all are," said Aunt Constance, her eyes filling with tears again. "What a lovely party this is turning out to be after all." Her fingers fumbled with the ribbon. She tore the paper, exposing a white jeweler's box. "What can it be?" she said, opening the lid, and there nestled on purple velvet was a small, heart-shaped pin.

I looked at Gabrielle. She stood in front of Aunt Constance and she was smiling. "Do you like it?" she said, and she licked her lips.

"How beautiful," I said, wondering where she had borrowed the money to buy it.

"Where did you get that?" said Helen Warren, her voice rising. "Constance, don't—"

Constance Bellingham opened her mouth, but no sound came forth. The box fell from her hands and rolled across the floor. The little pin lay in her lap, the stones winking in the light.

"I think they are sapphires," said Gabrielle. "I really think they are."

"Gordon!" said Helen Warren.

Gordon leaped forward and caught Aunt Constance in his arms. His fingers closed around her wrist.

Gabrielle began to laugh. She leaned over Gordon's shoulder. "Happy birthday," Gabrielle said, still laughing. "Happy birthday, Consuela, darling."

"It's Alarice," said Aunt Constance hoarsely. "It's Alarice's pin." She tried to free herself. Her mouth twisted. "It was buried with her," she said, and then her mouth went slack and she lay quiet in Gordon's arms.

 *Alarice*

THEY CALLED ME, AND WHEN I ANSWERED, THEY DID
not hear. They called me, and when I came, they did not see.
They called me, and my name echoed throughout the house,
joining all the other echoes, the words meeting in the rooms,
bumping into each other in the passageways, in the upstairs
hall and in the downstairs hall, in the front parlor and in the
back parlor, all the words that had been said lying dormant,
waiting to be brought to life again, there to be found by those
who searched, those who could hear, those who could see.

My name was called and the other sounds listened and
stirred, too, rustling softly at first, then louder, louder—Papa
shouting, "Janet, where are you?" and Mama answering from
the kitchen, her hands covered with flour, and Consuela saying
desperately, "Jotham, is that you?" and "Alarice," said Mama,
and "I'm coming," I cried, and Mama saying, "A lady always
wears gloves," and "I'll marry you," Jotham said thickly, and
"Don't you love me?" I cried, and, once again, "Why don't you
love me?"

The sounds settling once more, startled for a moment like
dust motes dancing in the sunlight, and "I'm almost finished,"

said Julie Sanders. "I'll clean better next time. We've been here long enough," and "Long enough," agreed the echoes.

The sunlight lay in patterned squares on the floor of my room and the front door closed "Because I can't live here," said Consuela. "I can't live here," said the strangers; one stranger, two strangers, three strangers coming and going, moving in and moving out, the front door closing behind them and the days and the nights and the months and the years going by with the sounds subsiding, softer than the murmur of the sea, the sounds more distant and farther away. Sunlight and shadow, moonlight and mist, rain and snow, and "Long enough," I said. "It's been long enough," I said, listening. "Did you call me? I thought you called my name."

The door to my room opened and there stood a child in a thin, pink nightgown.

"Mother?" she said.

Mother? I thought.

"I don't want this baby," said Jotham bitterly.

"I love you," I said. "I've always loved you."

Tell me you love me, I pleaded silently, begging. There was the thrust of your flesh within me. There was joy when you entered me. Have you forgotten? Tell me you love me.

"You can't stay," said Consuela. "There's no reason for you to stay here any longer. Is it not enough that I have buried Mama? Do I have to stand by and watch you take over my house?"

"This is my room," I said. "It might be your house. Mama might have thought she was leaving you the house, but this is my room and my child will be born here."

"I'm sorry," Jotham said.

"Why are you apologizing to her?" I screamed. "Why don't you apologize to me?"

"Mother," said the child crossing the threshold and the door closed behind her.

"Mama," I said, weeping as she moved away from me. "Mama, you came to meet me. You knew I would be frightened and you came to meet me. Please don't go. You can stay here with me."

"But I don't want to stay," she said. "I have been on the other side. I don't want to stay here when I don't have to."

"On the other side?" I said. "Where are you going?"

"Mother?" said the child standing in the dark.

"Mama, don't turn away from me," I said. "I can't help it."

"Alarice, Alarice," she said sadly, saying my name over and over again, and I put aside the book I was holding, the wire-bound notebook that ended with my name just the way I began with my name, and it seemed to me that this was fitting and proper, the book and I somehow one and the same.

I went over to the small table that served me as desk. There were the scattered papers I had been working on all afternoon, the papers I had turned from in despair. I looked at them, not caring, knowing that there were others, knowing that I had accomplished what I had set out to do, knowing I had guided the hand properly in the dusk, in the twilight, in the night.

I looked at the hand that now truly belonged to me and flexed its fingers. I walked over to the mirror and saw the face that now was mine, the dark eyes (how strange to see through dark eyes), and the hair, dark as well, cropped too short, so that it would take a long time to grow.

Meanwhile I groomed it, standing in front of my mirror, brushing it with steady strokes, using the old gestures on this new body, the head flung forward and back so that for a moment I could almost feel the weight of what used to be, the hair that had been mine heavy on my shoulders. The pain, the aching sense of loss, was gone now just the way my own body was gone, the long, fair hair dry and crumbling, the disintegrated flesh dust that was not my concern.

This was a beautiful body, an obedient and beautiful body, the breath moving in and out of the nostrils, the mouth opening and closing at my will, the heart beating quietly, functioning so well that it was unobtrusive. The breasts were round and firm, the legs slender and strong and the flesh was smooth and sleek, the skeleton sheathed by softness. This body was young, a fitting abode for one such as me.

And in the drawer of the dresser where these hands had

placed them were the pages that had been written, the pages the woman called Maggie had searched for while she shivered in this room that was mine.

And knowing where they were, remembering what had been written and seeing so clearly what would be written, I walked over to the window, pushing aside the organdy curtains.

The night was dark and still. I raised the sash and leaned on the window sill, smelling the scent of the dead leaves lying in the flower beds, this year's leaves rotting, a compost holding warm the dormant seeds in the earth, while on the trees, even now, even before the long winter began, even before the spring was in sight, the buds swelled, the next year's leaves beginning at the moment these ended.

I heard the woman, Maggie, groan as she rose, the bedsprings creaking, and I knew she was restless tonight as she had been last night, exhausted, weary, and yet unable to sleep. Last night she had come into this room, but tonight she moved down the hall, and there was water running in the bathroom, the woman taking care of the needs of her own aging body.

There, leaning on the window sill with the chill autumn air sweet in these nostrils, I heard the sounds of the woman, Maggie, die down again, mingling with the other muted sounds of this house, and I thought of Consuela, who slept across the hall, and the sounds she had made.

"It's Alarice," she had said, falling back, crying out my name, recognizing me before she fell back, white and still, and I had looked at her and I had shaken with laughter knowing that her punishment was what I had intended, not a whit more or less.

"Will she be all right?" the girl, Elizabeth, the sister-flesh of my body, had asked.

"Poor thing," said Maggie, "and on her birthday, too."

On her birthday, too, I had thought, and she hadn't been fortunate enough to go through what was called death. She would live and they would poke and pry at her, twisting and turning her, subjecting her body to every indignity, and she would know, locked within, she would know what they were doing, and she would have to submit without protest, the tongue flaccid, useless and lolling, the limbs without feeling, but the sight and the hearing still there, the eyes registering, seeing the faces bending above her, hearing the voices that reached her, and no way for her to answer, no way for her to communicate, locked in her own loneliness, the brain constantly working, the mind remembering with nothing gone, all the years that had been still there, and the few years that will be wished away, Consuela a prisoner in her bound, rigid flesh, her flesh locked against her before she was ready to leave it.

The way the door had been locked against me, the way the key had been turned in the lock stealthily, quietly as I moved toward the door, trying to follow Consuela as she carried my child in her arms, the flames licking the wall behind me, the room filled with smoke and the key turned in the lock so that I beat against the door, weeping with my cheek against the door and hearing the footsteps going down the stairs.

"She's had a stroke," said Helen Warren. "I told her not to come here," she said, twisting her hands. "I begged her. She wouldn't listen to me."

Who will listen to the warnings of witches? I thought then as I left the room. Who will heed the prophet, obey the seers and listen to the sermonizing of sorcerers?

I walked up the stairs and closed the door to my room behind me. I prepared for bed without waiting for the report of the doctors, the men of medicine, old and young, reaching for the pulse, counting the heartbeat, measuring the pressure of the blood, taking the temperature, and nodding their heads at each other to mask their own fears.

Now the night lay still around me. The woman, Maggie, went back to her bed and I stood quiet next to the window and knew that Consuela slept peacefully across the hall.

When they had gone, when the guests had departed (even my own child only a guest in this house), the girl, Elizabeth, had come to me, opening my door without knocking, walking into my room without an invitation.

"I know how upset you must be," she had said. "I came to tell you that Aunt Constance will be all right. It was just a faint."

I didn't answer her. I kept the tongue still in my mouth and I peered through those eyes that were now mine and I said not a word.

"Please, darling," said Elizabeth. "Don't look at me like that. I can't stand it when you look at me like that. It's not your fault. You've been through enough without having this on your mind, too. How were you to know about the pin? What I don't understand," said Elizabeth, shivering, "is where you got it. I know you must have found it somewhere in this room. Aunt Constance must have thought that it had been buried with Alarice, and all the time it had slipped in back of one of the dresser drawers and you found it and admired it and thought you'd surprise Aunt Constance with it."

I turned. My hands moved and I stared at them in surprise. They were mine. They were part of this beautiful new body that was mine and they had no right to move without me.

I ran my fingers across the top of the dresser.

This was the way I had stood that first day. I touched the Bible. The place of sapphires, I thought, and the book was heavy in my hands. I've looked everywhere and I can't find it. Is it in here?

"I don't know what you're talking about," I said.

"The pin," said Elizabeth.

"What pin?"

"The one you gave Aunt Constance tonight," she said, her voice rising. "Gabrielle, you must remember."

Who were they to order me around? *You must be Gabrielle.* Who were they to command? *You must remember. You must be Gabrielle and you must remember.*

"Oh, that," I said indifferently, making the tongue and the lips move.

"We're going to leave here tomorrow," she said desperately. "Do you hear me?"

"Yes," I said. "I hear you."

"Gordon says Aunt Constance can be moved then, and we can leave."

Leave here, I thought.

"Come with us," they had said, standing shining and straight. "Come with us," they had pleaded, their voices soft and sweet, and they were beckoning, shimmering columns of light. "You cannot stay here."

"Come with me," Mama had said, part of the others and yet separate, recognizable and separate, but her voice blending with theirs as though they sang together.

Leave here? I had turned away from the light. I had stayed in darkness, waiting for Consuela, and I would remain in the dark until my waiting time was over.

"I'll help you pack in the morning," Elizabeth said.

"I don't need any help," I said craftily. I turned around. "I can do it all by myself," I said.

"I know you can," said Elizabeth, and she closed my door behind her.

You must remember.

What must I remember? Must I remember going down the stairs in the night, searching for my love in the night and finding instead the smell of decay, the thick, sweet smell of lilacs, cloying in these nostrils, and then the notebook hard in my hands, and knowing now it was all for nothing, the agony of removing the pin, the effort of transporting the pin through space and time, the pin that was the perfect gift for Consuela, the pin that she herself had put in the coffin like an offering to the gods, Consuela supplicating, placating the powers, and then the moment of contrition past, the coffin buried in a lonely grave and Consuela lying warm in Jotham's arms.

Now she was across the hall, in her own room across this hall, and tomorrow she would leave here forever as they hoped to take this body that was mine away forever, and where would I find her again if I let her leave me now?

And the sister-flesh asleep in this quiet night, the sister-flesh, too, across the hall, satisfied and relaxed, the nerve endings brought to a point of anguished, quivering joy before the sweetness of sleep, and tomorrow she, too, would leave, the sister-flesh going its own way, and this body of mine left abandoned, deserted, this body of mine left without its love.

Across the hall. There were two women across the hall. One was young and one was old and yet they belonged together, the old and the young sharing the same murderous guilt.

243

And where there is guilt, there is retribution, and the punishment was waiting as I was waiting.

Across the hall. Now I was across the hall. I opened Consuela's door and went into her room. She lay in her bed, her eyes closed, her breathing ragged, her breath whistling through her nostrils, her breath wheezing in her throat, and I bent over her, listening to the life running in and out of her body and I turned on the light so that she would waken and see me, so that she would know who it was who placed this pillow over her mouth and nose, who stopped this breath, who held her with young strength while she fought futilely, feebly with the old.

She opened her eyes. "Gabrielle?" she murmured sleepily. She turned her head. She tried to sit up. "Gabrielle?" she said again. "What are you doing here? Is anything wrong?"

I began to laugh. "Don't you know who I am?" I said. "You should know who I am, Consuela."

She shrank back.

"Answer me," I said.

Her eyelids fluttered. She closed them and then opened them wide. "I'm dreaming," she said, her voice quivering.

"You're not dreaming," I said.

"Oh, my God," she whimpered, her voice too soft to be a whisper, her voice too frightened to be a cry. "Who are you?"

"Have you forgotten me then, Consuela?" I said softly. "Was it so easy to forget me? Do you remember how you stood on my wedding day, watching as Jotham put the ring on my finger? Do you remember the dress you wore, the blue dress with the embroidered collar and cuffs and how Mama wept and how spiteful Helen Warren was, saying Jotham had to marry me, that I was carrying his child? Neither one of you knew I had heard. You denied it, but I walked into the room and I said it was true, that I was having a child, and I just stood there and taunted you both, that mealymouthed old maid and you."

"Alarice," she said, her mouth working hard to form my name.

"Alarice," I said.

Her eyes reddened and the tears rolled down her cheeks. "I'm

244

dreaming," she babbled. "I know I'm dreaming and it's the same dream. Why is it always the same dream? Each time I explain it to you all over again and you won't believe me. It was not me. I swear it. Dear God, am I going mad?" She tried to sit up and I pushed her back. "It was Jotham," she wept. "How many times have I told you it was Jotham? When I reached the top of the stairs, I found the door locked. I tried to reach you. I swear I tried to reach you. It had to be Jotham. He was in the house. He said he came into the house looking for me, but there was no one else and I didn't lock your door. I came back for you. God knows I came back for you."

Jotham, I thought.

"Mother," the child had said, searching for me and then the door had opened. It was Jotham. It was Jotham who had given my child to Consuela. It was Jotham who had impregnated Consuela and I poured my hate upon him until he cowered under it.

"Didn't you love me?" I had cried to Jotham that night while he writhed on the floor, still not seeing me, never seeing me. "Why didn't you love me?"

"No," I said, and I leaned on the pillow. Her hands waved in the air, her hands beating the air, and I remembered the way my hands had beat at the door, my hands bruised beating at the door while my lungs fought for air, while my lungs were seared and I told her while she struggled that she was lucky, that this was a fortunate thing for her, an easier, gentler death than the one she had given me, that I was treating her with pity and with compassion.

"Not Jotham," I said, pressing down. "Jotham would have loved me. If it weren't for you, he would have loved me," and I stayed a minute longer than necessary until I saw the essence leave her body, until I saw the lights in the distance, the shining columns approaching to take her away, and within me there was regret that there was so much beauty waiting for her. It would have been better the other way, if she had lived imprisoned in her dying, disobedient flesh, bound by sorrow and fear. If they had given me enough time, I would have tried again, but they wanted to take her away and I needed the joy of witnessing at least her moment of death, of her agony at the moment of death, and now I had that and it was enough.

I left her room and there was Elizabeth standing in front of her open door, her sleepy eyes blinking in the light, her cheek creased from the pillow.

"Oh, it's you," she said, relieved.

"Who did you think it was?" I said, wanting to laugh.

"I didn't know. I thought I heard a sound. Is Aunt Constance all right?"

"She's fine," I said. "Why don't you go to sleep? You'll be tired in the morning."

"I'm tired now," said Elizabeth ruefully.

The sister-flesh, I thought, looking at her. If it weren't for you, he would have loved me.

I went into my room and closed my door. I leaned against it, my cheek pressed against it. It would be a while before Elizabeth fell asleep again. It would be a long time before I dared to go to her, before I dared to bend over her while she slept. She was young and strong as I was young and strong. She would fight me, her strength not feeble, not depleted with the years, but the equal to mine. I would have to find another way to reach Elizabeth. I would have to remain in the dark and find my own way to Elizabeth.

I locked my door. I always kept the key on the inside of my door now and I locked it, turning the key slowly.

The lock clicked and I backed away as if by moving away I could muffle all sound, but the house was filled with sounds that would not die, and although they were muted now, they were there for those who listened.

As I listened.

And I heard footsteps in the hall. I heard a door open. I heard a cry in the night, the sister-flesh crying out in the night and more footsteps racing up the stairs and the thump as the woman, Maggie, left her bed, her hand, in her haste, striking against the wall, and the voices, the present voices louder and clearer than those of the past, and "Is she dead?" Elizabeth cried. "Oh, Gordon, is she dead?"

"I can't bear it," said Maggie loudly. "How can any of us bear it?"

"Where is Gabrielle?" said Gordon.

"In her room," said Elizabeth, weeping. "She said Aunt Constance was all right. She closed Aunt Constance's door behind her and she said that everything was fine."

"We waited too long," said Gordon.

I walked across the room. I lit my candle and set it upon the small table. I sat down in the chair and folded my hands in my lap.

"We waited too long," he had said, but he was wrong. It was not they who had waited too long. It was I. I had waited too long. If I had gone down the steps, if I had tiptoed down the steps, I would have found the knives lying sharp in the kitchen drawer. With a knife in my hand I would have been stronger than Elizabeth. With a knife in my hand I would have cut into the sister-flesh until it was no longer sister and no longer flesh. Now I sat there and watched the knob of my door turn.

"Gabrielle," said Elizabeth, still weeping.

"Gabrielle," said Gordon, his voice sharper than the sharpest knife.

"I can't let anything happen to her," Elizabeth said, her voice thick with sobs. "What will they do to her?"

"Open the door," said Gordon.

I sighed. I stood up. The room was cold. The time had come for this room to be warm again, warm the way it once was. On long winter nights I had sat on that red rug in front of the fireplace, my legs curled under me, a book open on my lap. The flames leaped high and the logs crackled and the sparks flew. How warm my room was then.

I knelt on the hearth. Absorbed, intent, I arranged the logs to my liking. And then I reached for the candle.

"Gabrielle," screamed Elizabeth, bruising her hands on my locked door. "Please answer me. Gabrielle, Gabrielle, I won't let anyone hurt you. You know I won't let anyone touch you. You know I love you."

Gabrielle. Who was she? Had she ever paced this floor? Had

she slept in this bed? Had she lived and loved and wept in this house?

"Gabrielle," they cried. "Gabrielle. Gabrielle."

I sat back on my heels and watched as the flames caught, the fire leaping high. I held out my hands, sitting in front of my fireplace, feeling the blessed warmth, happy as I have never been before.

"Gabrielle," they cried foolishly, futilely, and I did not answer. I was silent. If they had spoken my name, I would have answered them, but they did not speak my name. Who was Gabrielle? I didn't know. I only knew I was not Gabrielle. I was Alarice and I was not afraid.